# DESTINY'S RUIN

Books by Philip S Davies:

**In the *Destiny's Rebel* trilogy:**

*Destiny's Rebel (Book One)*

*Destiny's Revenge (Book Two)*

*Destiny's Ruin (Book Three)*


**In the *Immortality* series:**

*Cave of Immortality (Book One)*

*War for Immortality (Book Two)*

# DESTINY'S RUIN

Book Three in the *Destiny's Rebel* Trilogy

## Philip S Davies

First published by Books to Treasure 2018
This updated third edition by Brittain Fisher 2026



www.philipsdavies.com

ISBN-10: 1-916767-03-6
ISBN-13: 978-1-916767-03-4

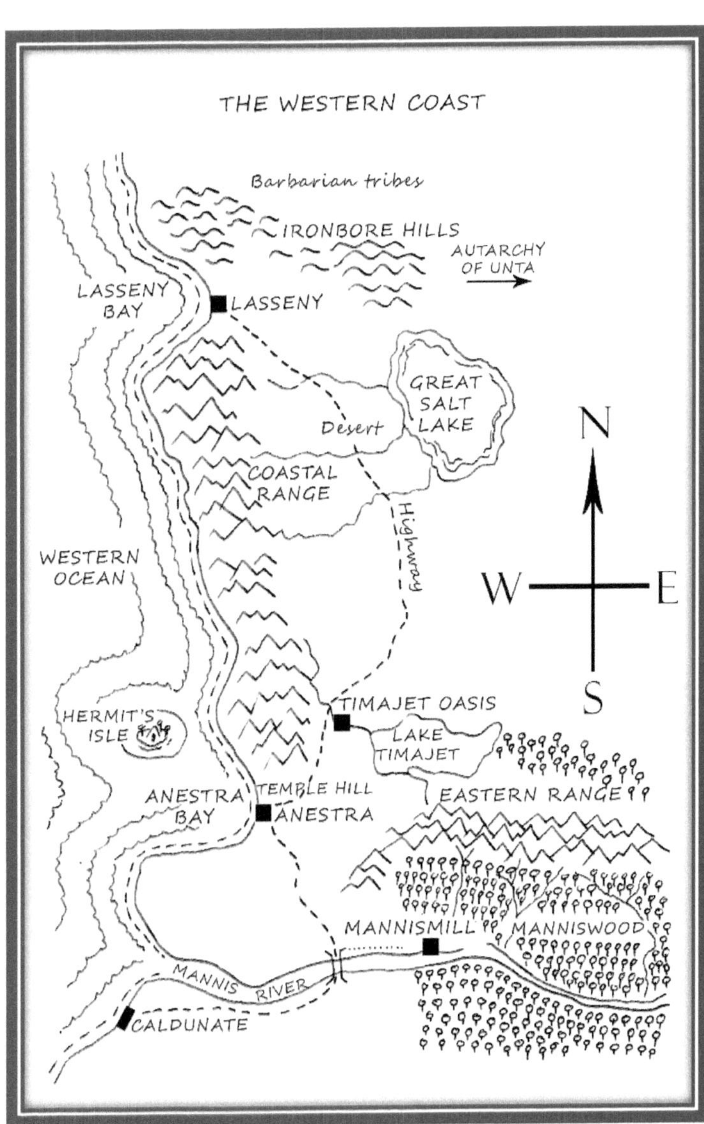

THE WESTERN COAST
Barbarian tribes
IRONBORE HILLS
AUTARCHY OF UNTA
LASSENY BAY
LASSENY
GREAT SALT LAKE
Desert
COASTAL RANGE
Highway
N
W
E
S
WESTERN OCEAN
HERMIT'S ISLE
TIMAJET OASIS
LAKE TIMAJET
EASTERN RANGE
ANESTRA BAY
TEMBLE HILL
ANESTRA
MANNISMILL
MANNISWOOD
MANNIS RIVER
CALDUNATE

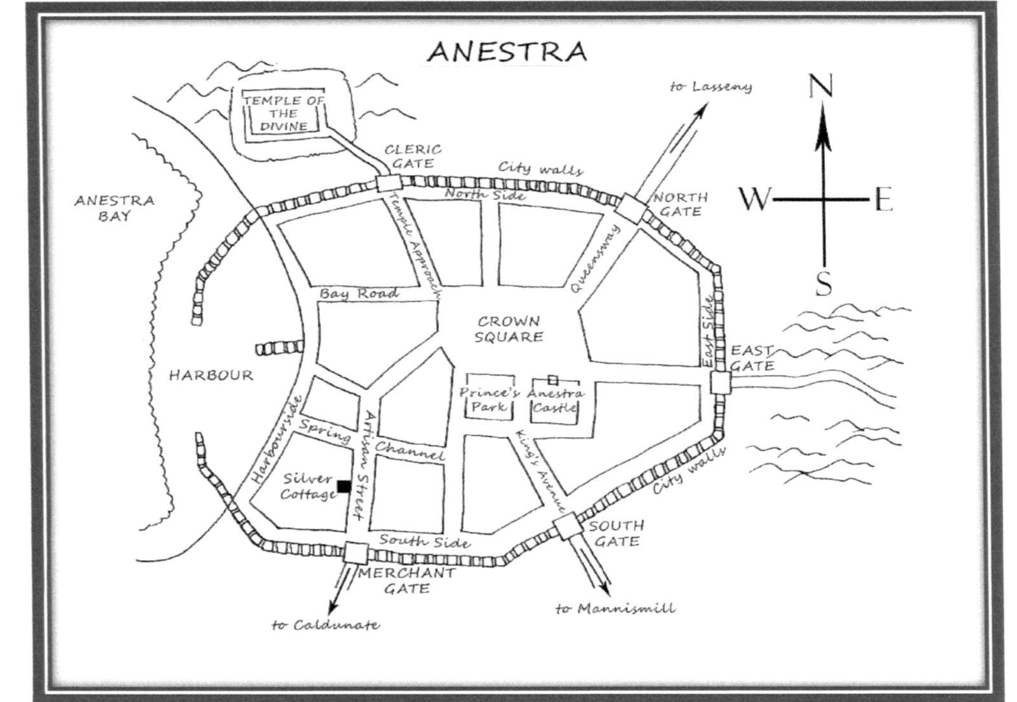

ANESTRA
N
E
W
S
to Lasseny
to Mannismill
to Coldunate
TEMPLE OF THE DIVINE
ANESTRA BAY
HARBOUR
CLERIC GATE
NORTH GATE
EAST GATE
SOUTH GATE
MERCHANT GATE
City walls
City wall
North Side
East Side
South Side
Queensway
Temple Approach
Bay Road
Harbourside
Spring Channel
Artisan Street
King's Avenue
CROWN SQUARE
Prince's Park
Anestra Castle
Silver Cottage

*For Ann,*
*for Mark, and for Rachel*

## 1

## DINNER

Mannismill. Katelin's least favourite place. Home of the detested aunt who had made her life a misery.

Since becoming Queen of Anestra a year ago, Katelin had got on better with her aunt, but only because they'd had nothing to do with each other. She wouldn't be here now, but her aunt's fiftieth birthday dinner was not something she felt able to ignore.

She paused before the polished wooden doors of the dining room and steeled herself for the ordeal. Aunt Sirika had never forgiven her for taking away the power she had held as Regent for so many years.

Katelin glanced sideways into the hall mirror to check she looked presentable after the ride from the city. She'd released her dark brown hair from its usual ponytail, but had no time to do anything fancier with it. She straightened the ruby necklace and smoothed down the burgundy gown into which she'd changed from her riding tunic and trousers. It was plainer than she wore for a banquet in the Hall of the Court, but good enough for dinner with Aunt Sirika. But anyway, it wasn't how she looked that mattered: it was who she was about to meet.

At her nod, the servants opened the hall doors, and she swept in.

A wall of windows on Katelin's left bathed the dining room with late afternoon sunshine. The room faced the wide Mannis River, and a low, gentle roar came from the waters churning through the nearby mill buildings which gave the estate its name. Comfortable armchairs and bookshelves filled the corners of the spacious room, and a plush, patterned carpet surrounded the long mahogany table where the other five of the family sat waiting for her.

At Katelin's entrance, three of Sirika's children—Princess Rashelin and the younger two of her three brothers, Agabos and Ethnir—stood up from their chairs at the table. Katelin accepted this mark of respect for the dignity of the exalted office she held.

Rashelin glared at the eldest of her brothers, the slouching Prince Tajion, to tell him to stand too, and he managed a grudging levering of himself to his feet. That left only Aunt Sirika, skeletal and sour-faced, leaning back in her chair at the table's far end. Everyone watched what she would do as Katelin approached her place at the head of the table.

Should she make an issue of this? Katelin wondered. Could she make a noble concession, allowing her aunt to remain seated, or would that be taken as a sign of weakness?

Sirika's cold, grey eyes were fixed on Katelin's as she leaned forward, grasped the table's edge, and pulled herself to her feet.

"How gracious of your Majesty to join us," she said as soon as she was upright. "Such a noble, condescending gesture from one so great towards your humble servants."

Katelin bit back a retort. She should have expected a sarcastic comment. She chose to let it pass, allowing a servant to pull out her chair and help her be seated.

As the others sat, Katelin said, as pleasantly as she could, "Thank you for welcoming me to your country estate, Aunt Sirika. I'm glad I could arrange to be present with the family on your special day. My congratulations to you on your fiftieth birthday."

Sirika regarded her with narrowed eyes along the length of the table, and Katelin returned the look steadily. Perhaps the woman was assessing whether Katelin's words held the same level of sarcasm as her own. No, she'd meant them sincerely. She doubted they could ever be friends, because nineteen years of antagonism might prove too much to forgive, but there was no excuse for lack of civility.

Sirika nodded to the servants, who began filling wine glasses and serving the first course, a delicious braised salmon.

"No doubt your room here is less grand than you've come to expect as Queen of the Western Coast," Sirika sneered.

"I'll be honest with you, Aunt Sirika," Katelin replied. "I always liked the cosiness of my childhood room, because growing up I didn't need anything spacious or fancy. But you're right that the Queen of Anestra needs larger accommodations."

She chose not to mention that her room had often been her sole place of refuge during a long childhood of bullying and abuse from her guardian aunt.

Feeling the need of a conversation with someone other than her aunt, Katelin turned to her cousin and best friend, Princess Rashelin, seated on her right.

"How was your ride from Anestra yesterday?" she asked in formal tones: the presence of the rest of family made it impossible to talk in her usual relaxed manner. "I hope you didn't get too wet in the rain."

Rashelin pulled a face, but the blue eyes under her blonde hair were bright. "Yes, very wet, I'm afraid, but nothing that a warm bath couldn't solve."

Silence fell around the table, broken only by the clink of cutlery. What else could they talk about?

Katelin hadn't visited Mannismill since Uncle Ethabos's funeral in the winter. His unexpected death had stirred in her heart a touch of sympathy for her bullying aunt. No matter who you were, it was hard to lose your husband or wife, hard for children to lose a parent. But she couldn't think what to say to them about that.

Then she remembered something else.

"Rashelin, after you left Anestra yesterday, a letter arrived from Initiate Prento."

Her cousin smiled at the mention of their friend.

Katelin had spent a lot of time with the young man over the last year, and missed his company now that he'd moved away. "He's adjusting to life in Lasseny," she went on, "and resuming his studies with Brother Armus. He asked to be remembered to you."

Rashelin nodded, but from the far end of the table came Sirika's disdainful voice. "At least that one was a trainee cleric, an Initiate of the Divine. That's more than can be said for your current one."

Katelin frowned as she faced her aunt. "My current what?"

"Yes, please tell us," Sirika replied. "How do you describe him? That 'special friend' of yours, or whatever he is, by the name of Zane." She spoke his name with a sneer.

Katelin bristled inside, but kept her voice level. "I fear you have given mere gossip too much credence. I consider him my friend. It's no one's business but my own who I choose as my friends."

She glanced at Rashelin, the only one who knew her feelings for the man.

"So you're *not* engaged, then? Thank the Divine for that," Sirika said. "Can you imagine what a disaster it would be for the Kingdom if the Crown were to pass to the children of someone like Zane?"

Katelin's knuckles whitened as she gripped her cutlery. "What do you mean, 'someone like Zane'? He saved my life more than once when I journeyed to Lasseny to negotiate the end of Ilbassi Plague. Everyone in Anestra should be grateful to him."

"But he was an outlaw," Sirika cried. "Aren't the fine sons of our Court's noble families good enough for you, that you go scouring the forests for vagabond friends instead?"

"He has a heart more noble than some I could mention. His only crime was to steal a loaf of bread to feed his starving brothers and sisters, and I pardoned him and his men because they'd more than repaid whatever wrongs they had done. The city's poor people had hard lives during the sixteen years of your Regency."

Katelin laid down her knife and fork, and the servants came to clear the plates. Soon she was enjoying the main course of pheasant in a delectable orange sauce, grateful for the friendliness of Rashelin's company on her right in contrast to the frostiness down the table. But she didn't like the way Prince Tajion, seated on her left, kept allowing his eyes to stray to look her up and down.

Sirika leaned back in her chair. "You mentioned our Regency. I understand why you might try to cast yourself in a better light by misrepresenting our recent history, but in reality, the years when your uncle and I ran the Kingdom were a golden age for Anestra. Under our rule, the people had peace and prosperity, instead of the string of disasters since you came to the throne."

Katelin almost choked on her pheasant, and was thankful for Rashelin's intervention.

"On the contrary, Mother; many at Court say that Queen Katelin has served us remarkably well in leading us through such difficult times."

"I accept that most in Anestra have survived the awful traumas of your first year as Queen"—Sirika's words were grudging—"but too many have been lost. Just consider: Lasseny invaded on your Coronation Day, followed only months later by an outbreak of Ilbassi Plague and the death of King Edgaran. We can't be surprised when people start asking questions."

Katelin sipped her wine and chose careful words. "What questions are people asking, then?"

Sirika licked her thin lips, as though savouring the chance to spread this gossip into the ears of its victim. "Well, no one can deny that you *appear* to be the rightful Queen of Anestra, by virtue of your birth and the ancient laws of succession. But that's not all we must consider for the rule of Anestra and the Western Coast, is it? We must listen to the Divine, our beloved White Goddess, and who *she* favours to be Queen. In the past, Kings and Queens have been removed from the throne as 'unfit to rule'."

Katelin recognised Sirika's attempts to provoke her, but she had known this was likely and had resolved to stay calm, no matter what. "I agree that the wishes of the Divine are paramount in these matters. She has revealed her glory through our sacred relic, the Crown of Anestra, when it's placed on my head."

"Yes, she has," Sirika conceded, "or at least she has so far. The Divine *has* been known to withdraw her glory. But there are other signs as well as the Crown; signs that anyone can read. Do you deny that the fortunes of Anestra worsened as soon as you became Queen, at eighteen? When the first year of a reign includes invasion, Plague and the death of the King, one wonders whether that reign enjoys Divine favour. In fact, one almost wonders whether that reign isn't cursed."

The silence around the table was different this time. Agabos and Ethnir, more interested in their food, kept out of the discussion. Prince Tajion smirked, as though enjoying the entertainment. Rashelin's mouth fell open in shock.

This was unacceptable! Katelin let her voice betray some of the outrage she felt. "None of last year's events were my fault. I didn't cause the Lassenite invasion, or make Ilbassi send his Plague against us. King Edgaran sacrificed his life to save our people from that Plague. And besides, from my experience, the Divine is not in the business of cursing anyone or anything. She is a loving Goddess, generous and merciful."

Sirika gave a small, dangerous smile, and Katelin berated herself for having fallen into her aunt's malicious trap.

"Now, now, my naïve young Queen," Sirika purred. "I can see you're in danger of becoming all defensive and upset. Let's pretend we're not talking about you, shall we? I trust you won't object to a rational discussion about the principles of Divine favour for the ruler of Anestra."

Katelin drew a deep breath to calm herself. "No, I'd be happy to have a reasoned conversation about that, free from personal animosity."

She glanced at Rashelin and received an approving nod.

"Excellent," Sirika replied, stabbing her fork into a slice of pheasant. "Let's suppose that during Anestra's history, a bad King comes to the throne. He is proud, selfish, greedy, cruel and violent. He rejects all the ways of our White Goddess and acts as a tyrant. Would the people be right to want rid of him, and to ask the Divine for a better ruler?"

Katelin gave a cautious nod. "If he's as bad as you describe, then yes, Anestra should ask the Divine to give them a ruler after her own heart, one who will listen to her and follow her ways."

"How might the Divine show her displeasure during the reign of such a King?" Sirika pressed. "Bad weather, poor harvests, war, disease, natural disasters? Isn't the Divine able to bestow or withdraw her blessings through all such things as these?"

Katelin shook her head. "No, I don't think that's right. The disasters you describe sound like a punishment for the whole people, rather than for the failings of the King. The Divine would find ways to show her displeasure for the unworthy King alone, perhaps through withdrawing her glory from the Crown."

"Very well," Sirika conceded. "But suppose this tyrant of a King had a younger sister, altogether the opposite of her brother: wise, gentle, selfless, brave, kind, generous and devout. Wouldn't the people ask the Divine to replace the brother with the sister?"

"Yes, they would," Katelin agreed. "The people would be much better off under her rule, and the Divine would see that."

Sirika leaned back. "So, we have the suggestion from you that the Divine should vent her displeasure against the King alone, not the mass of the people. If our imagined tyrant of a King should fall gravely ill, for example, or have a fatal accident, then the Divine would be justified in withholding her healing or protection, and let that bad King die, so the sister could become Queen?"

Katelin felt a chill down her back as she recognised where Aunt Sirika was going with this. Furious, she didn't trust herself to speak.

"Or even further," Sirika went on, "would the faithful, Divine-worshipping people of Anestra be right to pray for such a disease or accident for their tyrant King? Could they even be excused for assassinating him, to spare them his lifetime of misrule and abuse?"

Katelin slammed her cutlery onto the table. "You cloak your thoughts behind a veneer of reasonable, civilised discussion. I am no tyrant. And I advise you, my noble aunt, to be careful with your words, and remember to whom you are speaking. I *am* your Queen, and to suggest my reign is cursed by the Divine could be considered treason."

Sirika's voice rose. "Are you threatening me? In my own house and at my table? In the middle of my birthday dinner? Come, come, my girl. We agreed we weren't talking about you, didn't we? You say you want us to be open and honest with each other, speaking our minds face to face instead of whispering in corners. That's all I'm doing."

Katelin looked down at her plate, gathering her thoughts. Should she stay and listen to this, or get up and leave? She felt her aunt's eyes on her and looked up.

"You can take it as a threat, if you wish. I certainly advise you not to repeat those words elsewhere than in front of our immediate family."

She returned to her pheasant, and silence resumed around the table. Self-control, Katelin. Just finish the dinner and get through the night, then head back to Anestra in the morning.

The servants cleared the table again and brought in a summer fruit cheesecake.

"My friends at Court tell me," Sirika began again, as they tucked into the dessert, "that you're working hard, my young Queen. Very commendable. But have you considered you might be working hard to take Anestra in a wrong or dangerous direction?"

"And what determines a wrong or dangerous direction, Aunt Sirika?"

"There you go, getting all defensive and upset again." Sirika forced her lips into what might have been intended as a smile. "I hear that at every turn you champion the rights of the poor and common people of Anestra against the nobles and ministers of the Kingdom. By doing so, you endanger the social fabric that underlies our prosperity."

Katelin paused with her spoon poised halfway to her mouth. Was it possible to reason with this woman?

"If you mean that I challenge injustice, and the exploitation of the poor by the rich, then yes, I do. But I am very careful, my noble aunt, to investigate each situation fully, and judge with fairness every case that is brought before me. I know I'm a young and inexperienced Queen, so I draw on the wisdom of my Council and advisers, and together we lead our Kingdom in the ways we consider to be right."

Sirika snorted. "From what *I* hear, you've declared war on your own Court, picking fights with any noble or minister who crosses your path. The prosperity and smooth running of a kingdom depends on the goodwill of its leading citizens, you know. We can only pray that the Divine is merciful to us and keeps your reign short. She'll see the dangers of you setting nobles and people against each other, and that we won't survive any more of your disasters. A reckless and foolhardy Queen could soon get herself killed in an accident."

Katelin couldn't restrain a note of sarcasm. "Oh, what is this, aunt, dear? A sudden concern for my wellbeing and safety? Have no fear. When I tackle what needs to be done for the good of everyone in the Kingdom, I am always careful. I hope to lead a long and full life, striving to fulfil what the Divine asks of me."

Sirika's smile remained cold and thin. "Not at all, not at all. Your safety is of no concern to me. Others attend to that. But perhaps you misunderstand me. You see, as we discussed earlier, if the Divine is displeased with a ruler then we might see one disaster after another. In that case, for the good of the Kingdom, that ruler having a fatal disease or accident might be not just likely, but … desirable." She took a long drink of wine.

Katelin stared at her aunt down the length of the table. Even the young Princes paused in their eating at this.

Katelin glanced at Rashelin. "I cannot believe what I just heard."

"Eat up, eat up," Sirika said. "Don't waste good food."

Rashelin laid her cutlery down on the table. "Mother, I think I've lost my appetite. How dare you insult such an important guest when she's travelled all this way to be with us? Apologise to her."

Sirika turned to regard her daughter. "How dare I? I dare more than you know. Apologise to her? Dignity and respect are earned, not given away by unfortunate accidents of birth and succession."

Rashelin touched Katelin's arm. "Please forgive Mother's rudeness. Have you finished? Shall we retire to our rooms?"

But Katelin had been thinking over Sirika's words. Her aunt had implied that it was desirable for Anestra to be rid of her. She drew a deep breath.

"I've no mind to stay the night with those who insult their guests. I'm going to ride home to Anestra tonight."

Prince Tajion's head jerked to look at his mother, and

Katelin caught a frown from her to silence him.

"Oh, must you go tonight, Katelin, dear?" Sirika asked. "The boys like having their important cousin with them here."

The looks on the Princes' faces told Katelin this was far from true.

Rashelin was shaking her head. "If the Queen is leaving, then I shall accompany her. I, too, will ride back to Anestra tonight. Mother, sometimes you make me ashamed to be your daughter."

Katelin shoved back her chair, and Rashelin rose also.

"Goodnight, Aunt Sirika, and goodbye." Katelin spoke coldly. "The food was delicious, but you should learn from your daughter, who outshines you in courtesy, good conversation and good company."

## 2

## RIDE

The last light of evening was fading from the courtyard as Katelin adjusted the saddlebags on her white stallion, Novita. After the discussion in the dining room, the cool night air calmed her thoughts. It would be past midnight before she reached Anestra's city gates, but the clear sky promised an evening of glorious stars. Her escort home from Mannismill consisted of six of the Knights of Anestra, who waited nearby on their horses, three of them with flaming torches to light the way.

Princess Rashelin was frowning as she led her light grey mare, Whisper, from the stables.

"Don't let your mother upset you," Katelin said. "Her comments this evening were outrageous, but let's leave her behind, get back to the Castle and resume our real work of serving the Kingdom."

"You're more used to her bullying than I am. I saw little of what went on as you were growing up. Father's death has removed any restraint on her wilder notions, and now she's as eccentric and outspoken as she likes. But I'm puzzled, Katelin: the grooms say that while we were changing, Mother sent a fast rider up the highway ahead of us."

Katelin tried a small smile. "Do you think she's sent a messenger to Anestra Castle about preparing my bed for the night?"

Rashelin shook her head, and her brow remained furrowed as she stepped up into Whisper's saddle.

Katelin adjusted her shortbow to be comfortable across her body, and tightened the straps on her quiver and pack before swinging up onto Novita's back. The Knights took their cue from her and moved off, out of the courtyard to the front of the building, where a wide, tree-lined avenue led to the road. Katelin glanced back at the twinkling lamps in the house and outbuildings, as the horses' hooves thudded on the gravel and packed-earth drive. A mist was rising from the river, and the trees, her silent honour guard, receded steadily behind her.

Katelin was grateful for Rashelin's company on the journey, although they were lost in their own thoughts. They trotted along the highway as full night fell, with four Knights in front, and two following.

They rode in darkness for an hour until Katelin noticed the torches of the riders ahead slowing down. The highway had swung around into a narrow space between the wide Mannis River on their left and a dense wood on their right. She eased back on Novita's reins, even though her guards were still a hundred yards or more ahead.

"Clear the road." A Knight's call drifted back to them through the night air. "In the name of the Queen, make way."

Katelin slowed her stallion to walking pace, and Rashelin did the same with Whisper. They took the chance to stand in their stirrups and shift in their saddles while the Knights moved away whatever was impeding their progress.

Other torches flickered in the half-light ahead, and there were voices. Katelin glanced back and saw that the two following Knights had stopped.

A prickle of unease crept up her neck to her scalp.

"Rashelin, stop," she said.

Their horses stood in the middle of the highway, breathing steam into the dark.

"What is it?" Rashelin asked.

Katelin peered forward, but could hear little of the conversation between the Knights and those who stood in the road. Then she caught the unmistakeable glint of torchlight on the drawn swords of her guards. Why would they need their weapons? A chill washed over her skin, and hot blood coursed through her veins.

By instinct she dropped her reins, unslung her shortbow and whipped an arrow from the quiver. She was nocking it to the string when she remembered her role was as Queen, not as archer alongside her Knights. Could she leave Rashelin on her own on the highway, unarmed, while she investigated what was happening?

"I think you'd better wait here," she said to Rashelin, and trotted Novita forwards.

Carrying back to her through the stillness of the night came a Knight's clear voice: "Get back south of the river, Malgosian."

Katelin's insides clenched with dread. Malgosian? They weren't allowed to be north of the Mannis. She spurred Novita forwards to where the four Knights faced a line of about twenty men. She stopped a little way back from her guards, her shortbow ready.

Her ears caught the familiar twang of a bowstring nearby, and then the thud of an arrow into flesh. One of her Knights cried out.

At once the line of twenty surged forwards, swinging swords at the mounted Knights. Shouts, cries and screams erupted in front of her, and the clash of steel on steel.

The Knights blocked her aim at the attackers, but Katelin sent one careful arrow, then another, into their enemies.

Then a cry cut through the air. "There she is! The archer on the horse. Dark-haired, she's the one. Get her!"

Katelin hadn't registered that the flames of the torches illuminated her.

The four Knights obstructed the narrowed road, but two men slipped between them and sprinted towards her. She loosed an arrow into the first, but then the second was on her. He grabbed her boot and heaved to dismount her.

In pulling away, Katelin wrenched on Novita's reins. The stallion reared and kicked the man in the chest. He fell back to the road.

A Knight whipped his head around and screamed over his shoulder, "Go, milady. It's you they're after. Flee!" The Knight turned back to parry a blow.

Katelin hated to leave the Knights to face their enemies alone, but had already hesitated too long. They were the Queen's guards and fought to keep her safe, to give her the chance to escape. She must use the time they bought her.

She yanked Novita's reins to turn him on the highway and spurred him back the way they'd come. As she went, she slung her shortbow onto her shoulder. She needed to ride, not shoot.

Princess Rashelin and Whisper were silhouetted against the torchlight behind them.

"Back towards Mannismill," Katelin called, and Rashelin turned Whisper alongside her.

"But we're surrounded." Rashelin's voice shook with horror. "They've caught us front and back."

Ahead of them now, on the road towards Mannismill, the two Knights who had followed them were also confronting a shadowy group of perhaps a dozen men. Torches had flickered into flame, and again Katelin saw the glint of sharpened steel.

But here the confrontation had not yet come to blows. For the pair of Knights were retreating up the road before the ambushers. Katelin skidded Novita to a halt and Whisper stopped beside her. The group of a dozen men approaching them seemed content for now to corner the Knights, Queen and Princess into this narrow stretch of road.

"We need to escape," Katelin urged, her heart pounding. She jerked her head to left and right. Wide river on one side, dense wood on the other—their ambushers had chosen this site well.

She gripped her reins, needing to choose. Plunge into the river? What about the horses? Splashes would give them away, and the far bank was Malgosian territory.

Then the second group of attackers saw her. "It's their Queen," one shouted. "There, on her horse. But only the dark-haired one, remember?"

The wood? She and Rashelin knew this road; they had ridden here often over the years. The wood was large and dense, but there were tracks.

One of the retreating Knights shouted to her, "Fly, milady. Save yourself. We'll hold them off."

Katelin gulped at their self-sacrifice, but needed to act.

"Into the wood," Katelin ordered, and spurred Novita towards the trees. From both sides of them came shouted orders and the crash of weapons on shields. Could the Knights hold off the ambush while they made their escape? Would her guards survive?

She forced Novita towards the widest opening between the trunks, and behind her Rashelin urged Whisper to follow.

The leaves instantly robbed them of torchlight and the undergrowth was thick. Novita struggled to step and trample forwards in the near-complete darkness. Branches and twigs scratched at Katelin's face and clothes.

"A track, Novita, find a track," she said, hoping the stallion would sense the urgency in her voice, if not the meaning.

Novita veered to the right, and the sounds of weapons, cries and battle faded behind them. The blood throbbed in her ears as she strained to listen. Were they making too much noise in crashing through the trees? Could the Malgosians—if that's who they were—follow them? Or would they have guarded the other side of the wood?

Katelin's eyes had adjusted enough to see when Novita passed two trunks and turned left onto a clearer way. Yes, this was a track. She slapped his neck in thanks, and heard the hooves and breaking twigs of Whisper coming behind them.

She tried to steady her breathing, calm her panic, decide

what to do.

The ambushers had known who rode with the Knights. No band of highway robbers would tackle half a dozen Knights without good cause. How far would their pursuers go to finish their task, to catch their prey? Where could she and Rashelin go, now separated from their guards? Could they get away from here under cover of darkness? But then what?

They trotted with a quieter tread along the darkened track, until the thinning trees announced the edge of the concealing wood.

Katelin slowed Novita to a stop and Rashelin drew Whisper up beside her. In the starlight filtering through the leaves she saw the scratches on her cousin's arms and face. Strands of her blonde hair were coming loose, and Katelin knew she must look the same. But a light was in her cousin's blue eyes—a fire of anger and of fear.

Katelin swallowed hard before she whispered. "The ambushers might have overwhelmed the Knights by now, so we can't risk going back there. It's me they're after, because they said 'the dark-haired one'. We should draw up our hoods to hide who we are."

Rashelin nodded, and they covered their hair.

"We need to keep moving," Katelin went on, "but they'll watch our most obvious routes to safety, the roads to the city or back to Mannismill. No one will miss me until I fail to return to the city tomorrow, so we've a night and a day before anyone sets out to search for us. I suggest we ride in the other direction, through the night and into the Manniswood, and hide there until Anestran soldiers can find us. Agreed?"

Rashelin nodded again, and they turned to peer out from the trees towards the darkened land before them.

Katelin patted her stallion's neck. "Quietly now, Novita, but be ready for a burst of speed if we need it." He shook his mane.

The horses stepped forward, the Queen and Princess listening hard, scanning the darkness for lights or movement. But there was nothing: no flicker of torches, no voices, no thud of hoof or footfall.

Had their ambushers considered the wood an impenetrable barrier, like the river, that couldn't be crossed except with difficulty? Or perhaps there weren't enough of them to block both ends of the road, as well as to watch the length of the river and the edge of the wood.

They emerged from the trees and the land felt too open. Their dark-adjusted eyes made out rolling farmland of hills and valleys, fields and hedges, dotted with occasional trees. Katelin glanced back at the swaying treetops silhouetted against the stars.

At that moment, a bowstring twanged.

By instinct Katelin threw herself flat on Novita's neck and dug her heels into his flanks. The stallion leapt forward as an arrow whistled past her ear.

"Ride!" Katelin called, but Rashelin needed no urging. Their horses sprang away as a second arrow flew towards them. Their breath came in fitful gasps as they galloped into a dip between two slopes.

They thundered up the valley, with every stride leaving the wood behind them. The seconds grew into minutes, and they began to hope they'd ridden out of sight or range of the archer. Katelin willed the darkness to swallow and hide them.

The minutes passed and no more arrows came near.

Soon Katelin slowed enough to ask, "Rashelin, are you all right?"

"An arrow nicked my arm. It's bleeding, but I can carry on."

"That archer must have been another of the ambushers, watching this side of the wood. He might have been alone, but they'll soon know the direction we've fled. It's a vast country, but we need to stay ahead of them."

"Couldn't we find a barn or something to hide in?" Rashelin asked.

"I'd rather keep moving than sit somewhere waiting for them to find me."

They kept to the valleys and made good speed through the darkness, jumping stone walls and gates, and skirting around crops and livestock.

To Katelin's relief, they met no further sight or sound of people.

A few hours passed, and the energy of flight faded. Lack of sleep weighed heavily on Katelin's limbs, and at one point she almost nodded off in the saddle. She woke with a start, thankful for Novita's sure-footed progress.

Later in the night, the moon rose in the east before them. Katelin had questions she wanted to discuss with Rashelin, but feared their voices might carry and be heard. So they rode in silent thought, their cloaks pulled tight around them. Their breath, and that of their horses, wafted pale in the moonlight, mingling with the mist that rose from the grass. It would be dark for a few hours yet, so they were careful to keep a quiet and hidden pace.

## 3

## FOREST

At last they crested a rise and saw the first greying of the eastern horizon. The massive blackness of the Eastern Range jutted into the first lighting of the new day, and its buttressed shoulders blocked their view towards the Manniswood.

They trotted on, and the daylight grew. The sun's rays appeared in the pale blue sky above them, although they were still in the shadow of the great ridge that separated the coastal plain from the Manniswood. The horses slowed as they climbed. At last the warming sun was in their eyes as they reached the ridge's summit and walked a short way down the other side. They reached the cover of the Manniswood and entered among the first trees, the perils of the open country blocked from view behind.

Katelin called a stop. They found a hollow among the trees near a stream and dismounted. They tethered Novita and Whisper, who shook their manes, drank from a pool, and began to crop the grass. Katelin washed the arrow cut on Rashelin's arm and tied a handkerchief round it as a bandage. They had nothing in the way of breakfast, but refilled their water bottles from the stream. They sat opposite each other on the grass and sipped in silence.

Rashelin spoke first. "I need to tell you something I overheard before we left Mannismill."

Katelin looked up. "What did you hear?"

"I'd changed and was ready to go, and went to say goodbye to Mother. Before I reached her study, I heard Tajion's voice. He asked, 'What have you ordered the Baron's men to do?' Mother shushed him as I entered the room, and at the time I didn't understand what he meant."

Katelin stared at her, the blood draining from her cheeks. "The Baron's men? And one of the Knights called out: 'Get back south of the river, Malgosian.' Does that mean…?"

Rashelin's voice was small. "Baron Malgosy."

Katelin's world tilted. Since last night, she'd tried to forget that word 'Malgosian'. But to think it might be linked to her Aunt Sirika and cousin Tajion…

Everything she'd previously assumed to be decent and acceptable now needed to be set aside. There were steps that reasonable people did not take, and lines that the civilised did not cross. Beyond them lay cruelty and torture, madness, murder and evil. This was the name that Rashelin had uttered: Baron Malgosy. That someone in the Royal Family might associate with such was unthinkable.

Her anger burned hot. "From what you say, your mother and Tajion knew about the ambush. So what order did she need to give to the Baron's men?"

"I've been thinking about that while we rode," Rashelin replied. "You remember the fast rider the grooms said had left the Mannismill stables?"

Katelin nodded.

"That could have been Mother's messenger, telling the ambushers you were riding back last night instead of this morning. Or the order could have been about me being with you. Or both of these. Neither of us was due to ride home last night, and we only decided to do so during dinner. And it was supposed to be just you and the Knights. So, the Malgosians might have had orders to kill the Knights and capture you, but now Mother and Tajion needed to order them not to harm me. Or to capture me too, I don't know."

"Capture us?" Katelin thumped a fist into her palm. "Rashelin, we both know what Baron Malgosy and his men are like."

"What do you mean? I know he was a nobleman of the Kingdom until the Court banished him for life because they could no longer cover up his crimes."

"And you remember what his crimes were?" Katelin prompted.

"Um … I heard he was training and using assassins."

"Exactly. As well as trying to capture us, his men might have had orders to assassinate us."

Rashelin was staring at her, shaking her head. "No, not 'us'. I wasn't supposed to be there. They had orders to assassinate you."

The blunt statement stunned Katelin into speechlessness.

An icy chill ran down her spine and she shuddered. She'd always known the possibility of assassination, but been reassured by the constant presence of guards around her. But now, out here at the edge of the forest, there were no guards anywhere.

Her voice was small. "You're right. They said, 'Just the dark-haired one.'" Katelin adjusted her thinking: this was a fight for survival. "So last night those Knights gave their lives to save mine. Without them, by now I'd be lying by the roadside, or thrown in the river, poisoned, strangled or with a dagger in my heart."

Rashelin was frowning. "But why would Mother and Tajion have anything to do with Baron Malgosy and his assassins?"

A grim memory surfaced. "Your mother said it herself yesterday at dinner. She considers me 'unfit to rule', and my reign cursed by the Divine. A fatal accident for me is not just likely, but desirable."

They sat in silence until Rashelin asked, "But what does Mother gain by arranging to murder you? She's not next in line for the throne. I am."

"You're right that she's never been in the line of succession and never will be. That's what's made her so bitter. She joined our Royal Family by marrying Uncle Ethabos, and had sixteen years of ruling the Kingdom with him as Regent. But then I came of age and stole away her title and authority. Now that he's died, her plans must revolve around you becoming Queen instead of me."

"You think she hopes to rule the Kingdom through me? But I've always been loyal to you, and will never agree to do what she says, not after this."

"She must think that if she can kill me, then you won't dare oppose her anymore."

"But what about Tajion? Why does my brother know about Mother's plans?"

Katelin frowned. "Hmm. Maybe Sirika has enlisted Tajion to put further pressure on you to do as they say. He is next in the succession after you. If anything happens to both of us, then Tajion becomes King."

"She wouldn't order for me to be assassinated. I'm her daughter." There was an angry sadness in Rashelin's voice that Katelin couldn't answer.

They sipped from their water bottles, Rashelin looking as wretched as she felt. "What can we do now?" she asked at last.

Katelin drew a deep breath and said, "We must assume that Baron Malgosy's assassins are still searching for us. They'll want to complete their task by killing me. Anestran soldiers won't come looking for us until tonight, so the Malgosians have a long head start. Now that we're here, I suggest we stay hidden in this forest for as long as we can. If we hear anyone coming today, then we need to flee. They're more likely to be Malgosian than Anestran, and the consequences of getting caught by them are catastrophic."

"Is that all we can do today, run and hide?"

"No, we also need some protection. The only people I can think of are Zane and his band of former outlaws. They live here in the Manniswood, and if we can find them, we'll have a fighting chance of survival until the Anestran army catch up with us." She raised her water bottle and forced out a smile. "They also have food to go with our water."

Rashelin smiled back, and said, "I'm sorry you needed to

listen to all Mother said about Zane last night. But you know, some of the Court *are* concerned about his intentions."

Katelin hesitated, but said, "I don't know his intentions either. I think we both have feelings for each other, but I need to be in the city, and he prefers the forest. I'm Queen, and he's uncomfortable with everything to do with the Castle and Kingdom and Court. We spend more time in different places than we do together. I can't even call him more than a friend, because we've never managed to have a conversation about it. I'm afraid that if I raise the subject it will scare him away."

Rashelin's face had softened into a smile. "But you care about him."

Katelin shrugged and looked away. "Yes, I do. He treats me as a person first, with feelings and fears, and hopes and dreams, and not just as 'The Queen'. I think he's funny, and handsome, so how can I not like him? Yes, I know I need to worry about the way things appear to the Court, but I can't stop myself being attracted to someone. No one chooses who they fall in love with, anyway."

"No, we can't. And I'm pleased for you, Katelin, to have found a friend like that. And not a bit jealous. I wish I could find a hero like Zane to care about myself."

They both smiled, and in the midst of everything else, Katelin had time to be grateful for the presence and understanding of a best friend.

Without warning, the horses snapped their tethers and bolted.

The two girls leapt up as Novita and Whisper thundered past them and out of the hollow. They both swayed from standing up too quickly, as though a rug had slipped beneath their feet, and stared after their mounts, galloping out from under the trees. They looked around, and listened hard, but sensed nothing unusual.

They ran after the horses, who were beyond the edge of

the forest before they calmed themselves enough to stop. They were munching grass again by the time Katelin and Rashelin caught up with them.

"What was that, eh?" Katelin said, as she stroked Novita's flank. "Did you see something? Hear something?"

Rashelin said, "Maybe they saw a snake in the grass. That always spooks them."

Katelin looked back into the trees. "In which case, I'm glad we're away from there. Or perhaps they felt something we couldn't. Like a change in the wind. They're more sensitive to such things than we are."

Rashelin frowned. "Perhaps. That might make them nervous, but not so as to bolt. Maybe they heard something we couldn't."

They both looked around, listening, scanning the crest of the ridge behind them that shielded them from Anestra. But there was nothing save the breeze through the nearby trees and a twitter of birdsong.

At once Katelin felt vulnerable on the hillside, afraid of a horseman appearing over the crest of the ridge. Or that each curve of the land might hide an enemy. She shook herself. She mustn't give in to these fears, but try to stay clear-minded. Yet her unease remained and she turned and mounted. "Come on," she said. "Back into the forest."

Rashelin swung into her saddle as Katelin urged Novita towards the trees. It was only once a few rows of trunks, branches and leaves were between her and the open country that Katelin began to feel hidden again.

They pressed deeper into the Manniswood. At first the trees were well-spaced, with grass between them. But soon the trunks pressed closer together, with tangled undergrowth. Animal tracks and paths criss-crossed the forest floor, so the horses had no difficulty in picking their way along them.

They rode in silence, with care rather than speed. Katelin tried to remember to listen. Although the trees provided cover for her, they would also conceal any pursuers until they were close enough to be heard. But it was only the rustle of leaves and the carefree chirp of birdsong that surrounded them. At times they startled birds into flight, or disturbed some small, scurrying rodent of the forest, but they saw and heard no one.

The morning wore on, and Katelin's thoughts turned to what might be happening back at Mannismill or in Anestra. How would Aunt Sirika react on learning she and Rashelin had escaped the ambush? No doubt she would be furious, and order the Malgosians to track them down. Would she have the means to contact Baron Malgosy about this outcome, at his castle south of the river? Of course she would.

But Sirika and Tajion would struggle to control the Kingdom from away at Mannismill, now that the Queen and Princess were both missing. Would they move in haste back to Anestra Castle? They might even do that today, to control or delay any search for them by the Anestran army. Katelin shivered, and rode deeper into the forest.

Prince Tajion stretched his stiff limbs as he dismounted from his carriage in the courtyard of Anestra Castle. It was time to be at the centre of events again, instead of away at the estate in the south. Sirika had left Mannismill early this morning, straight after the events of last night, while he followed later with more of the guards.

He swaggered towards the entrance to the Keep, and smirked as he entered, because he'd spotted two servant girls. If they were pretty enough, he always made his advances. In fact, even if they weren't pretty. Very few were bold enough to rebuff him and risk losing their positions.

He was handsome, and he knew it. That, and being a Royal Prince, gave him his air of smug cockiness. It helped, of course, having a mother who thought he could do no wrong. He worked hard to cultivate that.

He knew one of the servant girls, but the other he didn't, so she must be new. He ran a hand through his dark, wavy hair. As he did so, the girl he knew grabbed the new servant by the arm and dragged her away, a look of shame and disgust on her face. He frowned: his reputation had been shared around. Still, it was only mid-afternoon, and he might see the new girl again later at supper in the Hall.

His mother had said to come to her study as soon as he arrived, so he climbed the Keep stairs, knocked and entered at her call. He hoped her fury at last night's failed ambush had turned into a plan of what to do next.

Lady Sirika was sitting in her carved wooden chair. No, her throne, thought Tajion, with a sudden flash of insight. That's how she sees it. She perched upright on the edge of the seat, looking even skinnier than normal. The bright eagerness in her cold, grey eyes accentuated the prominent bones in her face.

Tajion was relieved: her seething bitterness had been transformed by the threshold of an opportunity, a plan for their advancement.

"You wanted to see me as soon as I arrived, Mother?"

"Ah, yes, Tajion, my dear. Come in, close the door, sit down. On the way here, I've formulated our next steps."

Tajion did as he was told. He'd learned that to do so in the little things worked wonders when larger matters were afoot.

"Now then," Sirika began. "I've ordered the Baron and his men to redeem last night's failure by finishing the task we gave them. Your cousin may have evaded the Malgosians, but our plans are delayed, not thwarted. We can work towards a different accident to replace the ambush by robbers on the highway."

"Did the Baron say his assassins have found their trail?"

"They have indeed, and it seems the two girls have ridden for the Manniswood. They may have made things easier for us, because the Queen having an accident in the forest will be widely accepted. Now do you see my wisdom in bringing the Baron to stay in secret and hidden at Mannismill instead of away at his castle? We lost no time in ordering the pursuit as soon as we learned the ambush had failed. Already his men are conducting a sweep through the forest."

"When will we hear that they've found them?" Tajion didn't share his mother's blind faith in the skills of the Malgosians, but it suited him at this stage to agree that the capture of the girls was merely a matter of time.

"Maybe not until tonight," Sirika replied. "When I arrived, I informed General Bolas that the Queen and Princess appear to be missing, and he ordered Knights to ride out and search for them. But I didn't tell him where the girls went. We need the Baron's men to keep their head start and find them first."

"What about Rashelin? What will we do, since she was caught up in the ambush?"

"Yes, she brought that on herself by choosing to accompany that girl on her ride home. But it may turn out to our advantage. We can assume neither of them knows the identity of last night's ambushers, or their connection to us, yet. But after this experience she won't dare cross me again."

"You still think she'll give in to you once Katelin is dead?" Tajion couldn't keep the concern from his voice. His hopes rested on his sister proving difficult and refusing to go along with their plans. Then they would force her to renounce her place in the line of succession, and he would become King.

'King Tajion of Anestra': he liked the sound of that. He would let his mother attend to the tiresome business of running the Kingdom, sitting through all those boring meetings, while he signed a few papers and lazed around in his luxury and prestige. She wouldn't be there for ever, of course, but later he would choose a few noble friends to advise and look after everything for him. Yes, it was a good prospect.

Sirika waved a dismissive hand. "I'm sure Rashelin will see the sense of not opposing us. And I've been thinking. While the Queen remains missing, we can take steps of our own. To discuss our developing plans, I'd like the Baron closer at hand. We shall arrange for him to be re-accepted at Court."

Tajion's eyebrows rose in surprise. "So soon? That will take some persuading. The Court's distrust of him is deep-seated."

Sirika shook her head. "Not at all. It is only a matter of the way things are presented. In extreme circumstances such as these, many things can change: opinion, position, fortune and favour."

"What do you have in mind?"

Sirika gave a small smile, seeming to relish her own brilliance. "Since Katelin has fled to the dangerous Manniswood, I think our noble Lord Malgosy—once the deed is done—could be the one who undertakes the sad but necessary task of conveying the Queen's body back to Anestra. He can describe how he fought to save the young lady's life after her tragic accident in the forest. He will earn the sympathy and thanks of all in the Court …"

Tajion allowed his smile to spread into a grin. His mother had her uses. When it came to devising plans for their advantage, she was without equal.

In the early afternoon, Katelin decided to pause in a small glade among the trees. They had nothing to eat for lunch, but needed to exercise their legs after the long morning's ride.

As they drank from their water bottles, she took the opportunity to ask, "Rashelin, if it's true your mother enlisted Baron Malgosy to assassinate me, what are you going to do now? You're her daughter, and next in line for the throne, but you're at risk because you know about her connection to the ambushers."

Rashelin looked away into the trees, and then met Katelin's gaze at last. "Yes. This morning I made a decision. For too long I've tried to be loyal to both sides, to you and my mother. I hoped the two of you might find some way to get along and work together. Or at least avoid fighting each other." She paused, and tried to smile.

Katelin asked, "And after last night?"

"Tajion's mention of the Baron's men, and the Knight calling the ambusher 'Malgosian', changes everything. Mother has declared war on you, and there's no way I could side with her. Her plans are illegal, murderous and evil. I can't keep out of it or remain neutral. I'm in the Royal Family, next in the line of succession, and whatever happens to you affects me deeply. I must be on your side." Her voice broke as she said, "Queen Katelin, my fate will now be the same as yours."

Katelin reached and held her cousin in a tight embrace, the fear and tension trembling through their bodies. This morning, the world had changed for them both.

At length they pulled back and wiped their eyes. They laughed to stop themselves from crying.

"I hope no Anestrans or Malgosians are watching," Katelin said, "or they'll imprison us as silly little girls, never mind anything else." She resumed a serious tone. "But suppose something does happen to me, will you cope with being Queen?"

Rashelin was knotting her hands. "I can't contemplate anything happening to you, Katelin, because of what it would mean. You know how I feel about being next in line for the throne. I don't like to be out in front, leading, speaking, everyone looking at me. I prefer to do my work behind the scenes, talking with people in the Court one to one, or in small groups."

Katelin nodded. "And you do that very well."

Rashelin drew a deep breath. "If anything does happen to you before you have children, then of course I will accept the responsibility of being Queen. But after the events of last night, I think Mother and Tajion will give me an ultimatum. They will insist I keep quiet about what I know, by threatening a fatal accident for me too. Either I go along with their plans, become Queen, and rule as Mother wishes, or else sign a Deed of Abdication, renounce my place in the line of succession, and let Tajion become King."

"Rashelin, I'm sorry. You're in an impossible situation too. I'll try my hardest to stay alive, if only to spare you all of that."

They were silent for a while, until Rashelin said, "I was pleased to hear Mother acknowledge yesterday that you're working hard. You have so much responsibility, and I wish I could help you more. Sometimes it feels as though you're running the whole Kingdom by yourself."

Katelin swallowed. "Does it seem like that? I'm sorry. I guess it's my inexperience, that I don't know who in the Court I can trust yet."

Rashelin's voice was tentative. "Governing a Kingdom involves many tedious chores, meetings and paperwork, that help everything run smoothly. Why not share your load and delegate some tasks? You can trust me. I'll help you, and the courtiers will too if you'll let them."

"I trust you of course, Rashelin, but I don't know the nobles and ministers as well as you do. I hope I don't view them as enemies anymore, to battle and defeat all the time, like Sirika said. But I still wonder about some of them, whether they're more concerned with their own position and influence than the good of all the people."

"That discernment will grow with knowing them better over time," Rashelin replied. "You might even discover you like them. But in the meantime, we have work to do and a Kingdom to run."

Katelin nodded. Her cousin had so much valuable wisdom and experience she could draw on, especially in dealing with everyone in the Anestran Court.

"I've been meaning to ask you," Rashelin went on, "why won't you make more use of the Crown? It's your sacred relic, and such an ancient and precious heirloom of the Kingdom. Through it you have access to all the Divine's wisdom and guidance, her glory and power, to help you rule our people. And yet you seem reluctant to wear it."

Katelin sighed. It was true. She'd always hesitated when it came even to touching the sacred Crown of Anestra. "It's hard to explain. It's as though each time I touch it, and Divine glory shines forth, it confirms that the responsibility of ruling the Kingdom is all up to me, and there's no escape. It makes me feel trapped and on my own. I still feel too young to accept all of that yet."

Rashelin leaned forward and touched her arm. "The Crown is a blessing, Katelin, not a curse, and is meant to help you. Please don't struggle on, trying to do everything in your own strength. Accept the Divine's wisdom and power for your reign. You don't want it to appear as though in rejecting her Crown you are rejecting the Divine herself."

"No, it's not like that at all," Katelin protested. "Or at least, I don't think it is."

Rashelin smiled. "Anyway, here we are in the forest, and you said we should find Zane. But isn't he the first person they'll look for? If the Malgosians follow us into the Manniswood, they'll head straight for his old outlaw camps."

"Yes, I know. So we need to warn him, as well as enlisting his men as our bodyguards. We might have only a few hours' head start on our pursuers, so Zane needs to know that Malgosians, and then Anestrans, will come looking for him."

"He won't like that. He's been a free man for only a few months since you pardoned him, and now he'll be a fugitive again."

Katelin sighed. "I cause trouble for everyone around me, don't I? First you and now him. Well, he needs to know what's happening, and we can only survive for so long on our own out here."

"All right. Do you know where he is?"

Katelin shrugged. "Not exactly. We'll check the various places in turn where he used to camp as an outlaw. When we last met, he spoke about venturing deeper into the forest this time, so he may be quite some distance."

Rashelin was staring at her. "Deeper into the forest? But Katelin, the Manniswood is vast. Some say it goes on forever, right to the edge of the world. Or at least to the Far Oceans, wherever they are. How far away are we planning to go?"

Katelin chewed her lip. "I don't know. We'll try to find Zane and his companions, and in the meantime, I'll work on a plan to find the Anestran soldiers before the Malgosians catch us."

"But how shall we find our way? We both know the paths at this end of the forest, but the deeper we go, the more lost we'll become."

Katelin smiled. "Zane had a good answer for that one. He said not to look at the trees."

"Not look at the trees?" Rashelin threw up her hands in joking disbelief. "Oh yes, we're in the middle of a forest. Don't look at the trees. Of course."

Katelin laughed. "I think what he means, or the way he tried to explain it, is to look beyond them. If we glimpse the mountains of the Eastern Range, then they're to our north. Find the direction of the sun at different times of day. Watch the lie of the land and the flow of the streams as they run down to the Mannis River valley in the south. That sort of thing."

"Oh, I get it." Rashelin's teasing tone remained. "Don't look at the trees, but beyond them. It's not as though all the trees look the same, is it? There are different species, shapes and sizes, but we don't need to notice those at all. Let's ignore these non-identical trees and study the lie of the land instead."

Katelin couldn't help but chuckle. "Okay, you navigate by remembering every single tree in the forest if you like, and I'll use Zane's method."

But her joking stopped when a chilling thought occurred. "Baron Malgosy's castle is deep in the Manniswood, isn't it? But south of the river. Zane will know to stay on this side of the Mannis. It still feels like we're heading towards danger, though."

Rashelin's nod was sober. "We didn't have anywhere other than this forest where we could hide." They fell silent after that.

It was time to be moving. As Katelin mounted, she found she was saddle-sore. She'd become soft. This last year as Queen had robbed her of riding time, and her muscles were no longer used to a full day's ride. She wondered if she might get the chance to rectify that now.

They both pulled up the hoods of their cloaks again, to hide their hair. It was as they began to move off that they heard the tell-tale crack of a branch behind them.

## 4

## SEARCHERS

They stared at each other in alarm.

"Go," Katelin urged.

They spurred their horses through the trees before them. Katelin was torn between stealth and speed. Had they been noticed?

She couldn't tell. She guided Novita along a narrow path between the trunks, and held her breath at the thud of each hoof-fall and as the leaves brushed against her.

But on her left Rashelin's mare, Whisper, was forcing her way through undergrowth too thick for her. Katelin winced at each thrash and crack, and hoped the pursuers' own noise might mask it. For the sounds were of several horses or people moving through the forest behind them.

Rashelin made it through onto a clearer track and Katelin breathed more easily again.

Then came a shout.

It was answered by other calls to their left and right. Some were closer, some farther away.

Their dilemma was resolved, and Katelin and Rashelin spurred their mounts into a gallop. Novita was strong, sure-footed and fast, and leapt away through the trees. But Whisper was less experienced in the forest, and hesitated too much in the confined spaces. She was in danger of falling behind. And being caught.

All secrecy gone, the pursuers were crashing through the trees on all sides. Katelin tried to weave an erratic path to confuse those behind, but this slowed her down. She could only think of one way to avoid them both being caught.

She swerved closer to Rashelin and hissed one word as they flew between the trunks.

"Separate."

Rashelin stared at her, but then pulled Whisper to the left. Katelin veered back towards the right, and their tracks diverged. The sounds of Rashelin's progress receded into the distance.

Katelin gulped with fear, as much for Rashelin as for herself. Had she consigned her cousin to capture? She tried to shake off the guilt of selfishness, but couldn't. She rationalised it: Rashelin would want to save her Queen before herself. But a wretched sickness churned inside her about the order she'd just given.

For a minute her conscience cleared. Their separate paths caused confusion among the pursuers. There were shouted questions, orders called and answered, and the pursuit stopped, or at least paused. They couldn't know who to follow as a priority.

Katelin took advantage of the brief reprieve, and prayed that Rashelin would do the same. She spurred Novita to a new burst of speed, and the stallion appeared to relish the challenge. He almost seemed to be playing a game with himself: the straightest path, the fastest route and the closest to each passing trunk. As a result, twigs and leaves whipped at Katelin, stinging her face, arms and legs. The lower branches made her throw herself onto Novita's neck, burying her face in his mane. She abandoned all attempt to steer him by rein, trusting to his direction and step.

The ground began to slope downwards, and Katelin recognised it. They were approaching a deep gully that she and Novita had jumped before. Their track came to a ledge, with a firm landing place opposite. She urged Novita onwards, hoping he remembered it too.

She needn't have worried. Novita was showing off. He galloped to the ledge and made a perfect launch into the air. Deep below them the stream gushed down its channel to join the River Mannis. They landed easily and shot forwards into the trees on the other side. Katelin couldn't help but grin and slap his neck with pride.

Behind her, the pursuing horses whinnied and reared as they reached the brink. They quailed, snorted, stamped, were whipped and shouted at, but with every second Katelin was making her escape.

She galloped on, but knew her pursuers would soon cross the stream further up and then quickly find her trail. How long could she keep this up, staying a short distance ahead of them? She needed to shake them off for good, to throw them off their pursuit. How could she do that?

A terror surged upwards as she remembered what they'd discussed earlier. These pursuers had orders not just to catch her, but to kill her. If they overtook her, they would delight to arrange a 'fatal accident' for her, and then carry her bloodied and mangled body back to Anestra. It wasn't merely her freedom at stake, but her very life, and with it the whole future course of the Old Kingdom.

She dug her heels into the stallion's flanks. Fly, Novita, fly. I need you to save me.

But speed and skill alone might not be enough. She felt a sinking in the pit of her stomach at the thought of trying to hide and hoping they'd pass her. Could that work? But what about Novita? There was no way to hide a horse.

She formulated a rapid plan. Acting on an instinct she couldn't have explained, she leaned forward and whispered her intentions to Novita, as though he could understand her. Then she selected an approaching tree and guided him underneath it.

She loosened her boots in the stirrups and rose from the saddle. As a low branch passed close above, she dropped the reins, caught hold, and swung herself up.

Novita hesitated. He slowed, turned his head, but then pressed on. Now he could play his game of racing through the forest without the burden of a rider. Maybe he'd understood what Katelin had told him. He disappeared out of sight, and Katelin hoped that instead of coming to an early halt, he'd have the sense to continue his flight from the pursuing riders. The longer the Malgosians thought Novita's saddle was occupied, the longer she'd have to elude them.

With all speed, Katelin scrambled upwards. She'd chosen well. It was an ancient elm, in full leaf, with sturdy branches. She climbed as high as she dared, and tried to find a secure, comfortable, hidden perch. But she wasn't as well concealed as she'd hoped. Looking down, she could still see the ground, which meant that anyone looking up could see her.

She froze, holding her breath. They were coming.

Hooves thudded on the forest floor. Two horses thundered past beneath her, trying to keep pace with the fleeing Novita. Others came past, some trotting, some walking. They were all following her trail, but she couldn't see them clearly until a man on a charcoal grey horse rode under her elm tree, and stopped.

He wore the dark green and grey of Malgosy, an excellent camouflage among the shadowed trees. He had close-cropped hair, bare on top. His face was hidden, turned to the ground, scanning for traces and tracks. Badges on the man's shoulders, of crossed grey daggers on green, confirmed for Katelin his allegiance.

All they'd heard, and what Rashelin had told her, was true: Malgosian assassins.

She held her breath. Could he tell that Novita's hoof-prints were lighter without a rider? Could he see where the stallion hesitated, slowing before continuing? Katelin thanked the Divine she hadn't left any boot-print between horse and tree. The man dismounted and studied the leaf-strewn ground.

An ache in her chest forced her to breathe. She let out, and drew in, the shallowest of air through an open mouth.

An ant crawled onto her finger. The tickle of its legs was excruciating, but she dared not move. With her attention fixed below, she hadn't registered the ant highway that ran along the branch beneath her left arm. She held still. The ant was no danger compared to the Malgosian.

The man on the ground motioned silently to another. Katelin couldn't make out the signal, but willed and pleaded for his ugly bald pate to go. A second Malgosian appeared and examined the tracks.

The ant crossed the back of her hand, her wrist, and onto her forearm, manoeuvring through its own forest of hairs. It was a big one. A biting one. What were such ants doing up here in the tree top, so far from the ground?

Katelin was transfixed, her muscles tensed, as the ant raised its proboscis and plunged it into her arm. It took all her self-control and willpower not to flinch, cry or move. She gritted her teeth, steeling herself against the pain of the bite. A second ant approached her fingers.

The Malgosians raised their heads. But they were looking around and ahead, not up. They re-mounted their horses and began to move, following Novita's tracks away.

Katelin flicked her fingers, and the second ant stopped. The first had sucked blood and was preparing for a further incision. What were these ants doing? They were helping themselves to a dinner of Queen. In the circumstances, she hoped the Divine would forgive her. She reached across and smashed the beast into a bloody mess on her forearm.

The tree creaked. Her shift of movement transmitted into a groan of protest from the elm. Katelin froze again, breathing harder now than she'd have liked.

The sounds of the Malgosians receded, but she couldn't be sure they'd all gone.

She waited. The seconds became minutes and she began to relax.

She felt no qualms now about brushing away the approaching ants. She shifted her body, to ease the cramps and numbness.

She listened hard. There was nothing: only a breeze through the leaves and an occasional bird. The minutes mounted, and she decided to stay in the tree. In the daylight it was safer to stay up here than to risk stumbling into one of her pursuers.

She flicked the entrails of the ant from her left arm, and gazed at the blood there.

A few months ago, she'd learnt something about the blood that flowed around her body. She'd always known she had royal blood, and that the Royal Family of Anestra had been chosen long ago by their White Goddess, the Divine, to rule their city and Kingdom.

But now she knew a secret. The Divine hadn't merely chosen her ancestors, but had given birth to them. It was many generations past, but Katelin now knew herself to be a direct blood descendent of the Divine. It was knowledge that still bewildered her: that the blood of the White Goddess flowed within her.

And an ant had bitten her. Was she wrong to begrudge an insect a taste of Divine blood? Katelin sighed. It had hurt, and she couldn't be found or caught, and now the ant was dead, so that was that.

The minutes turned to hours, and the sunlight slanted lower through the forest's branches. The snuffling and rustling of animals on the forest floor confirmed that no people were near. Katelin wondered about Rashelin, and Novita. Had they escaped, or been caught? There was no way for her to know.

She couldn't trust herself to sleep in the tree, for fear of falling out. So as dusk fell she eased herself gingerly down from the elm. She looked about, and it felt good to be on the ground again. She stretched and flexed her aching muscles. Before it became completely dark, she wrapped herself in her cloak and found the deepest of thickets. Soon it made no difference whether her eyes were open or closed, for she could see nothing in front of her face. But as she curled up in the undergrowth, waiting for sleep, the noises and calls of the forest night grew about her.

Rashelin reined in her mare. It was no use. She was cornered in a hollow with deep undergrowth, and Whisper had baulked at the steep bank to escape it.

She turned to face her pursuers. She'd led them on a wild chase through the forest, giving time enough, she hoped, for Katelin to make her escape, but there was no way to be sure. What would her fate be now? Could she trust her mother to have ordered these assassins to spare her life?

There had been plenty of thundering hooves and crashing through branches and undergrowth, but she'd seen no more than glimpses of those chasing her. The dark green and grey uniforms, though, told her these were the Baron's men. No blue and silver of Anestra. She was in Malgosian hands, but determined to face them down.

A tall man rode into view from between the trees. He had a narrow face and sandy hair, with eyes of cold, grey steel.

Rashelin lowered her hood to reveal her long blonde hair, and the Malgosian cursed.

"It's the blonde one, you fools," he shouted. "Three of you stay with me, and the rest of you get after the other, the dark-haired one."

Rashelin heard the trampling of horses turning and riding off, before three other horsemen appeared, encircling her. She studied the man before her, her eyes catching the emblem of crossed grey daggers on his shoulders. There could be no mistake: the mark of Baron Malgosy's assassins.

She glared at him with anger and defiance. "What do you mean by this?"

"Oh, do forgive me, your Royal Highness," the Malgosian said with a mocking sneer. "We're here to drag your pampered backside to Anestra city."

"How dare you speak to me like that? You know who I am, then, and what trouble awaits you back in the city." Too late Rashelin realised she had few meaningful threats to use against them.

"Oh, yes, and what trouble would that be?" The Malgosian chuckled, and his companions grinned. "Going to report us to your mother? When it's her orders we're following?"

Rashelin noticed he'd confirmed his connection to Lady Sirika. She had one last try, tossing back her hair. "As Princess of Anestra, I order you to let me go my way. To hinder or restrain my passage within our borders breaks the laws of the Old Kingdom."

The Malgosian held up a finger. "Ah, but your stinking laws don't apply to us, do they? Since your pathetic Court saw fit to banish our kindly master, we humble servants of the Baron are outside of your control. So you will come with us."

"No," Rashelin declared. "I won't."

The Malgosian's eyebrows rose. "We have orders to use force if you won't comply." He examined his fingernails. "There was no mention of bringing you back unhurt, so the boys here will enjoy it if you choose to resist."

A thrill of fear shuddered through Rashelin's body at the thought of their hands all over her. She couldn't fight them off, so she needed to think of other ways to defy them. Her skills weren't with a bow or dagger, as Katelin's were, but she could still muster her courage and strength in the Queen's cause.

Go, Katelin, go. You must evade capture by these men.

She didn't trust herself to speak in case her voice betrayed her trembling. Without meeting the Malgosian's eye, she urged Whisper forward and rode out of the thicket. Her captors followed, one on either side, and two behind.

Rashelin took her time as they picked their way through the forest and out into the open. She reasoned that the longer it took for these four Malgosians to escort her back to Anestra, the later they would return to the Manniswood to search for Katelin. Allowing the Queen to hide and escape was paramount.

It was a long afternoon's ride back across the fields to Anestra, the only encouragement being that the Malgosians didn't appear to have captured Katelin yet.

As she rode, Rashelin tried to think. The Malgosian had confirmed he was acting under her mother's orders. But they hadn't been after her, only 'the dark-haired one'. And she was to be escorted back to Anestra city. Last night's order to the Baron's men had been to kill Katelin and the Knights, but not to harm her. Once she was back in Anestra Castle, perhaps she still had some place in her mother's plans. She could try to use that.

Whether or not her mother had travelled from Mannismill to Anestra by now, she'd soon need to face her. Rashelin might know more than her mother expected: that the ambushers were these very Malgosians, and that the assassination attempt had been ordered by Sirika. But did it make any difference what Rashelin knew, without any proof of it to present to the Court?

Yes, it made the difference that Rashelin knew whose side she needed to be on. Any residual loyalty or affection for her mother had been squashed, in view of these malicious, evil orders. The Princess was on Katelin's side.

How could she help Katelin now? If the Queen was alive and free in the forest, Rashelin could do little to affect that situation. Katelin was the one with the skills of escaping, riding, hiding and fighting, anyway.

What were her own skills? Did they lie with the Court? She was still a Princess of Anestra, and could command their attention because of it. Yes, that must be it: to oppose her mother and maintain loyalty to Katelin inside the Castle and Court.

But she felt terribly alone. Was there anyone she could trust as an ally? The nobles and courtiers were too preoccupied with their own positions to stick their necks out for Katelin, especially if she were absent or out of favour. Rashelin felt sick at the thought of how quickly support for the young Queen might vanish once her wily old mother declared Katelin unfit to rule. Could she dare to contradict her mother in public, and make the case to the Court that the Divine had not abandoned the Queen?

The Divine. That was it. The clerics. The clerics of the Divine were led by Under-Father Ruis, who was sufficiently loyal and detached to see Rashelin's side and help her. She would arrange to see the Under-Father on her return.

It was evening when Rashelin and her escort arrived back at the South Gate to Anestra city. She was exhausted, needing nothing more than to collapse into bed. She hadn't slept the night before, and had spent all night and all today in the saddle.

But she was alert at once when she saw the city guards gathering at the Gate, torches in their hands. She rode up, and the guards stared at her and her companions, a few of them drawing weapons.

"Halt," the sergeant commanded, and they did so.

Was this her chance to escape her captors? Yes, she could deliver herself into the hands of loyal Anestran soldiers. But how would the guards react to these Malgosians? She decided to keep quiet for the moment. Despite her capture and night-time flight from assassins, she would return to the Castle as a Princess and face her mother with dignity.

"Let us pass," the sandy-haired leader of the Malgosians said.

The sergeant blocked their way. "You wear the badge and colours of the Baron Malgosy. Is it him you serve?"

"You are correct that the noble Baron is our lord, so get out of our way."

The sergeant stiffened, and his men lined up alongside and behind him. "Then you know that your 'noble lord' is banished from this city. You, as his followers, are also not welcome. Be gone."

"You fool. The unjust sentence of banishment applies

only to the Baron, and not to his men. You should check your facts before obstructing law-abiding citizens of Anestra." He said this last with a sneering tone that turned Rashelin's stomach.

The sergeant's eyes flicked to Rashelin and back to the Malgosian leader. "You have the Princess Rashelin in your midst. Why do you, of all people, escort her here?"

"We are ordered by her mother to conduct the Princess back to Anestra Castle. Unless you wish to incur Lady Sirika's displeasure, you will clear out of our path."

Some guards exchanged glances, but the sergeant was resolute. "I will not take a single instruction from you, Malgosian. However, whatever the Princess Rashelin commands, that I will perform." He marched between the horses to stand beside Rashelin's mare. "Your Highness, do you require our assistance? What is your command?"

Rashelin drew a deep breath, aware how muddy, sweaty and dishevelled she must look. The tiredness weighed heavily on her as she broke her silence. Did she have the energy for one last note of defiance? Yes, of course she did.

She raised her voice so all could hear. "Thank you for your concern for my welfare, Sergeant. Yes, I require your assistance. These Malgosian thugs apprehended me on a ride in the Manniswood. They threatened me with violence, and I order you to arrest them."

As she spoke, she urged Whisper forward, away from the Malgosians and towards the Anestran guards. There was a scuffle behind her, a ring of swords, and the Anestrans surged forwards. She looked back in time to see the four Malgosians turning their horses and trying to ride away before the city guards could stop them.

"After them," the sergeant shouted, and in moments mounted city guards galloped past after the cursing, sandy-haired Malgosian and his men.

Rashelin sighed and turned to the sergeant. "Thank you for your help. I'm exhausted, and would appreciate an escort to the Castle."

"My pleasure, milady. No Malgosian tells me what to do at my own gate. I don't believe a word of his threats concerning the Lady Sirika." The sergeant stepped aside, and motioned to four guards to accompany the Princess.

No doubt her mother might try to get the Malgosians admitted to the city, but Rashelin would try to prevent that. And for now, she'd made her point.

She couldn't ask Whisper for more than a walking pace up King's Avenue. The city guards escorted her past Princes' Park and into Crown Square, where heads turned to watch the dishevelled Princess ride by. At the Castle gates, Rashelin wanted only to go to her room and sleep. She dismounted in the courtyard, gave Whisper a grateful pat, and handed the reins to a stable boy.

Without looking back, she entered the Keep and mustered her remaining energy to climb the stairs. She kept her eyes down, and continued past anyone who greeted or tried to talk to her. In a weary blur she closed the bedroom door behind her and collapsed, fully clothed, onto her bed, until exhaustion gave way to sleep.

*5*

## WANDERERS

Katelin jerked awake at sounds nearby. The moon must have risen, for she could see the outlines of trees around her. To her ears came the crack of breaking twigs and stems, of movement through the forest with the thud of heavy footfalls.

Her heart pounded. Malgosians? A chill washed over her skin, but it didn't sound like men.

It was much worse: a loud snuffling followed by an unmistakeable sniff. A large animal that had caught her scent?

Katelin forced herself to keep still, desperate to remain silent in the undergrowth, straining her eyes. In the moonlight filtering down through the canopy above, a huge, dark shape was moving towards her thicket.

From its size and outline, it could only be a bear.

Katelin let out a slow breath. So, this was it. The bear had smelled her. It would maul and kill her. She would end her days here, in awful pain, a mess of blood and flesh, and her bones might be found in some far distant future.

If she reached for her dagger, would it make any difference? Could she hurt it, kill it, fend it off? She inched her left hand towards the hilt.

She knew she must not meet the bear's gaze, for fear of antagonising it, but what difference would that make now? It might make her end swifter.

She felt its breath. Katelin turned her head, and looked straight into the creature's eyes as it lowered its muzzle towards her. It bared its teeth, emitting a low growl, drooling saliva to the ground. Its muscles rippled under the fur of its neck and shoulders.

It gave a definite sniff. Its head turned towards Katelin's bare left arm, where the ant bite had left dried blood. Of course. She'd been foolish not to clean it, for the bear had smelled her blood.

Her fingers closed around the dagger hilt.

The bear looked back at her, leaned forward and trapped her arm under its paw. Her arm that held the dagger. It closed its jaws, licking its muzzle with a long tongue. If she hadn't known better, Katelin would have guessed it was thinking.

What was it waiting for? Couldn't her death be swift and painless, instead of this agony of delayed dismemberment?

It licked her arm.

Katelin stared at it. Rather than biting, it was licking her wound clean. With its rough, wet tongue, it tasted every last drop of dried Divine blood.

Her whole body shook with fear. If the bear hadn't trapped her arm, she'd have leapt up and fled. Now it had tasted her blood, it wouldn't be able to resist tearing her to pieces with those sharp claws and powerful jaws, slashing her flesh to drink every last drop of her life.

The bear looked at her again, and then bowed its head.

To Katelin's astonishment, it released her arm, backed away, turned aside, and lumbered off among the trees.

Katelin clenched her teeth to keep from crying out. Relief and incomprehension flooded her, her heart hammering, her breath coming in shuddering gasps.

How had she survived? Katelin couldn't fathom it. Could the bear possibly have recognised her Divine blood? And then spared her life out of respect for the White Goddess, its creator?

But the experience of seeing her life so endangered and then spared shook her to the core. She was too fragile, too easy to kill. What was the answer to that? To live every minute to the full, as though her last?

She curled into a ball, locking her limbs into a tight

huddle to quell the shaking, and tried to deepen and slow her breathing. But she couldn't stop the tears from coming.

She told herself she needed to sleep, to rest. If every minute now was to be a fight to survive, then she needed to be alert, at her best.

She must have slept again at last, but fitfully. The night wasn't cold, but she couldn't get comfortable or calm. She'd woken in the darkness several more times with the feeling of an insect in her hair, or an imagined tramp of boots on the edge of hearing.

At first light she ventured from her thicket of undergrowth, her cloak damp with dew. The breaking of the day revealed a thick mist curling between the tree trunks. Katelin didn't like it. Although it concealed her, it also hid her pursuers. She wanted to be able to see, to know what was coming.

What should she do? Where should she go? She stood among the trees, feeling small and alone in the vast quietness of the forest. The trunks seemed to stretch in all directions, further than she could imagine. Could she be any more lost or insignificant?

How many times had she brushed with imminent death since Mannismill? Three? She couldn't keep on living like this. Something needed to change, but she couldn't think what.

Part of her wanted to run away. To keep going, hiding and running, away from the troubles of the throne of Anestra and the pursuing Malgosians, to find a new, safer, unknown life. Was that the answer? To find an easier life, where no one would be chasing her, no murderer intent on killing her? Let someone else rule the Kingdom, she didn't care who.

Tears stung her eyes again, as she leaned against a trunk. That was the problem. She *did* care. She loved Anestra city and its people. To think they might be misruled or oppressed made her rage inside.

She straightened up and shook herself. It was no good to feel lost or despairing. She needed to find someone – Rashelin, or Zane, or at least Novita. But which way?

She wouldn't follow the direction of the Malgosians, who'd been sweeping through the forest eastwards. She would head north, keeping the growing light of day on her right, and climb the gradual slope from the river towards the mountains. That was the way Rashelin had gone, and it would leave Malgosy Castle, south of the river, far behind her.

She set off, but her stomach grumbled in protest. She'd had nothing to eat since the dinner at Mannismill two nights ago. Could she trust her knowledge of berries to know which were edible?

Soon she heard a trickle of water, and made a diversion to slake her thirst at a tiny rivulet. At least her insides now had something to fill them, but it was still too early in the year for most berries.

She washed her face and arms, and then walked on. The upward slope left her puffed out and sweating. She'd become unfit since becoming Queen. Must do something about that, she determined. She paused frequently to catch her breath and listen, but the forest seemed undisturbed by any human sounds.

The morning wore on and the mist cleared. At last she came to a path, running east–west. She debated, but decided to follow it, away from Anestra. Rashelin might have found it and ridden along it. And the further she went, the more she began to think she recognised it. Was this a path that led to one of Zane's old camps?

She trod as lightly as she could, always straining her ears for movement in front or behind, and always checking which way she would run if she needed to.

She rounded a bend and came to an abrupt halt. A man with curly blond hair sat cross-legged beside the path munching on a loaf of bread. Katelin saw him first, but was too startled to react before he looked up.

He grinned, his blue eyes sparkling. "Morning."

A surge of recognition overwhelmed her, for he was one of Zane's band of former outlaws. Katelin ran up to him and grabbed his arm. "Rish!"

"Hey, hey," Rish said. "What's the matter? Calm yourself." He eased her grip from his arm. "What is it, Kat?"

Again, she tried to pull him up. "Come on, Rish, we need to go. It isn't safe. We need to get to Zane."

"Okay." Rish stood. He bent to pick up his bag, but Katelin had already seized his loaf and water bottle and was starting off along the path.

"Wait, Kat," he said. "Can't you tell me what's going on?"

"Hush," Katelin hissed. "Keep your voice down. I'll tell you as we go."

Rish shrugged and then ambled after her. She kept pulling ahead, her pace urgent, while his was more of a wander.

"Keep up," she said. "We're in danger."

"Danger?" Rish frowned and stopped. "Hold on, what do you mean? From who?"

Katelin turned back to him. "Listen, I escaped an assassination attempt on the road from Mannismill back to the city. My Aunt Sirika sent Malgosians to kill me. I only just evaded a search party of the Baron's men yesterday, so we need to get to Zane. I'm sorry to bring my troubles to his men, but I need some armed protection. I can't be on my own out here because everyone in Malgosy Castle is after me, until some searching Anestrans can find me. Got it?"

Rish's mouth dropped open and his eyes widened. Katelin could almost see his mind working as he gave a slow nod. "Right," he said. "Let's get moving then."

Katelin was thankful to find that his pace along the path improved, although it was too slow for her liking. But that was not her only concern. "I'm starving," she said. "May I have some of your loaf?"

"Finish it, if you like."

Katelin tore off a chunk and chewed gratefully. A thought occurred. "Were you heading east or west?"

"East. I'm on my way from Anestra back to camp."

At least she wasn't dragging him back the way he'd come, or out of his way. "Did you have some business in Anestra?"

"Buying supplies. The forest meets most of our needs, but some things it's easier to buy in the city. Some of our group like carving wood and crafting things, so we trade them in Anestra for leather and rope. We take hunted meat to swap for other foodstuffs: salt, sugar, things like that."

Katelin nodded, reminded that she had things easy in the Castle: she could take for granted so much that others needed to work or trade for. "So, where's your horse? Why are you walking, not riding?"

Rish gave her a look. "Riding gets there too quickly."

Despite her situation, Katelin smiled. She'd forgotten the different view on life of these former outlaws. "You'd rather spend a week walking to Anestra and back than a couple of days by horse?"

"Yes." Rish was definite. He spread his arms wide. "What's the hurry?"

Katelin struggled to answer this, and Rish continued: "You city folk are always rushing about. You seem to think you need to do twenty things every day, like the world's ending tomorrow. As a result, you don't do any of them well, and you don't enjoy any of it."

Katelin spluttered. "But … but the more we get done each day, the more we'll accomplish in the end. We only have a limited number of days to live, you know."

Rish chuckled. "Listen to yourself. Are you really making the most of life, or simply rushing through it? Do you get the chance to enjoy each day, and what you do in it, or are you only thinking about all you haven't done, and what's on for tomorrow? I reckon you never have your mind on today and enjoying each moment because you're too busy with yesterday, or next week, or five years' time. None of us know how long we have, and from what you've said, you least of all."

Katelin sighed. He had a point. But she didn't dare slow her pace and grabbed his arm to make him match hers.

"Look at this forest," Rish said. "It's the greatest forest in the world, vast, bountiful, magnificent. I bet you look at it as no more than somewhere to hide in, or run through, or find someone in. No thought of appreciating the diversity, the richness, the beauty—"

"All right, all right," Katelin interrupted him. "One day—when I'm not being chased for my life—I'll stop and smell the air, and stroke each trunk, and touch each leaf if you want me to. But today we need to hurry."

Rish nodded and then smiled. "When the need arises, we can hurry just as well as you city folk."

Katelin thought of something else. "I've always described your group as outlaws, but since I pardoned you, that's not the right word any more, is it? What do you call yourselves?"

Rish laughed. "Yes, we talked about that too. The best we could come up with was 'wanderers'."

She nodded. "Wanderers you are, and wanderers I shall always call you."

As they chatted, he told her of the trades he'd made in Anestra, and the different places where their band had moved. It was refreshing not to talk about thrones or kingdoms, or Malgosians or murder. But she made sure they spoke in low voices.

By mid-afternoon, Rish had led her at a good pace along forest tracks towards their current camp. She had begun to feel calmer under his guidance, but Katelin now began to feel twinges of nervousness. She recognised that it was the prospect of seeing Zane again, and hated her own reaction. She hadn't seen him for a few weeks, and had thought about him far too much in the meantime. She shouldn't dream or fantasise about this man, who might view her as no more than a friend.

"Look who's here," Rish announced to the assembled company, as they entered a large clearing.

About thirty men and women were scattered across the camp, working alone or in groups. The other half of the band were probably away gathering or hunting. Katelin was always struck by the poverty of their clothing, but knew these to be good and honest people.

Her heart stuttered. Zane was here. He was strolling across from one side of the clearing, a broad grin upon his ruggedly handsome face. His dark, wavy hair was brushed back, and a few days' stubble shadowed his jaw.

"Hey," he answered Rish's announcement. "A royal visit. We're honoured." He bowed low.

Katelin smiled at him. She never knew what to expect from Zane, but he always managed to avoid being the romantic hero of her dreams. No running to embrace her or lifting her off her feet. Katelin berated herself for ever having such thoughts, because it always led to disappointment.

Instead, Zane tended to joke. Katelin laughed with him to keep her feet on the ground, and to avoid pomposity and self-importance. But sometimes she needed him to respect the seriousness of her role as Queen.

This afternoon she forced herself to continue his joke. "Yes, I decided I'd better check whether my pardoned outlaws are behaving themselves. We can't have naughty subjects roaming the forests of the Kingdom, can we?"

"Ah, my Queen," Zane replied. "That depends on what sort of naughty behaviour you're looking for." With that, he leapt forward, swept her up into his arms, and swung her around in the air, her legs flying.

Katelin clung to him, gasping, squeezing his shoulders. By the time he'd landed her back on her feet and planted a bristly kiss on her cheek, she'd forgiven him any imagined hurt or disappointment. His unpredictability was exactly why she liked him.

She found herself laughing. "Yes, that sort of naughtiness will be fine."

Zane was regarding her steadily. His hand felt heavy and warm on her shoulder. She thought she saw a sparkle in his dark brown eyes that made her blush. What did this welcome mean, then? More than a friend?

"It's great to see you again, Kat," he said. "As always, we are at your service."

She looked away from the intensity of his eyes, took his arm and led him to one side of the forest clearing. "Thank you, Zane," she breathed. "I'm glad to be here, and it's good that you offer your service." She fixed her gaze on him. "I need the protection of you and your men as my bodyguards. And you need to move camp. Now."

Zane hadn't caught her seriousness. "Well, of course, we're all more than happy to obey royal commands, but first may we know why we're required to do so?"

"Because soon there will be pursuers coming looking for me. And you."

Zane sighed. "Have you run away again, milady?"

"Yes. But with good reason this time. My aunt is trying to kill me."

Zane smile vanished. "You're joking, aren't you? I know you've never got on with your Aunt Sirika, but she wouldn't harm you. And no Anestran soldiers would think of injuring you."

Katelin looked down at her hands, and realised she'd been twisting her fingers. She'd tried to keep her explanation brief to prevent the seriousness of it sinking in. But it was no good. The mortal danger threatened to overwhelm her again.

She drew a deep breath and tried to keep her voice level. "Aunt Sirika has decided to remove me as Queen. She considers me unfit to rule and says the disasters of invasion and plague show the Divine has abandoned me. She arranged to assassinate me and for Rashelin to ascend the throne instead."

Zane was staring at her. "But … how do you know all this? Are you sure?"

"Yes, I'm sure." Katelin sniffed. "Rashelin and I were riding home from Mannismill to Anestra two nights ago when the Knights guarding us were attacked. We escaped the ambush and rode here to the forest, but got separated. You haven't seen her, have you?"

Zane shook his head. "So, you've fled into the forest for your safety. But when Anestran soldiers find you, they'll follow your orders rather than Sirika's."

Katelin held Zane's gaze. "It's not Anestran soldiers that concern me, because yes, they're loyal to their Queen. Sirika has enlisted the help of Baron Malgosy."

Zane's eyes widened. He thumped his fist into his other hand. His voice became low, as though afraid of alarming any within earshot. "The Malgosians have always stayed south of the river, while we keep to the north of it. Are you saying that's no longer the case?"

Katelin also made her voice conspiratorial. "Yesterday afternoon I climbed a tree to escape a Malgosian search party. On this side of the river."

Zane's nod was slow. "I've had no reports of anyone seeing them, but that doesn't mean much. The Malgosians are experts at keeping themselves hidden."

"With a band the size of yours, they'd think twice about confronting you. I wouldn't expect them to show themselves until they were sure of winning a fight."

"Which means they may have done no more than keep an eye on us, track our movements, that sort of thing. It's harder for us to conceal a whole camp than it is for them to follow and watch us."

Katelin found herself scanning the trees around the

clearing, half expecting to see a Malgosian spy among the leaves or behind a trunk. "It won't take them long to guess I'm with you, and once they gather themselves together into a small army …"

"… we'd better not be caught in the open forest," Zane finished for her. "We need somewhere more defensible, where we can't be surrounded. And with a means of escape for you, if necessary." He straightened his back. "Ryebald's Cleft."

Katelin nodded. "Zane, I'm sorry to have brought this on you and your people."

Zane forced a smile. "We'll talk about it later. But you know we'll do what we can for you." He swung an arm across her shoulders, and she welcomed the chance to lean into him. "Before we do anything else, let's get you something to eat."

He led her across the clearing to where some logs circled a campfire, and then went to order the packing up and moving of the camp. Katelin sat, and a large woman with ruddy cheeks handed her a bowl of thick vegetable soup and a wooden spoon. The soup was good, she decided. While she was eating, Katelin recognised a small, dark-haired man named Arch coming across the clearing. And he was leading Novita.

Katelin almost dropped her bowl, but set it down before she jumped up. She jogged across and embraced her stallion around the neck. Novita tossed his head.

Zane came across to meet them. "Thanks, Arch."

"Found him wandering in the forest, Kat," said Arch. "Thought we recognised him as yours."

Katelin nodded and smiled at him. "Yes, thank you. When I get the chance, I'll explain what I'm doing here and how I became separated from my horse."

"Another thing, Zane," Arch said. "The horses are nervous today, jumpy and restless. And yesterday too. They've been pulling up their tethers for no obvious reason."

"That happened to us yesterday morning too," Katelin said, "as we entered the forest. The horses bolted all of a sudden. What is it?"

Arch scratched his chin. "Well, a couple of the girls said they felt a trembling of the ground, like when horses gallop past. A sort of … shaking of the forest floor. Horses can be more sensitive to that kind of thing, so maybe that's it."

Zane shrugged. "Not much we can do about that then, but thanks. We'll try to keep them calm."

Katelin was stroking Novita's flank, and she patted his side before Arch led him away to where they'd picketed their horses. She returned to finish her soup, as around her Zane's band of wanderers prepared to break camp.

Rashelin was woken by a servant girl bringing in breakfast on a tray. The sun was shining through the curtains, so she'd overslept.

"Oh, you didn't need to do that. I'd have come down to find myself some breakfast."

The servant girl stopped. "The Lady Sirika told me to bring it to you."

At once Rashelin remembered the Malgosians. And her mother.

Her hackles rose, but she controlled herself. She forced out a smile. "Oh, yes, thank you."

The servant girl curtsied and left. So Sirika was here. She'd come from Mannismill to take charge. Well, Katelin was still Queen, and it was time for Rashelin to make clear where her loyalties lay.

As she breakfasted, she gathered her thoughts about what to say to her mother. She reminded herself to approach the situation with calmness, firmness and dignity.

After she had washed and dressed, a messenger arrived. What Rashelin had been waiting for. And dreading. The summons to her mother's study. She had always hated arguments and confrontations, and the biggest of her life was imminent.

The guards outside her room, and those who escorted her along the corridors and down the stairs, were Anestran rather than Malgosian. Her moment of defiance at the city gate last night had put the Baron's men in their place. There were still plenty of people loyal to the Queen, Rashelin reminded herself.

Lady Sirika watched her as she entered the study and Rashelin quailed a little under the gaze. There was no warmth in her mother's eyes. In fact, she looked more skeletal than ever, bolt upright in her 'throne' behind the desk. The guards stayed outside the door, so the two of them were alone in the room, and Rashelin sat in the chair facing her.

"Are you all right, Rashelin, my dear? I was so sorry to hear of your ordeal on the road and in the forest."

So Sirika was pretending ignorance and concern. Assuming her daughter knew nothing.

Rashelin decided to come straight to the point before she heard any more lies. But her trembling inside made it difficult to keep her voice level. "Katelin and I were lucky to survive, Mother. Those who ambushed us on the road were Malgosians."

She watched her mother's face, and saw a flicker of alarm before Sirika masked it with raised eyebrows. "Malgosians? Are you sure? How do you know?"

"One of the Knights called out: 'Get back south of the river, Malgosian,' before he was attacked. Were all the Knights killed?"

Sirika nodded. "Yes, I'm afraid they were. This is a shocking development on Baron Malgosy's part—"

Rashelin had had enough of the pretence. "Do not lie to me, Mother. Before I left Mannismill, I heard Tajion ask you, 'What have you ordered the Baron's men to do?' And yesterday afternoon, the Malgosian who caught me confirmed he was acting on your orders. So, admit it, you arranged for Katelin to be assassinated, and I was caught up in it."

She'd said what she needed to, but felt sick inside at the antagonism, at being betrayed. Part of her still longed to surrender, to forgive, to try to make everything right. But the time for conciliation and appeasement had passed. Her mother had crossed too many unacceptable lines, and could now only be resisted.

Behind her impassive expression, Sirika was thinking hard, choosing careful words. "Do you have any proof for these outrageous accusations?"

"Only what I heard," Rashelin replied. "I'm sure the Malgosians were careful to remove any evidence of their identity from the scene of the ambush."

"You are correct," Sirika declared. "The ambushers left no clue as to who they were. So, this comes down to your word against mine. I caution you not to repeat what you have said here to anyone. You are a Princess, but you are young, and I have decades of experience and can count on much loyalty here. Understand well that I carry considerably more weight at Court than you do."

Rashelin could only accept the truth of her mother's words. Without clear evidence, no one in the Court would believe the Lady Sirika capable of such misdemeanours, because she'd worked hard to preserve the appearance of integrity. "As the rightful Queen of the Kingdom, Katelin escaped and survived your ambush. So, what are you going to do now?"

"Putting to one side the circumstances of the ambush, I wish to offer you an opportunity."

"An opportunity for what?" Rashelin tried to hold her mother's gaze, but glanced downwards again.

"To see sense. To change your mind. To choose the winning rather than the losing side."

"Sides? Winning and losing? What are you talking

about?"

Sirika leaned forward. "Very well. You said not to lie to you, so let's be honest with each other. It will save time. We're talking about the changes that are coming to Anestra."

Rashelin drew a squirming breath. Being open with her mother now was like a pitched battle erupting between them.

"I see no changes coming," Rashelin said. "When Queen Katelin returns from the Manniswood—"

"When?" Sirika snorted. "When? I wouldn't even say 'if' she returns to Anestra. For that girl is never coming back here, you know. Not alive, anyway."

Rashelin stared and swallowed, and couldn't utter all she wanted to say.

"In due course I will arrange for the Court to make me Regent," Sirika went on. "While the former Queen is missing, I am running the Kingdom anyway. Once her death is announced, we will make it official."

"She is not dead," Rashelin blurted out. "Katelin is still the rightful Queen."

"Oh, she may be dead by now," Sirika purred. "It's merely that the happy news hasn't reached the city yet."

Her mother was doing this on purpose. Tormenting Rashelin, provoking her to anger. And Rashelin's self-control was nearing its limit. She hesitated, then struck back with the one fact that always rankled with her mother.

"If anything happens to Katelin," Rashelin managed to say, "then the succession falls to me. You have no royal blood in your veins, Mother. You weren't born into this family. You married into it. You have no royal authority whatsoever."

Sirika had clearly anticipated this argument, because her counterattack was smooth and unruffled. "Hence my role as Regent. But I still give you a choice. You will do everything I tell you, or you will forsake your place in the succession and the Crown will pass to Tajion."

"Tajion?" Rashelin spluttered. "He has no desire or aptitude for ruling the Kingdom."

"Which is exactly as it should be. He can be King and get on with whatever he wants, and delegate all his royal authority to his capable mother and Regent."

"No, I won't," Rashelin stated. "I will neither follow your wishes nor abdicate."

Sirika's eyebrows rose. "Consider what you're saying, my dear. You would defy me, make an enemy of me? You would try to rule this Kingdom on your own? Without any friends or allies? With me, and Tajion, and all the Court against you? Come, come, my girl. You're no Queen, and we both know it."

Of all the things her mother had said, this stung the most. Because Rashelin feared it was true. Her eyes filled and she blinked hard. She quailed at the prospect of holding her own against everyone in the way that Katelin did. She simply didn't have her cousin's independence and defiance.

"What about Baron Malgosy?" Rashelin accused. "You would find an ally in an exiled murderer and his thugs? I suppose you heard I prevented his men from entering the city last night."

Sirika nodded. "Yes, dear, I heard about your last, spirited act of rebellion at the city gates. But don't worry, I've brought plenty of Mannismill guards here with me whom I can trust, who answer to me rather than to their former Queen."

Rashelin had had enough. She stood up to leave. "There is no 'former' about Katelin. She is still Queen. I see that we need to pray to the Divine for the Queen and her Kingdom. I trust you have no objection to me meeting with Under-Father Ruis to do so?"

Sirika considered for a moment. Then she shrugged. "Very well. Ruis may visit you. Although I can't see why you seek solace in the goddess who has abandoned your cousin.

I suggest you ask the Divine to grant you some wisdom and sense."

Rashelin was overcome by an unexpected desire to understand her mother. "You of all people were always so tied to tradition. Everything must be as it always has been. Why are you doing this now?"

Sirika sniffed. "Circumstances demand it. The future of the Kingdom is at stake. I've learned there are times when we need to dispense with the more, shall we say, inconvenient traditions. When it comes to that dangerous cousin of yours, my experience teaches me that we need to take matters into our own hands. There are times when the Divine relies on her faithful servants to do her will."

Rashelin's rage surged back. "You are no servant of the Divine," she spat.

Sirika's response was calm. "Be careful, my dear. I gave birth to you, my firstborn, my only daughter, so at present I am inclined to be patient with you. But don't presume to oppose me, for you will not succeed. Once Katelin is dead, I don't mind whether it's you or Tajion who wears the Crown. You're more capable than your brother, but I will get rid of you if necessary. Because make no mistake, the rule of Anestra will be mine. I trust you will decide you want to keep your place in our Royal Family."

"You can plot and scheme all you like, but I trust our White Goddess to be just in ordering the future of her Kingdom. And when it comes to my place in this Royal Family, that is up to the Divine, not you."

Rashelin turned and flung open the door. She stormed along the corridors and up the stairs to her room, the guards hurrying to keep up. She barely managed to restrain her shaking and the flood of tears until her bedroom door slammed and she slumped into a chair.

## 6

## RYEBALD'S CLEFT

Guilt nudged at Katelin that the wanderers needed to pack up and move their camp in the late afternoon, but she saw no ill will in the faces of those busily bundling their belongings. She supposed they moved so often that it became little hardship.

The large woman with ruddy cheeks handed Katelin a bun of sweet bread to follow the soup, and she chewed it as she went to where Novita was picketed. She rearranged some items in the saddlebags, expecting to wait a while before the wanderers moved.

But everyone else was ready before she was. The process of moving camp had become a practised and efficient art. A few of the group stayed behind, hidden, to send the returning gatherers and hunters on to Ryebald's Cleft.

They set off through the trees, leading horses, carrying packs, singly, in twos or small groups. Katelin found and walked with Zane, each of them holding the reins of their horses. She wanted his company, to chat with him, but struggled to think of anything to talk about other than thrones or kingdoms or escaping from danger. What did ordinary people discuss? She refused to be the shy, tongue-tied little girl in front of this man.

Novita was showing off, tossing his mane, and Katelin realised it was for the benefit of Zane's chestnut mare. She indicated his horse. "I've never asked you her name."

Zane grinned. "Conker. Want to know why?"

Katelin nodded.

"Well, she's a horse, and she's chestnut coloured. So, what do we call a horse chestnut?"

Katelin laughed. "A conker. I get it. Very good. I think

my Novita has taken a shine to your Conker."

Zane chuckled, but at that moment the dark-haired man Arch came up.

"We think someone's following us," he said.

"Malgosians?" Katelin said in alarm.

"We didn't see him," Arch replied. "He fled as soon as we approached."

"But we need to make sure he stays away," Zane said. "A few of us will see if we can find him and drive him off."

"I suppose I'd better remain hidden among the rest of your company," Katelin said with a sigh.

Zane touched her shoulder. "It would be better if he doesn't see you."

She watched Zane and Arch disappear into the trees, and then walked the rest of the way on her own. The company were around her, but moving silently and dispersed, to avoid a mass of tracks. They headed northwards, towards the mountains, and from Katelin's left the golden light of the setting sun slanted through gaps between the leaves.

She could see why the wanderers lived here. A yearning blossomed inside her for this place, these people, this life. They were kind and generous, and could afford to be because the forest was so bountiful and their days so unhurried. Their only responsibilities were to each other, to care, protect and provide for one another. Katelin found herself wondering if she could learn the woodland life, learn which plants and fruits were edible, medicinal or otherwise useful. She envied their ability to live off the forest, and the everyday beauty of their surroundings.

Here there were no Castles, Crowns, Kingdoms or thrones. There was no Court, no Hall, no nobles, ministers, courtiers or officials. Katelin accepted that as Queen she spent much of her time with such things, but it didn't stop her being a touch jealous of these people's freedom.

Darkness crept over them before they reached the mountain foothills, but they lit no torches. Their eyes adjusted to starlight as they picked their way between the trees, climbing steadily. Katelin's muscles ached, but she refused to admit that she was weaker and less fit than the others. This time in the forest was doing her good, she was sure.

They came to an abrupt halt at the foot of a sheer cliff face. Zane had brought Katelin to Ryebald's Cleft once before, so she knew why he'd chosen this as a defensible position.

The Cleft was a deep valley between two massive granite bluffs with sheer sides. The mountains had thrust forth two towering, rocky buttresses which sheltered a narrow, flat space within. At the entrance, the cliff-faces almost joined, forming something like a gatehouse to the valley, with space for only a few men to walk through abreast. Winding paths upwards had been carved into the rock of the cliff-faces near the entrance, and at the head of the valley, but these could only be climbed with difficulty, and in single file. It was a forbidding place of scree and grassy tufts, a castle of the Eastern Range.

Katelin led Novita towards the gap in the cliff, and spotted wanderers who had already taken up lookout positions in the trees nearby, and others who were scaling the paths to guard the ways to the cliff-tops. A phalanx of archers and swordsmen was ready to hold the gatehouse to the valley against incursion.

The Cleft was dark. The towering walls robbed the valley floor of the light of star and rising moon, and there were neither torches nor fires. Katelin picked her way forwards, trying to avoid stumbling into those setting up the camp. Novita seemed to have no difficulty in finding sure places for his hooves, and Katelin marvelled at everyone's keen, night-adjusted sight. Or maybe they were better at hiding their groping and staggering about in the darkness. Around her the air hummed with a murmur of whispered conversations.

Someone took her arm and Zane's face came close in the gloom. For an instant she thought he was about to kiss her, and hurried to dismiss the distracting fantasy. But her nose was filled with his woody, smoky aroma.

"Kat, I found you," he said in her ear. "We couldn't find whoever was following us, so it's impossible to know whether someone tracked us here. But there are over fifty of us when we're all together, so it would take a small army to risk attacking us in the Cleft."

Katelin nodded. "Where's safest for me to camp?"

"I thought you and I could climb the ridge above the head of the valley, which will be safer for you than down on the Cleft floor. There's a flat, grassy space up there for us and the horses, and escape routes if necessary along the paths on top of these foothills. It may be more exposed up there, but we could get away quicker, and the Malgosians will have to come through all of my men to reach us. Will Novita manage the narrow path up the cliff face?"

It was as though the stallion understood the question. Novita tossed his head and stamped a hoof as if to reply, 'Of course.'

Katelin smiled and patted his neck. "I'm sure he'll manage. He's in a showing off mood today. Aren't you, young man?"

"Good. If you and your young man would like to head up there, I'll follow as soon as I've arranged things down here."

"Thank you, Zane." Katelin squeezed his arm, and didn't want him to move his face away. But she let him go, and he disappeared into the darkness.

She led Novita between packs and people towards the rear of the valley, and the ground climbed steadily. The walls beside them narrowed and rose until they faced a near vertical cliff face. The path up it was rocky, winding back and forth, and often little more than a precipitous ledge.

Katelin went first, and more than once skidded as she

dislodged loose stones. At times Novita's nose bumped her back. Was he telling her to stop being such a sissy and get on with it, or giving her gentle encouragement to overcome her fears? When a touch of his head restored her balance from a danger of slipping over the edge, she concluded that his nudges were the latter. He was a good horse.

The light improved as they ascended. More starlight fell on the path than filtered down to the gloom of the valley floor, and the moon was rising in the east. Katelin's legs and feet ached, and she wondered whether Novita tired in the same way when climbing mountains.

At last they reached the top. As Zane had said, there was a flat, grassy space before the mountains climbed higher in front of them. A faint path stretched to left and right as a route along this level of the southern side of the Eastern Range.

Katelin turned and gasped.

She let go of Novita's rein, and let him wander off to crop the grass. She stepped forward to the rim of the ledge.

The whole forest lay below her. She didn't know how far she could see, but in a vast panorama to the south the Manniswood stretched into the distance. In places it was cut through by streams and river valleys, and it undulated with the folds of the land. But the movement of the breeze over the trees made the leaves ripple and sway like water.

It was as though she were a lookout up a mast on a ship, and the whole Western Ocean rolled below her. The trees were waves, swelling with tide and breeze, and it was all she could do not to imagine that a deck pitched and tossed under her feet. She sank to the grass to keep her balance. But the earth was firm, and the cliff face held her secure, and she wouldn't have been surprised to hear the trees breaking in waves against the rocks at her feet.

A tear rolled down her cheek, and she made no move to wipe it away. For moonlight and starlight bathed the trees, a heavenly glimmer, a pathway to the Divine across the surface of this sea. The forest was quiet, and the scene more peaceful and beautiful than anything she'd ever seen. She could stay here forever, to gaze and ache at the wonder before her.

Katelin didn't know how much later it was when she heard footsteps on the path below her. She hurriedly wiped her face, because it wouldn't do for Zane to discover her weeping herself silly over a view. She looked around, and made out the shadowed form of Novita on the grass behind her.

Zane appeared, panting only a little at the climb. "Enjoying the view, milady?"

Katelin smiled. She hugged her knees and rested her chin upon them. "I love it up here, Zane. When you brought me to the Cleft before, why didn't you bring me to this ledge?"

"Aha." Zane grinned. "This is my own special place. I can't show it to just anybody. It wouldn't be the same with crowds up here, would it?"

"I'm honoured to be let in to your secret."

Zane sat down next to her and they were quiet together for a while.

At length, he said, "Are you all right, Kat?"

It was rare for someone to ask her how she was. She was touched, and wanted to tell him the truth. "No, I'm not."

He leaned in and reached an arm across her shoulders. They shuffled together so that she felt his warmth down her side. She rested her head against his shoulder, and was grateful that he didn't press her with questions, but waited until she was ready.

"Something's different now," she said. "I've always known there might be people who wish me harm. Being Princess and now Queen of Anestra means my guards have sworn to protect me, because my life has always been valuable to be captured and ransomed. But it's worse now. Bands of men are roaming this forest, searching for me, to take my life. I've been close to death too often in the last couple of days. People want to kill me, Zane, and I don't like it."

Zane squeezed her shoulders. "I'm sorry, Kat. I can't imagine what that's like." He paused a moment, then continued, "So, let's consider your options. They're only after you because you're Queen. You've never liked the responsibility of that, so one thing you could do is to abdicate."

Katelin pulled a face. "Yes, I've always known that was an option, but it's what happens to Anestra if I do. I couldn't live with myself, leaving them in the clutches of Aunt Sirika."

"But it wouldn't be Sirika," Zane pointed out. "It would be Rashelin, and your cousin has a good heart for the people of Anestra."

"I couldn't do that to Rashelin. I'd be putting her in the same impossible situation I'm in: standing up to the bullying of Sirika, and the ambition of everyone else in the Court, to chart her own course. That wouldn't be fair of me."

Zane nodded. "I understand. So that leaves you as Queen, and as a fugitive, until we can work something out."

Katelin turned her head to look at him. "Can you give me some lessons? You were an outlaw for years before I pardoned you. How did you live with that? Didn't you have a constant fear of being caught and taken for punishment?"

Zane chuckled, and there was a sparkle of moonlight in his eye. "Only at first. You learn to live with it, and start to take each day as it comes. When each day of freedom feels like a gift, you make the most of it, and stop worrying about tomorrow."

"I'd love to live like that," Katelin murmured.

It was Zane's turn to look at her. "Well, now you can. Stay with us, Kat. I realise you need to defend yourself against the Malgosians for a while, but since you're Queen, why can't you choose the sort of life you want? Why can't you rule the Kingdom from here in the forest?"

Katelin's smile was grim. "Oh, yes. I can see the Court would love to trek out here to see me. All those ministers and officials plodding along the Manniswood paths to consult their Queen. That will never happen."

Zane looked away. "It would be good for them. But you'd know more about that than I do. In the meantime, we're your friends, Kat, and we'll help you if we can."

"But the simple fact of my presence here endangers you. If the Malgosians track me down to this Cleft, then there will be a fight, and some of your people will get hurt or killed. I feel bad enough that you've moved camp, let alone anything worse."

"Kat, we move around all the time. And I know you don't like it when I say this, but you're our Queen. You're special to us, and we're your subjects. We love you and are happy to serve you."

Katelin rolled her eyes, but spotted the opportunity to broach a forbidden topic with him. She'd no time to think about it, but maybe that was the best way. Her nerves clenched her throat but she jumped in.

"So, you all love me," she said. "But what about you, Zane? I'm asking a lot of you, to risk your life for me. Before I make any decisions, I'd like to know where you and I stand with each other."

There, she'd said it. It had been blurted out, but she didn't think it too forceful or awkward. Zane gave a predictable lean away from her, to scan her face. Katelin managed to catch his gaze for a moment before feeling the need to inspect her boots instead.

She heard him breathe out. "That was somewhat forward of you, milady. You know I'm your friend, but I sense you mean something more than that."

Katelin nodded dumbly. She didn't trust herself to say any more.

He reached and touched her hair, so Katelin turned and rested her head sideways, able to see his face.

"I like you a lot, Kat," he breathed. "You have more spirit within you than anyone I know. But a friendship with you includes certain … complications."

"Because I'm Queen," Katelin sighed.

"Yes." Zane paused, and Katelin was afraid he wasn't going to say any more, that all her fantasies of a relationship with him would go unanswered. But then he leaned forward and kissed her hair. "But putting all that 'Majesty' stuff to one side, I would like the chance to get to know you better."

Katelin's heart leapt. This was the best she could hope for. Even knowing who she was, Zane was willing to consider something more than friendship. She couldn't stop the grin from spreading across her face, and her eyebrows rose. "Really?" she said, her voice a little higher than she'd have liked. When Zane nodded slowly, she hugged him and cleared her throat. She tried to calm her galloping heart too.

Her voice quavered as she said, "I ought to warn you that not everyone thinks it's acceptable that I'm friends with a former outlaw."

"Oh, yes, I cultivate that disreputable image," Zane chuckled. "The bad boys of Anestra, the bandits and vagabonds of the Manniswood, that's us."

"Yes, apparently some of the Court are most put out. How come that none of the young men in their noble families are good enough for me, that I should set my affections on a renegade in the forest."

"Oh, is that where you've 'set your affections'?" Katelin missed the note of hesitation in his voice.

"Yes, and Aunt Sirika is getting her grey hair all knotted about what might happen to the royal bloodline and succession when we have children—"

As soon as she said it, Katelin knew she shouldn't have. She'd been gabbling on, exhilarated by Zane's encouragement.

She felt him stiffen.

"What?" he whispered.

It wasn't her imagination. He was drawing away.

"When we have children?" His voice was louder.

"No … I mean … it isn't …"

But she'd said it.

Zane stood up and walked away. Katelin felt cold, and knew her shiver wasn't only because of his absent warmth at her side.

"Zane … wait, listen, please," she stuttered. She gave a nervous laugh, trying to make light of her mistake. Stupid, stupid, stupid.

But when Zane turned around, his face had darkened. Not only was he not laughing, his fists were clenched. "No, you listen, Kat."

The sudden anger in his voice, the clench of his jaw, shocked her.

"I thought you knew me well enough by now to know the things I can't stand." His finger was pointing at her. "I don't like people making decisions for me. They make assumptions, and try to run my life, and I won't have it. I thought we were the same that way."

Katelin's voice was small. "No, I don't like that either."

"So I'd appreciate it, *milady*, if you wouldn't jump to conclusions about who you might marry, or start a family with. You and your precious royal bloodline and succession. Do you think I care about that?"

"No, it's not that *I* worry—" She tried to answer him, but he'd stopped listening.

"And where's all this supposed to end up? With me as some sort of Prince Consort, always two steps behind you, bowing low, seen but not heard? Is that how you see me?"

Katelin's voice failed as her cheeks turned cold. She felt sick, and the tears had welled up. She turned away, burying her face in her knees. She hated crying in front of him, but couldn't stop her shoulders from shaking. Her fantasies had spilled out, and he was ripping them to pieces, and it was all her own fault.

"Get some sleep," Zane snapped, and stalked away.

Katelin stayed where she was. Curled up, hugging her knees, feeling wretched. She couldn't believe she'd spoiled everything. In a moment of hope, her stupid mouth had gabbled on, blurting out dream and fantasy. Why couldn't she have shut up, and enjoyed the moment, and given him the time he needed? No, she'd blundered in and scared him off, and now he'd never trust her again.

When the night air became colder, she crept over to Novita and pulled a blanket from a saddlebag. Zane was sitting a distance away, looking out over the forest, shredding grass with his fingers. Katelin's eyes were too blurry to take in the view, and it seemed to have lost its former beauty.

She curled up and longed for sleep to take away her stupidity and wretchedness. But when oblivion finally received her, pursuit and despair followed her into her dreams.

## 7

## BATTLE

In the early evening, Rashelin heard a muffled conversation outside her bedroom door, followed by a gentle knock.

"Come in," she called.

Around the door appeared the short, wiry form of Under-Father Ruis. He had pale blue eyes in a bony face topped with short-cropped hair, and wore a plain grey monk's habit. "You asked to see me, Princess?"

Relief surged through Rashelin. "Yes, thank you, Under-Father. Please come in and sit down." Apart from the servant girls who brought her food, his was the first half-friendly face she'd seen all day. Since the argument with her mother, she'd wrestled over what to do, how much to say, and to whom. Here was someone who could be her ally.

The Under-Father sat down opposite her and waited for her to begin.

"I need to confide in someone," she said. "I know some things, and need to decide whether to make them public. They concern Queen Katelin, and my mother, and the future of the Kingdom. We need to pray to the Divine for us all." She was in danger of gabbling, desperate to share what was tearing away at her heart.

Ruis held up a hand to calm her. "Yes, we always need to pray. I heard that the Queen is missing, and that Lady Sirika has returned to Anestra and taken charge. If you're willing to share with me what you know, we can decide what to do together."

Rashelin swallowed. "Two days ago, the Queen and I attended a dinner at Mannismill, but on our ride back here were ambushed by Baron Malgosy's men. We escaped into the forest, but our escort of Knights was killed. The ambush was arranged by my mother, trying to assassinate the Queen and then rule the Kingdom as Regent, with me or my brother on the throne."

The Under-Father stared at her. "I see. Do you have any proof of this?"

Rashelin shook her head. "My mother is too careful an operator to allow evidence of her involvement to exist. I know the ambushers were Malgosians, as were those who chased Katelin and me in the forest. But it's my word against hers, and she'll deny any connection. I'm trying to remain loyal to Katelin, Under-Father, and I need your help."

"Hmm." Ruis bowed his head and spoke to the floor. "Your mother is a dangerous enemy, because she has a network of strong support in the Court. We need to be calm and careful, and not act rashly, even when others are doing so. The Divine takes a long-term view, my child. She works out her purposes over lifetimes and generations, not in the rush of a week or two."

"Is there anything we can do, except pray?"

"I don't think we can reveal what you've told me without clear evidence to support the accusations, if that's what you mean. I fear we need to await your mother's next move. The guards in the corridor seemed reluctant to let me in here, so is she trying to restrict your movement and contacts?"

"I wouldn't be surprised. I left this room only once today, and that was to see her, and we had an argument."

"I'll make sure you attend any significant meetings in the Hall of the Court. You have a critical role here, Princess, because you're next in the succession. Sirika might prefer it otherwise, but she can't change that, and the Court has an affection for you."

"She's going to bully me and try to force me to abdicate. I don't know if I can hold on."

The Under-Father reached out and took hold of Rashelin's hand. "We need to hold on, Your Highness, for as long as we can. At least for as long as Katelin's alive. We must remain loyal to the Queen."

"But we don't know whether she's alive."

For the first time the Under-Father's grave face broke into a smile. "Don't we? What does your heart tell you? Ask the Divine to show you. Is Katelin dead or is she alive?"

Rashelin searched inside. Ruis was right. If the Divine wanted them to know Katelin's fate, then the White Goddess could enlighten their thoughts and feelings with the truth of the situation. So, which was it for Katelin at that moment – death or life? Divine, please tell us.

The unmistakeable glimmer of hope burned deep inside Rashelin. It was faint, but it was there. Slowly she matched the Under-Father's smile.

"She's alive."

"Yes, I agree," Ruis replied. "So, let's pray."

Katelin was woken by a cry from below. She jerked bolt upright. It was still dark, with shouting down in the Cleft.

Zane whipped the blanket off her. Katelin leapt up, rubbing her face.

His whisper was urgent. "Kat, go." He'd led Novita across to her, and was stuffing her blanket into a saddle bag.

Katelin looked at him, but he wasn't meeting her eye. She couldn't leave him with last night's argument unresolved. She longed to speak with him, to apologise, to explain, but they had no time.

Zane no more than glanced at her. "Come on, Kat, wake up. It must have been a Malgosian tracking us, and they've gathered in force to attack us. Get going."

Her heart clenched and her face felt hot. She busied herself tightening Novita's tack and harness.

"Take your escape route along the path to the east," Zane was saying. "I must get down to the Cleft. And remember it's you they want, not us. We'll try to give you time to flee."

"Zane, I'm sorry," Katelin began. There was so much she was sorry for, but it would remain unexplained.

He waved her off. "Not now, Kat. Ready your bow, and get out of here."

She caught his eye for a moment, but he looked away first. Then he was gone, drawing his sword, and racing away down the steep path into the Cleft.

Katelin shuddered, and willed her limbs to move. She mounted Novita, and readied her shortbow and quiver. She loosened the dagger at her belt and forced herself to look down to where moonlight bathed the forest.

She caught glimpses of dark figures moving between the trees. In the Cleft, torches were lit, and a smell of smoke drifted up. There were cries below, of alarm and pain, the twang of bowstrings, a ring of steel. The wanderers were fighting for her. They fought in her defence, to let her escape.

She spurred Novita to move. The eastward path wound along this level of the mountainside, curving into gullies and around outcrops, often no wider than a ledge. Her hood was up, and she went as secretly as she could, but felt horribly exposed to view from the forest below. The moon was high, casting a clear wash of silver across the bare slopes. She hoped Zane was right.

Then came the cry that Katelin dreaded. A throaty bellow from the forest below: "Up there, on the ridge!"

She didn't stop to look, but urged Novita from his trot into the fastest canter he could manage along the narrow path. Gravel flew from his hooves, but he barely stumbled or faltered as they crashed between bushes and teetered along the edge of precipices. But even above the thud of his hooves and her gasping breath she could hear the sounds of battle below.

Katelin's heart came to an involuntary pause each time she rounded an outcrop, where solid rock blocked her view of the path ahead. Then at one such place, she yanked and screeched Novita to a halt.

There were men some distance ahead on the path. They were advancing slowly, ten or so, dark cloaked, swords drawn.

Malgosians. And they had seen her.

She scrambled to nock an arrow to her bow and let it fly. The Malgosians had no room to evade on the narrow path and it struck the first of them. But now they were running towards her.

She couldn't fight them all, and they'd be on her before she could fire more than a few arrows. She pulled Novita's rein to turn him, but it was tight on the ledge. He squeezed round, and set off back along the path out of sight of the Malgosians.

How had her enemies found her? Had they scouted in secret all the paths of the forest and mountainside to be sure of encircling her? How many of them were there, to assault the Cleft below and also to climb this ridge and intercept her escape?

Where to now? The mountainside above her was steep and exposed. Wherever she went upwards they could see and follow her. Downwards led into the midst of battle. She could try the mountain path westwards, back past the top of Ryebald's Cleft, and towards Anestra.

Novita thundered on, and Katelin sensed the Malgosians sprinting along the path behind her. She had a start on them, and a quicker, mounted pace, but they knew where she was, and where she was heading.

She glanced down, and the forest below her was seething. Dark shapes ran through the trees towards her, and scrambled up the slopes towards the path along the ridge. A few of Zane's men were holding them off, but for how long?

Then a great shout of many voices rose to her. It came from Ryebald's Cleft on her left, and could only be the wanderers. "For Zane and for Anestra!" they shouted. And also among them, "For the Queen!"

Katelin's heart cracked open, both leaping and sinking at the same time. Zane's band was sallying from the Cleft, to engage the Malgosians in battle. She longed to go and help them, to fight alongside each one, but she knew they fought for her freedom. They fought to give her a diversion and a chance.

Novita raced past tracks that led downwards, along ridges and into gullies, but Katelin's eyes were fixed ahead. If she passed Ryebald's Cleft, then she could escape down into the secrecy of the forest below.

And then she saw them. Malgosians were on the path ahead as well as behind. They were nearing Ryebald's Cleft from the west, to cut off her last possibility of flight.

Katelin stopped, frantic. Again, they had set their trap too well. What could she do? Where could she go? With a sickening dread she realised that not even surrender was an option. They didn't want her capture, but her death.

Tears stung her eyes, and she shuddered in desperation. Divine, help me! If this was to be her end, then she wasn't going to meet it alone. Not up here on the mountainside, but fighting alongside her friends. If death came for her tonight, then it would be in battle beside Zane's people.

She turned Novita to plunge down a track into a gully. The valley was darker, shadowed from the moonlight, and too late Katelin noticed the fall of scree beneath Novita's hooves. The stallion lurched as the pebbles slid, and then toppled heavily onto his side. Katelin's leg was crushed, but they were still moving, sliding relentlessly down the slope. Novita thrashed his legs, and at last Katelin pushed herself free of him. She clutched her knee as they both crashed into bushes and stopped. Stones pelted them, and then slid on past and into the trees.

Katelin gasped and swore. She was covered in dust, cuts and bruises, but the sharp pain in her right knee was the worst. Could she even walk?

Novita was scrambling back upright, snorting. He looked terrible. Was he snorting in pain, or in disgust at the indignity of falling? He came over to Katelin and bent his head low.

She reached out and touched him. "I'm sorry, Novita," she breathed. All she could do was apologise to everyone.

She looked back up the slope. She doubted the Malgosians would try to follow them down that way. But neither could she climb back up. That meant downwards into the bushes and trees.

Katelin tried to move. She levered herself onto her good leg, using Novita for support. Her teeth were gritted, but she couldn't mount him without putting weight on her damaged knee.

Then Novita knelt for her. She couldn't believe it. She'd never been able to get him to do this. He was far too proud a horse for kneeling. He tossed his head as if to say, 'Only this once, so don't think otherwise.'

Katelin leaned on him, and swung her crushed leg across his back. She held on as he lurched back upwards. She was on, she could move, even though her knee sent piercing pains all over her body.

Novita stepped forward between the bushes as an arrow whistled past Katelin's head. The Malgosians had reached the path above them, and got out their bows. Instinctively Katelin clenched her knees to urge Novita forward and cried out in pain. This brought a new volley of arrows. One nicked Katelin's arm. Another bounced off Novita's flank and a third thudded into a saddlebag. It must have penetrated to Novita's flesh, for he started forward with a grunt.

Katelin held on grimly as her stallion crashed through undergrowth and into the trees. By now they might be safe from aimed arrows from above, but this didn't seem to stop the Malgosians from sending wild missiles in their direction. One hit Katelin's quiver, but no others found their mark as they stumbled on downwards into the forest.

They rode into the midst of battle. The cries and blows had been muffled through the trees, but now Novita stumbled into a place where men fought hand to hand. Arrows flew through the gloom, swords flashed and rang, and screams and grunts surrounded them. Wanderers and Malgosians pitted their lives against each other on all sides.

Katelin dropped the reins and strung an arrow to her bow. Novita walked forward, hesitating. Katelin struggled to see clearly, needing to avoid her arrows flying into friend not foe. But she fired, and Malgosians fell, and Novita pressed ahead.

A few wanderers rallied to her. Katelin hardly recognised them, but she scanned their faces for Zane. He wasn't here.

Then the Malgosians were on them. With shouts of recognition, and calls for help, cloaked and shadowy figures swarmed out of the darkness. Zane's men flung themselves in the way, and Katelin was prevented from advancing.

They were outnumbered. The wanderers were pierced through, hacked back and tossed aside, and at this close range Katelin couldn't let her arrows fly fast enough.

A Malgosian reached her, grabbing her left leg. Katelin kicked, and whipped out the dagger at her belt. She stabbed, and the man fell back. Then another grabbed her right, damaged knee, and she screamed. Her wild, desperate dagger swing missed, and the man pulled. Katelin felt herself slipping, and she fell from Novita's back. She kicked with her free leg, and connected, but she was on the ground, winded, the Malgosian beside her.

Then he was on her, his hot breath in her face. She was pinned, helpless, and so this was it. She would die here, alone, crushed, friendless and in agony, her Divine blood to seep unremarked into the forest floor.

The Malgosian had a hand round her throat, choking the breath from her, and he leaned his weight into it. Katelin strained her arms to wrench up the man's hand, but she couldn't budge it. And now he'd drawn his knife.

The forest seemed to dim, and stars burst around the edges of her sight. She could hear the shouting, but made no sense of the boots and commotion around her. Katelin tried to grab his knife hand, but her strength was leaving her.

The Malgosian shifted. His knife came down and plunged into the ground by her head. The hand on her throat relaxed, but then the man's whole body fell on her. She still couldn't breathe.

Her body screamed for air, and it was too long before the weight was rolled away from her. A blow to her chest made her gasp. She choked, spluttered and coughed as much air into her as she could. She writhed into a ball, hacking the breath into her.

Someone grabbed her arm and turned her over. Then she was held, lifted to sit upright. Katelin forced her eyes open and it was Zane. She clung to him, but he was picking her up, carrying her. He dumped her into Novita's saddle, and she collapsed forward against her stallion's neck.

Katelin tried to look around. Her eyes struggled to focus, and the sounds of battle continued nearby, but were muffled. She looked to Zane, and he drew his two-handed sword from the back of the Malgosian who had tried to strangle and stab her.

Zane lifted the sword and struck the flat of it against Novita's rear.

The stallion jumped forward, neighing and rearing, and bolted off through the trees. Katelin had no control over speed or direction, and closed her eyes against Novita's neck as they crashed through the forest. Branches whipped her arms and legs, and more than once hands grabbed at Katelin. But Novita was galloping too fast for anyone to stop them, as they careered through the Malgosian lines.

She heard pounding feet, shouted orders, and the swish of weapons missing.

Then an arrow plunged into her arm.

Katelin screamed. She let go of Novita's neck and clawed at the shaft through her flesh. It had missed the bone in her upper left arm, but the point protruded through. She clutched Novita's mane and only just held on as they swerved on their headlong course. The blood was flowing down her arm, but Novita carried her on, and away.

Then Novita stumbled. Katelin heard the arrow thud into his flesh, as her stallion too was hit. His pace became irregular, and swaying, but he pressed on.

Katelin closed her eyes and twined her fingers through the hair on his back. She rested her head on him, dropping her wounded arm to his side.

Divine, Hedger, anyone, help us. Ease our pain, stem the blood, give us strength. Divine, help, Divine, now.

She realised she could no longer hear the battle. Only the thud of hooves, and the gasping of her and Novita's breath. And finally the darkness took her.

Katelin woke to a jolt of Novita's neck. He'd made a small jump, but now walked on. She opened her eyes and tried to sit up.

The forest was growing light around them. Dawn had broken, but she had no sense of how long she'd been out, or how far they'd come. Or even at what time in the night the battle had occurred.

The battle! The cold grabbed her gut, and a sombre weight pressed her down onto Novita's neck. How many had been killed? Had the Malgosians wiped out the wanderers ... including Zane?

She shook herself. She couldn't consider it. She looked at her arm instead. A crust of blood had congealed around the arrow wound, and all the way down to her fingers. She touched her right knee, and cried out at the stabbing that went with it.

Novita turned his head at this, and she looked down at

him. Her blood was all over his mane and back. She peered around, and saw the arrow sticking from the top of his right leg.

Her heart twinged and she patted his neck. He'd saved her. Shed his own blood, but his strength and speed had carried her through and away from the battle.

She tried to heave a breath, but her whole body ached. Her chest still felt crushed, her throat mangled, and all her muscles screaming for rest. Every inch of her skin felt bruised and slashed.

But worse than the physical agony was the anguish of her heart and soul. Novita walked on, and Katelin fought to keep at bay the enormity of last night, and of the last few days. Zane could be dead, and all his band. Rashelin had probably been captured and was at the mercy of Aunt Sirika, who now ruled unopposed in Anestra. Bands of murderous Malgosians roamed the Manniswood, and it was only a matter of time before they found her. Even now they were no doubt tracking the daylight trail of blood, both hers and Novita's.

Katelin's shock and numbness gave way to racking sobs. They entered a clearing, where a stream from the mountains flowed down past a stretch of grass. She pulled Novita to a halt, and slid from his saddle. Her knee gave way at once, in a crunch of agony and a scream. She collapsed face down on the grass.

Death had come too close again. She couldn't do this anymore. If only death could take her, then she'd be free from grief and fear.

This was as good a place as any. Let them find and kill her here.

And she sobbed her tears into the earth.

## 8

## HAVEN

Katelin didn't know how much later it was when she stirred. The grass tickled her face and she opened her eyes. She was looking straight at a flower: yellow, a buttercup. It swayed in a gentle breeze.

Then she remembered, and groaned. They hadn't found and killed her yet. Why couldn't they have come upon her while she slept and done away with her then? She could have been free of this agony of body and despair of heart and anguish of soul. So she still had a few more hours to face. Her last few hours.

She tried to sit up, but everything hurt. Her arm and knee most of all, but she managed it. She looked around.

The warm afternoon sun slanted across the clearing, brightening the grass and flowers. She hadn't noticed the flowers before. Not just buttercups, but daisies, dandelions, forget-me-nots, and too many others she didn't know. This stretch of grass was a wild flower meadow. When she and Novita arrived in the early morning, the flowers must have been closed, but had now opened to drink in the warmth of the day.

Novita. Katelin turned and saw him cropping the grass behind her. But his leg! It was a mess of blood and matted hair, the arrow shaft still sticking out of it. He lifted his head to see that she was awake, and she tried to fathom the look in his eye.

Pain. She couldn't hold his gaze, for her tears had sprung up. She'd brought all this on him too. This danger, flight, injury, exhaustion and pain. But not death yet. What would the Malgosians do with Novita, after they'd found and killed her? He was strong and intelligent, so they'd make use of him, but they wouldn't care for him like she did. That didn't bear thinking about either.

Katelin sighed. She was parched. And starving. She hadn't eaten or drunk anything since the evening before, at the wanderer camp. The nearby stream bubbled noisily alongside the clearing on its way down to join the Mannis River. She might as well spend her remaining minutes before the Malgosians arrived in satisfying her thirst. But she needed to get over to the stream.

With her one good arm and leg, Katelin began to crawl and drag herself across the grass towards the water. More than once she cried out, as she put too much weight on her crushed knee and arrow-pierced arm. But she made it, sweating and shaking, to lie face down on the bank.

The water was clear, with a tinge of blue. It would be melt-water from the Eastern Ranges, from the snow and ice at the peaks. Katelin braced herself for the aching cold of it as she plunged in her hand. Yes, it was cool, but not cold, and more refreshing than bitter. She cupped some water, lapped and slurped it, until she'd had enough. She splashed it on her face and neck, and even started to wash the dried blood from her left arm.

She watched the red tinges flow off downstream as her Divine blood washed away. She looked down, and caught the distorted reflection of her own face in the surface of the water. But despair prevented her from looking herself in the eye.

She rolled over onto her back on the bank, and gazed at the blue sky and clouds for a while. The water had revived her. It tasted sweet, and was clean and fresh and pure. She needed a wash all over, and not just her hands and face, but she couldn't manage to strip or get herself in or out of the stream. That would feel so good, but the last thing she would do was let the Malgosians stumble upon her naked in a stream.

Her next need was food. Novita had bread in his

saddlebags, but how would she get up to them? She needed some sort of prop or crutch. She looked around, and saw some fallen branches at the edge of the trees. With a sigh, she began to crawl and drag herself in that direction.

The first branch was too dry, and snapped as soon as she put any weight on it. She selected another that was strong and solid, and used it to lever herself onto her good knee, and then upright. She winced at every movement, gritting her teeth, but at last she was standing.

She began to hop and hobble towards Novita. But she couldn't win. Either her right knee gave way if she so much as rested that leg on the ground, or her left arm lanced with pain if she used that arrow-struck limb to support her. She needed both arms gripping the branch to stay up.

She stopped, gasping for breath, wiping her face. Novita looked up, and seemed to understand. He walked over, and Katelin collapsed against him. He held steady, and she worked her way back to the saddlebags. One was struck through with an arrow, but that had the blanket and clothes. She unbuckled the other and fished out the food bag.

Katelin dropped it to the ground and collapsed. A slight twist of her knee made her cry out again, and she clutched and massaged her thigh to assuage it.

Novita stepped away, and she looked again at the arrow in his rump. And then at the arrow in her own arm. Would she be able to rip those out of their flesh herself? She shuddered. It would be agonising, bloody, and might do more damage than leaving them in place. At least the wounds were sealed, crusted over, scabbed. In her current state she doubted her strength or will to do it. If the Malgosians were coming, it wasn't worth the agony or effort.

Katelin sat on the grass and nibbled a biscuit. Then she started on a small loaf the wanderers had given her. It was turning crusty and hard, but still edible.

As she ate, Katelin looked at the clearing. The lowering

sun now cast a gentle, restful light. The wild flowers appeared to be closing up again for the night, and the blades of grass rippled and swayed with each movement of the air. The constant murmur of the stream made a soothing backdrop to the occasional song of the birds.

She breathed deeply. There was a fragrance to the air she hadn't noticed before: pure, sweet, natural. She filled herself up with it, and it seemed to heal the crushed and bruised passageways of her throat and chest. Even the soil beneath her fingers seemed soft, warm, good.

Yes, she liked this place. How had she found it? Novita had brought them here and stopped, so she could thank his excellent taste and sense. Yes, this was where she'd let the Malgosians find her, if they were going to. In fact, if she could choose where to die, then this would be it, among so much natural beauty and peace.

She bit into another mouthful of bread and then noticed something. Two tree trunks on the other side of the clearing caught her eye, because they seemed to arch together to form a natural doorway. To one side of them, the branches forked into the straight lines of a window. She thought it strange how the mind saw man-made angles and structures of things even in the natural chaos of a forest.

Katelin stopped chewing and stared. Now that she studied it, there were more of those angles and lines on the other side of the tree-trunk doorway. This second semblance of a window was higher up than the first, but definitely there. The loaf dropped from her hand as she scanned the forest edge before her. The more she looked, the more she could see. The lines of walls to the sides, other windows higher up, a roof across the top, and screens of twigs and leaves to enclose the rooms. Either she was going insane, or the edge of this clearing concealed a complete woodland cottage.

How had she not noticed this before? Was it a trick of the late afternoon light, or the particular angle from which she looked, that revealed this marvel to her eyes? She'd never known anything so cunningly concealed.

Then she shivered. Could this only have been done by magic? How could anyone fashion the natural shapes and branches of trees into a home for themselves without supernatural aid? There were many forces and powers in the world that Katelin didn't understand, and not all of them were kindly and good.

But this place was beautiful. Could anything twisted or evil live here? Unless it was a ruse, a tempting trap for the unwary.

Then she heard the singing. It was a woman's voice, high and clear. It wasn't loud, but it carried, filtering through the trees from behind the cottage. Katelin couldn't make out the words, but the song sounded merry, reminding her at once of a farmer woman returning home after a long day in the fields.

The voice was approaching. Katelin had no prospect of running, or of hiding in time, so she sat on the grass where she was and waited. Novita heard the song too, for he lifted his head and stepped closer to see.

An old woman came into view walking down a path. As with the cottage, Katelin hadn't noticed the path until the woman appeared at the end of it. Her silver hair was tied back, and she carried a basket. Her dress might once have been white, but it had greyed through too many washings, and was frayed, and stained with berry juice and soil. Her plumpness told of a love of good food. The round face was wrinkled, and had the deepest blue eyes that Katelin had ever seen.

The old woman stopped, her singing halting in mid-phrase, and she dropped the basket.

"Oh, my dear girl. You poor thing." The old woman bustled across the clearing, her hands flapping in agitation. "Just look at you. You're in a right pickle, aren't you? Blood … and arrows … and your horse as well."

She stopped in front of Katelin, who said, "And my knee's crushed too, so I can't walk." She indicated the branch she'd been using for support.

The old woman knelt on the grass, and inspected Katelin's wounds with those piercing blue eyes. The hands that touched her were gentle and skilled, but looked strong, knobbly and worn. Katelin felt she would describe the intense look on that wrinkled face as that of a concerned mother. Or more probably a grandmother.

Her knee and arm began to go numb. The old woman must know the places to press to ease someone's pain.

The old woman's plump face broke into a smile, and a warmth of relief kindled deep inside Katelin. The blue eyes sparkled as she said, "Come on then, my dear. Not much use you sitting out here on the grass. Let's get you inside."

"What? To … to the cottage?" Katelin stuttered, as she indicated across the clearing.

"Yes, of course." The old woman began to help Katelin up, and she was surprisingly strong. "I call it 'The Haven'. My own little place here in the woods."

Katelin leaned her weight across the old woman's shoulders, and bent her good knee to lever herself to standing. "But … but why couldn't I see it when I first entered the clearing? It's almost … magical."

"Ah," the old woman chuckled, as they began to take their first steps together across the grass. "That all depends on how you look at things. There are plenty of things that folk don't see even if they're staring them right in the face. But magical? Not as such. Just hidden, except for those who most need to see it."

They made their careful way towards the arched tree-trunk doorway, Novita following behind. "What about my horse?" Katelin asked. "Have you anywhere for him too?"

"Yes, we do," the old woman said. "Plenty of room for young handsome round the back. I'll settle you down somewhere comfy, and then see he's let in to his hay and his straw."

They reached the doorway and Katelin stopped. "Thank you," she said. "You're being so kind. My name is Kat."

"And you can call me Gracie," the old woman replied. She lifted a branch to reveal the way into the cottage. "So then, Kat, what do you call the young sir with the arrow in his bum?"

Despite her pain, Katelin laughed. It was as much in relief as anything else, but the instant warmth and good humour of this old woman touched her deeply. Once she'd started, she found it hard to stop, and giggled for a while before she could cross the threshold. Gracie beamed, waiting with patience, seeming happy to share and enjoy the mirth.

At last Katelin managed, "That's Novita." Then some seriousness returned. "He's saved my life several times in the last few days."

Gracie's face wrinkled in understanding. "Aye. You've been in some battle, haven't you? Let's set you down, and then we can see to your wounds, and talk."

Katelin ducked her head through the doorway and shuffled into the cottage. She couldn't believe that anywhere natural could appear so comfortable. The walls of twigs and leaves gave the living room a warm, dappled light, both bright and shaded. The furniture had been built or carved out of logs or branches, with woven seats and baskets. There were cushions and blankets, and plant pots in the corners with living flowers. On one side, a family of hedgehogs was curled up asleep on a rug. Katelin adored the place at once.

Gracie helped her across to a long couch, and it was a relief to lie down. The old woman fussed for a moment, plumping the cushions and spreading a blanket over her, and then went to fetch some food and drink.

She came back with a wooden cup of stream water, flavoured with lemon juice. It was cold and delicious, the sharpness of the juice blending with the sweetness of the water. Then came a wooden plate with a roll of home-baked bread, a pear and cherries. The bread was a marvel: soft and tasty as Katelin bit into it.

"But Gracie," Katelin asked, "where in this forest do you get lemon juice, and the fruit, and the wheat for bread?"

The old woman's deep blue eyes twinkled at her. "Ah, my girl, it's always a case of knowing where to look. The forest is a whole market of foods, providing more than you or I could ever want. And as for the bread, I blend a variety of wild grains to make the flour. Do you like it?"

"It's wonderful," Katelin mumbled through a mouthful. "The best bread I've ever tasted."

Gracie beamed, and then sat down opposite, her face serious. "Now then, Kat, to tend to your wounds, I'll need you asleep. I have a drink that will make you sleep, but I want you to agree before I give it to you."

Katelin glanced down at her arm and knee. "Can you heal these?"

Gracie smiled. "They'll heal themselves if we help them. And yes, I'm quite good with things like this. I need to be able to look after myself out here."

Katelin nodded. "Yes, I agree, then. And for Novita too. I don't suppose he can give his consent, but you can see if he'll drink your sleeping draught."

Gracie chuckled. "Oh, I don't know. I think your young gentleman friend is cleverer than you think. I'll explain to him what I'm doing." She got up. "I'll bring the draught once you've finished eating. The sooner I attend to these wounds, the better."

The pear and cherries tasted as wonderful as the bread. Did all this natural goodness come from the forest? Katelin supposed it must do.

So who was this old woman, then? If she had some healing powers, maybe she was some sort of cleric, like those in the Temple of the Divine in Anestra. Gracie certainly reminded Katelin of those kindly woman clerics she'd known.

When Gracie brought it, the cup of sleeping draught was pungent and sharp, but it soon wafted Katelin's thoughts away on the gentlest of breezes.

## 9

## COURT

The following morning, a commotion in the Castle courtyard below her window disturbed Princess Rashelin. Riders were coming and going in a clash of hooves on cobbles, with shouts from the guards. Then messengers hurried up and down the stairs of the Keep. She longed to know what was happening, but could only watch it all from above.

At last her bedroom door opened, and she turned to face the guard. She didn't recognise him, so he was from Mannismill, and obedient to Sirika, not Katelin.

"What's going on?" she demanded.

"Lady Sirika says you're to go to the Hall." The guard was roughly spoken, and had none of the politeness of the Castle servants.

Rashelin jumped up, and grabbed an embroidered shawl to cover the bare shoulders of her gown. "Excuse me," she said, but the guard chose not to move out of her way. She squeezed past him out of the door, and hated to be so close to him, even in passing. He stank.

Others were racing up and down the Keep stairs: messengers, guards, servants, courtiers, nobles, but no one seemed able to explain the commotion. Rashelin resigned herself to finding out soon enough in the Hall of the Court.

At the foot of the stairs, a steady stream of people was filing into the Hall, both from the Keep, and from the doors that opened onto the courtyard. In the rush, no one was being announced, as this seemed an emergency assembly.

Rashelin joined the throng, smiling, nodding, acknowledging those she knew, and the crowds were careful not to jostle her. The morning sun filtered through the mullioned stone windows along each side of the Hall, but the high timbered roof was in shadow. Between pillars along the walls hung dark blue banners, each emblazoned with the silver emblem of the radiant Crown of Anestra.

The incoming stream of people parted to fill up the left and right-hand sides of the Hall, leaving Rashelin to make the final walk by herself, up to the Royal Family's dais at the far end. No one else was seated there yet, and Rashelin's gaze fell on Katelin's vacant throne of ancient wood, carved with berries and ivy leaves, with its red velvet upholstery. Where was their Queen now? Rashelin took her place and watched as the Hall continued to fill.

She tried to guess what the nobles and courtiers might know of the last few days. It would be little more than gossip and rumours: that Katelin and Rashelin had been ambushed a few nights ago on the road back from Mannismill, and escaped into the forest; that the Princess had returned but that the Queen was still missing. Of more local interest might be that Malgosians had appeared at the South Gate at her return, but been turned away from entering the city.

No one else would know of Sirika's murderous plans, except of course for Under-Father Ruis. Rashelin saw him now entering the Hall, summoned from the Temple of the Divine.

This must be important. Sirika had called together everyone of significance in the city. Rashelin tried to compose herself, with calmness and strength, for whatever manoeuvre her mother was about to make.

Rashelin's wonderings were interrupted by the Castle Steward, Yardles, knocking his staff on the threshold. Those in the Hall of the Court finished their conversations as Lady Sirika and Prince Tajion entered and paraded up to the dais. Tajion did so with his customary swagger, while Sirika seemed to be glaring at Rashelin the whole way. The look was one of warning, and Rashelin decided to bide her time before causing trouble in public. She could oppose her mother in private, but needed to plan and prepare before doing so in front of the whole Court.

It rankled, though, that her mother had arranged to make an entrance with her younger brother, and without her. It isolated her on the dais, both from her family and from the rest of the Court, but she guessed this was the point. Unlike his mother, Prince Tajion took his seat without giving his sister even a glance. Lady Sirika, instead of going to her accustomed chair, approached Queen Katelin's vacant throne. Rashelin held her breath at the thought that her mother might seat herself in it, but Sirika turned and addressed the Hall standing, positioning herself in front of it.

"Ladies, lords, courtiers," Sirika called, and the murmur in the Hall died away into silence. "Forgive me for calling you all here without due notice, but a situation has arisen which requires our urgent attention."

Rashelin conceded that if her mother wanted to make an impact about the seriousness of the matter at hand, she'd done so most effectively. Every ear and eye was focussed on her.

"I will come straight to the point. A city guard rode up to the Castle a short while ago with a message for us. He reports that the Baron Malgosy himself has come to the South Gate."

Sirika paused for the expected reaction, and Rashelin was not surprised at the concerned hubbub, the shouts of "No!" and "How dare he?" that erupted at once. Throughout the Hall, swift reminders of the Baron's past crimes and sentence of banishment were being shared.

Sirika held up her hands to restore order, which she achieved only with difficulty. Once all was quiet, she continued, "I share all of your concerns about this man and his past deeds."

No, Rashelin fumed, you don't.

"I see that I do not need to remind you that by order of

this Court, the Baron is banished from Anestra for the remainder of his life. So we have the right in law to turn him away from our gates, even though he remains a nobleman of the Kingdom."

There were nods and murmurs of agreement.

"However," Sirika said, and the silence became absolute once more, "the guard's message is that the Baron claims to have vital and urgent information for us. Under these circumstances, he begs leave to appear before us—on this one occasion only—so that he may deliver this news in person." Sirika paused for the whispers to subside. "He gives no more details, other than that it concerns ... the Queen."

Rashelin gasped. And the rest of the Hall with her. The stunned collective intake of breath was followed by worried looks and murmurs of consternation.

But Rashelin's heart had stopped. For some moments she couldn't breathe. One thought dominated her mind: they've done it. They've killed her. And now the Baron has come to gloat in person, and to share in Sirika's triumph. They will mask it under a pretence of shock and grief, but their goal has been accomplished.

And now, with Queen Katelin out of the way, the Kingdom would pass to her. Rashelin gulped. She focussed her vacant, unseeing eyes to register that too many in the Hall now looked at her.

But Sirika was speaking again. "Members of the Court," she called, to quell the continuing discussion, "allow me to explain the current situation." The Hall quietened.

"A few days ago, Queen Katelin and Princess Rashelin were ambushed by highway robbers on their ride back from Mannismill. Their escort of brave Knights died, allowing time for the Queen and Princess to escape into the forest. My daughter chose to return to the city the same day, leaving the Queen to fend for herself, alone in that vast and dangerous forest. That is the latest news we have."

It took some moments for Rashelin to register what her mother had said. But her outrage was immediate. *She's making this sound like my fault!* The accusation, or implication, of negligence was clear, and it was reflected in the frowns and glares that now came in Rashelin's direction.

It was all she could do not to leap up and protest. But what could she say? How could she explain what was going on, without the slightest evidence to prove it? To try to stop her body from shaking, she clenched her hands together in her lap, and fixed her gaze on the flag-stoned floor. *Divine, help me.*

Sirika addressed the Hall again. "I ask for the guidance of this Court. In these exceptional circumstances, I propose that we allow the Baron Malgosy, for this one occasion only, to enter the city and this Hall to deliver his message. We can insist that he comes alone and unarmed, for we need the opportunity to question him in person when it comes to the welfare of our spirited young Queen. Are there any here who oppose or object to that proposal?"

For some moments the Hall filled with shaking heads, sidelong glances, and murmurs of "Let him come".

When no one voiced an objection, Sirika declared, "Then let us record the decision of this Court. For this one day only, we suspend Baron Malgosy's sentence of banishment from Anestra. Please send for the Baron."

She turned to sit down. For a moment again it looked as though Sirika would sit in Katelin's vacant throne, but she stopped herself in time and veered away to sit in her usual chair, next to Prince Tajion.

Rashelin watched her mother and brother confer together in whispers. They were ignoring her completely, and leaving her isolated on the other side of the dais. Turning her head, Rashelin wished the rest of the Court would also ignore her, instead of giving her what felt like accusatory glances.

But it couldn't be true, could it? That Queen Katelin was

dead? Rashelin remembered what she and Under-Father Ruis had discussed, about praying to the Divine to learn the truth of Katelin's life or death. She closed her eyes now, and tried to feel for the answer, for the truth in her heart.

Her emotions were in too much turmoil: outrage, betrayal, sadness, loneliness and anger all vied for attention. But among them all, there was also … hope.

Yes, it was still there. That spark and glimmer of the Queen's life, that meant hope.

She snapped her eyes open and searched among the crowd for the Under-Father. She found Ruis at once, for his gaze was steadily fixed on her.

"Alive," she mouthed, and he returned a slight nod.

He gave her a small, forced smile, and then clenched his fists at his sides. She understood his message at once: "Be strong." She nodded back, and watched him draw a deep breath and close his eyes to meditate. She followed his example, while the Court waited for the Baron to arrive.

But Rashelin struggled to concentrate on prayer. The injustice of her mother's insinuation hurt deeply. There was nothing she wouldn't do to protect and defend the Queen, and she'd only left the forest under virtual arrest by Malgosian soldiers, who were acting on Sirika's orders. She should have expected this: a campaign to discredit her in public and in the eyes of the Court. Sirika wanted to establish Rashelin also as unfit to govern, so that any abdication proposal would be unopposed.

She wasn't going to give her mother that satisfaction. Not after this. And besides, Katelin was still alive, and as Princess her loyalty to her cousin would be unwavering and absolute.

The murmur in the Hall quietened. Then Rashelin heard it too: the clop of hooves in the courtyard outside, audible through the open doors of the Hall and Keep. And then the heavy tread of boots, accompanied by the repeated sound of a metal-tipped staff striking the flagstones. Rashelin could almost feel the rising nerves of the courtiers.

Baron Malgosy entered the Hall.

He didn't pause at the threshold to be announced, but strode in as though he owned the place. He was tall, dressed in black leather, riding boots up to his knees. Rashelin remembered him as a muscular, tattooed young man, but she'd been only a young girl at the time. The Baron retained his muscles, but had thickened around the stomach and neck. His head was bald, and his beard a greying black stubble. He swung his staff as though it were a weapon, seeming to delight in the cringing around the Hall each time he crashed it to the floor. He'd probably fooled the guards that it wasn't a weapon, but a walking stick, by feigning a limp as he dismounted. But there was no limp now. And he probably had a blade hidden in his boot.

Baron Malgosy strode the length of the Hall to approach the Royal Family's dais, and the Court backed away from him as he passed. But they clustered forward in his wake to hear what he would say.

The Baron's light blue eyes surveyed the dais and his surroundings, alighting for a moment on Rashelin, before he made a show of an elaborate bow to Lady Sirika. The Princess remembered that the lightness of his eyes had made him seem mild and gentle to her childish thoughts, until he'd proven himself a vicious murderer.

"Your Royal Highnesses," Baron Malgosy boomed, "Ladies and Lords of the Court of Anestra, Ministers of the Kingdom, courtiers and officials, I greet you. I express my humble gratitude at your gracious suspending of my deserved sentence."

He was mocking them. Rashelin could hear it in his voice, in his twisted half smile, but wondered whether others picked that up. They couldn't fault his words, but the tone said something else.

Sirika was formal and official in response, hiding the fact that the two of them had been in secret, friendly contact.

"Baron Malgosy, you have been admitted here for one purpose only: to deliver the information that you consider both urgent and vital for us to hear. You will proceed."

The Baron inclined his head, and the Court seemed to lean forward, anxious to miss nothing.

"Yesterday morning," he began, "one of my men rode to me in haste at Malgosy Castle. They had come across a young woman injured in the forest. It appeared she'd been in a riding accident, falling from her horse, and then attacked by a wild animal. She had broken bones, and was covered in blood from bite and claw wounds."

The Court stood in stunned silence, and an ache in her chest told Rashelin she wasn't breathing. The picture of a wounded and bloody Queen Katelin sprawled across the Manniswood floor sprang to mind, but she shoved it away, unwilling to contemplate it.

"I summoned my best physicians and rode out myself to the scene. We conveyed her battered body as best we could on a stretcher back to Malgosy Castle, where we set her bones and bound her wounds. It is years since I last saw the young Princess Katelin, but I recognised her at once. I considered it my duty to the Kingdom to ride here myself to inform you."

There came a silence, and Rashelin thought that the Baron was relishing this moment, with a tell-tale lick of his lips.

General Bolas stepped forward from among the ranks of the courtiers, stroking his walrus moustache. He was the old man in command of the Anestran army, and Rashelin had always respected him. Sirika nodded for him to speak.

"Baron Malgosy," he said in his gruff voice, and the Baron looked sideways at him. "You suggest a riding accident. Was the horse at the scene, and could you describe it?"

"We found a horse a short distance away. He may have fled as the wild animal attacked, or else helped to scare the beast off by kicking with his hooves. We're unable to say. But he's a white stallion. You need to tell me: is that Queen Katelin's horse?"

Rashelin sighed at the confirmation that it was Novita.

"And where in the Manniswood was this?" General Bolas asked. "North or south of the river?"

Rashelin heard the intake of breath from around the Hall. Everyone present knew the terms of the Baron's banishment, requiring him to remain south of the River Mannis.

"South," the Baron replied. "I don't know how or where she crossed the Mannis—fording the shallows or swimming, I guess—but that's where she ended up."

That's when Rashelin knew he was lying. Katelin would never have crossed the river, into the Baron's own territory, with the increased likelihood of capture. The Baron was pretending that he'd abided by the sentence of the Court and remained south of the Mannis, even though Rashelin had been chased by Malgosians on the Anestran side. She fumed, but couldn't think how to prove her word against his. If he lied about this, was any of the rest of his account true?

"Her wounds," General Bolas continued. "Bite and claw marks from wild animals, you say. From which beasts, would you guess? And no evidence of weapons causing injury to her?"

The Baron turned to face the General. He seemed needled, although he must have expected the questioning. He shook his head. "No weapon marks at all. The beasts I would guess as wolves or bears. Both are known to roam the forest."

Sirika interrupted from the dais at this point. "May we go and see her? Or is she well enough to be moved back here to Anestra? We must insist at the very least that Jemmorick, the Royal Physician, attends her."

Baron Malgosy turned back to face Rashelin's mother,

and raised his voice to be sure everyone in the Court heard him clearly. "Of course, you may send whom you wish to care for her. You will be most welcome at Malgosy Castle. But I regret there is no way that Queen Katelin should be moved."

The Hall became silent and still as the Baron went on. "Perhaps I haven't made myself clear about the serious nature of the young Queen's wounds. She has lost a lot of blood, and is weak and pale. It is a testament to the young lady's strength that she lives still. When I came upon her I thought I saw a corpse. And I regret to say that she is not far away from death. I must inform you that we consider her wounds life-threatening. She is gravely ill, mortally wounded, and I counsel you all to prepare for the fact that her injuries are likely to prove fatal."

The silence in the Hall was absolute, followed by everyone speaking at once. Rashelin leaned back in her chair.

Katelin was alive. She believed that. But for how much longer? And what parts, if any, of the Baron's report could she trust?

From the corner of her eye, Rashelin saw her mother rise to her feet. As though from a great distance she heard Sirika quell the Hall and propose that, with her previous experience, she would assume the role and title of Regent of the Kingdom. Rashelin couldn't concentrate enough to object to that. Or when her mother proposed that Baron Malgosy should remain in Anestra for the coming days, to liaise concerning news of Queen Katelin.

None of that mattered to Rashelin as much as her cousin's life.

Live, Katelin, live. You must hold on. You need to survive, because without you everything falls apart.

Divine, save her. Save us all.

## 10

## COUNSEL

First, there was birdsong. It twittered in the distance and chirruped nearby as it rose and fell in its timeless melody.

Underneath was the sound of the stream, as it rippled and burbled across rounded pebbles in its passage from the mountains to the Ocean.

Above it all was the breeze, rustling the leaves and sighing through the trees in its restful, joyful whispers of creation.

Katelin didn't open her eyes. She'd be content to lie here forever, listening to the sounds of the forest, for their beauty was such that she wanted nothing more.

She filled her lungs and smelled the wild flowers in the meadow outside. The air couldn't have been purer or sweeter. The bed was comfortable and soft, the blanket warm. The linen had been freshly laundered in the stream and then dried in this clean forest air.

At last she sighed. The sights would be wonderful too, so she opened her eyes to drink them in.

The shadows of leaves danced across her blanket as though playing a game. The sunbeams gave a green, filtered light as they came to rest inside the woodland cottage of the Haven. The bedroom was simple, sparsely furnished, with woven mats on the plank floor.

Katelin turned her head. A brown owl watched her with unblinking eyes from a perch in the corner of the room. She looked around, but there was no sign of the old woman, Gracie.

Through the twigs that made up the bedroom wall, Katelin saw that she was higher up than the ground. So this cottage in the forest had an upstairs, too. But how had the old woman carried her up here? Gracie must be stronger than she looked.

Katelin remembered her wounds. Her arm was arrow-free and bandaged. She flexed her knee and winced a little; it, too, was strapped up. There was no sharpness to these pains, only a dull ache. And she felt cleaner, as though all her sweat and dirt had been washed away along with the blood. If Gracie had done all this for her, she was the most attentive and skilled cleric-healer that Katelin had ever known.

She couldn't think of getting up yet, so what was she to do? She looked at the owl, and it gazed back at her with its dark eyes. "Hello?" she said, in a dry, croaky voice.

The owl gave her a slow, lazy blink, ruffled its wings and emitted a low hoot.

"All right, Tawnie," came the old woman's voice from downstairs.

Katelin heard movement below, as though Gracie stirred herself from a comfortable armchair. The old lady hummed as she climbed the stairs, and then pulled back the strips of cloth that covered the doorway.

"Ah, you're awake, my dear. How do you feel?"

"Much better, thank you." And it was true. It was almost miraculous how recovered she felt when compared with her arrival and collapse in the clearing. "Nothing worse than a soreness here and there."

Gracie beamed. "That's wonderful to hear."

"So, are you some sort of cleric?"

Gracie's eyebrows rose. "A cleric of the Divine? Yes, something like that." She chuckled.

"I'm thirsty, though," Katelin added.

"That's easily fixed. Let's sit you up a bit." The old lady bent and held Katelin under her armpits. With an impressive strength she pulled her up the bed into a sitting position against the pillows. For some reason, Katelin had expected the old lady to smell a bit stale, unwashed, or like boiled vegetables. But not at all: Gracie bore the unmistakeable fragrance of flowers.

She reached to a shelf above Katelin's bed and poured liquid from a jug into a wooden cup. "Here you are."

Katelin sipped, and then drained the cup in one go. It was the sparkling stream water, this time with a hint of raspberry juice. She could feel it soothing her throat as it went down. She held out the cup. "Is there more?"

Gracie laughed. "Thirsty, indeed. And I guess you'll be hungry."

As soon as the old lady said it, Katelin's stomach seemed one cavernous ache. How long had it been since she'd eaten?

"I'm starving. Have I been asleep for a while? And how is Novita?"

Gracie's face became grave. "Two days, I'm afraid. Your wounds were serious. And your young sir is fine, off grazing between the trees. You both lost a lot of blood, so we need to restore your iron. It's plenty of green vegetables for you, my girl, so I've some spinach soup to warm up for you."

Katelin pulled a face, but then smiled. "Only as long as there's some more of your bread to go with it."

Gracie laughed. "Coming right up."

Katelin sipped the cup of water while the old lady prepared the soup downstairs. Gracie sang softly to herself, but Katelin couldn't make out the words. It was peaceful here, and she sighed as she nestled herself among the pillows.

Soon Gracie reappeared with a tray. "Spinach and cream soup, with a hint of watercress," she announced. Katelin gazed into the bowl of dark green liquid as it rested on her lap, the curls of steam wafting the wholesome odours to her nose. It smelled good, and the first dip of the spoon confirmed the quality of the flavour.

Katelin licked her lips. "This is the best that I have ever

known spinach to taste."

Gracie chuckled. "But that's not saying much, am I right?"

Katelin smiled, and as she ate the old lady settled herself into a wooden chair against the wall. The owl flew down and gave a gentle peck at Gracie's hand. Katelin's tray had bread to dip in the soup, and a bowl of dried apricots and hazelnuts to follow.

After wolfing down the soup in silence, Katelin alternated the chewy sweetness of the apricots with the crunch of hazelnut, until Gracie spoke again.

"We should leave it a few days before you try to get up," she said. "Your knee needs some strength before bearing any weight. But I'll find you a crutch to help with your walking before you need to be on your way."

A chill crept over Katelin at the old lady's words. Before she needed to be on her way. A clenching dread settled inside as she remembered what waited outside this cottage and clearing. Couldn't she stay here, safe, quiet, hidden? For a short while she'd been able to forget about Kingdom and Queenship, and the upset with Zane, but now it flooded back.

Gracie noticed at once that Katelin stopped in mid chew. She'd bitten the inside of her cheek, a half-eaten apricot still in her mouth. The old lady's smiling, wrinkled face had tensed into concern.

"Oh dear," she said. "You poor girl. It's not my place to pry, but there's something about 'being on your way' that's made you look unhappy. You don't need to tell me, because your business can remain your own if you wish. But if you'd prefer someone to talk to about it, then my listening is as good as my bread."

Katelin managed half a smile as she caught the old lady's deep blue eyes. Then she looked down, resuming her chewing and crunching.

What could she say? Yes, she wanted to explain it all to

someone, and Gracie was the only person around. Perhaps she could tell the old lady her worries and troubles. She seemed like someone who would sympathise and understand.

But where could she begin, about the Kingdom of Anestra and being Queen of the Western Coast? How could this old lady in the forest possibly understand the challenges she faced? She might know about Baron Malgosy, but not Aunt Sirika, Prince Tajion and all the rest of the Court.

And then there was Zane. Did Gracie have much wisdom and experience in dealing with young men? Maybe she'd been married in her younger days, but Katelin couldn't be sure. But the understanding of a mother or grandmother was what Katelin needed right now. And the worry about a man was the easier option to discuss.

Katelin took a sip of water, swallowed and cleared her throat. "Well, there's this young man …"

"Ah."

"I like him, and I think he likes me. But before I came here we had an argument. We didn't get the chance to sort it out, and so I don't know what to do. Should I go and find him, or try to forget about him?"

"What did you argue about?" Gracie's voice was gentle, kind.

"Oh, um, about where our liking for each other might lead. I think my hopes and dreams have gone ahead of where he's willing to go at present."

"Hmm, I see."

Katelin risked a glance up, and Gracie's deep blue eyes were twinkling.

"It sounds to me, my dear, as though you're falling in love with this lucky young man. But he's holding back, uncertain, wary of where this might lead. He might have been hurt or disappointed in the past."

Katelin stared at the old lady and then tore her eyes away. She popped in another apricot. Was that true, that she was falling in love with Zane? Her thoughts had certainly got carried away about a future with him. And who knew what heartaches the wandering leader had suffered in the past?

"Why do you call him lucky?" Katelin muttered. "I wouldn't call him that with me following him around."

When she looked up, Gracie was frowning. "Why do you say that, Kat, my girl? There are plenty of young men who would feel lucky to have you interested in them."

Katelin shrugged at the compliment. After all, Gracie didn't know about the rest of it, that association with her meant Kingdoms and diplomacy, the complexities of the Court and the expectations of being Royal Consort. No, Gracie was trying to be kind, but didn't understand.

"If I were you," the old lady went on, "I wouldn't worry myself over what the young gentleman thinks of me."

"What do you mean?" Katelin spluttered. "Of course I worry about what he thinks of me."

"Ah, but you can't change his feelings, can you? Can you make him fall in love with you? No. So don't worry about what you can't change."

Katelin gulped. Was that possible? It made a sort of sense: while she could encourage or squash her feelings for Zane, him falling in love with her—or not—was beyond her power. "So ... what should I do?"

"Live your own life, my girl. Do what you must, make your own choices, and see what happens. He knows you're interested, so it's up to him now. If he comes after you, then well and good, and he deserves you. If not, then he wasn't worth bothering about anyway."

"You don't think I should try to find him, then?"

"Oh, you can seek him out if you need to, when you go on from here. But when you meet, apologise for upsetting him in that argument, and leave it at that. Then be yourself as you go about your work. Let him see what you're like. If he should fall in love with you, then you'll know it's with the real you."

A smile crept across Katelin's face. She liked the sound of that. Zane knowing the real her, and loving and chasing after her.

She'd always struggled to be herself, with the expectations that went with being Queen swirling around her. But if anyone were ever to be interested in her, it must be in her as Queen. That was her destiny, sure and unavoidable, it seemed.

But then … Aunt Sirika, Baron Malgosy, Prince Tajion and all the rest of the Court swarmed back into her thoughts. She faced a battle against all of them to be Queen at all, if she were ever to fulfil that destiny.

She slumped back against her pillows. She was too weak and tired to consider that battle now.

"Thank you, Gracie," she murmured. "I'll think about what you've said."

The old lady nodded, and roused herself from her chair. She patted Katelin's arm and lifted the tray of empty bowls. "From my experience, Kat, there's nothing to make a young man fall in love so much as a young woman who knows who she is and what she wants. Chasing love is like running after rainbows: the faster you run the further away they move. Let them follow after you."

Gracie left the bedroom and Katelin curled back down under her blanket, wincing at slight stabbing pains in her arm and knee. When at last she drifted back to sleep, it was with dreams of Zane wanting to find her.

In the days that followed, Katelin could sit up by herself, leave her bed, and finally totter downstairs. Gracie was the perfect nurse: attentive with food and drink, checking and changing bandages, and trying her best to bolster her patient's mood. She also provided plenty of quiet and solitude for thinking her own thoughts, which Katelin appreciated.

Katelin said no more to the old lady about Zane, but

warmed more and more to the idea of letting him chase after her. That prospect always made her smile.

The days drifted into each other, with little to differentiate them, for they were all filled with rest and healing, with excellent food and drink, and with as much company and laughter as Katelin wished.

At long last the day arrived for which she had been yearning: the day she could bathe in the stream. Gracie agreed that the waters would do her good, and deemed the wounds to be healed enough for the bandages to be removed and for a walk across the meadow.

A nagging worry remained at the back of Katelin's mind about the Malgosians. She didn't explain to Gracie about her pursuers, but begged the old lady to keep an ear and eye out while she was naked. She hadn't seen another living soul since arriving at the Haven, but didn't want to trust to luck that no one would pass by today.

Gracie supported Katelin, hobbling on her crutch, out of the cottage. Before venturing to the stream Katelin had another visit to make. She found Novita cropping grass between the trees beside the cottage. The stallion turned at once, as though to hide from her his bandaged rump. Katelin wanted to see how the wound was healing, but it soon became clear there was no way Novita would permit her to inspect his embarrassment. Gracie was chuckling.

Katelin relented and allowed him his dignity, but couldn't resist a tease. "You let Gracie here treat your wound, didn't you? So, what's the difference between the old lady and me?"

Novita gazed at her, as if to say, "You're my mistress," which apparently explained everything. Katelin laughed and hugged his neck. It was good to feel his warmth and strength. She stroked his flank. "Thank you, Novita," she murmured. "You saved my life again back there."

He turned his head and blinked at her, as though to say, "Yes, of course. What did you expect?"

Katelin smiled, and could have sworn he gave her the twitch of a smile back.

Gracie had washed the stallion's white coat clean of its matted dirt and blood, but Katelin still said, "I'm going to bathe in the stream, Novita. You should try it yourself."

He tossed his head, as though saying, "A bath? Only if I must, and only when no one's watching."

Katelin and Gracie left him and walked across the grass between the wild flowers. At the stream's edge, the old lady helped her to undress and then ease into the water. As promised, she then kept watch.

It was bliss. Katelin still couldn't understand how the stream of melt-water from the Eastern Range glaciers could be so warm. Yes, the flow was brisk and refreshing, but must be warmed by the sun along the whole length of its passage.

And it was cleansing and pure. The waters had a wholesomeness that seemed to wash away more than just dust and dirt. It was as though disease, infection, bruising, aches and tiredness were swept away in this healing stream.

Katelin lay back and let the waters flow all over her. She even lowered her hair and head until her entire body was submerged, floating to the surface only for an occasional breath.

She became more and more convinced that this stream was magical.

It was healing her spirit.

One by one, she felt the sensations of despair, and worry, and anger, and fear, and loneliness disappear off downstream. If only she could stay in this stream for long enough, Katelin was sure that all her troubles could be solved.

But eventually she began to feel cold. She couldn't live here in the stream, but needed to return to the light and warmth of sun, and air, and grass. With a fond farewell and a thank you to the stream, Katelin sat up in the water.

She hardly needed Gracie's help anymore as she stood up, dripping and shivering. The old lady caught her eye and beamed, stepping forward with a towel. "Was that good?"

Katelin's teeth chattered. "Your stream," she breathed, "is wonderful. There's so much about the Haven that is magical, but now I think I've found the best."

Gracie chuckled, picked up Katelin's clothes and they began to walk towards the cottage. "Let's get you dry, and warm, and inside."

Then without warning, the old lady's head snapped round. "Hmm. We need to move. Someone is coming."

* 11 *

## DECISION

Katelin's panic overwhelmed her. Whatever fear had been washed away in the stream now returned in full force. She couldn't limp fast enough towards the doorway of the cottage, and found herself cursing because the meadow was so wide. She struggled to listen for other sounds above her own footfalls and the gasping of her breath. The breeze that rustled the leaves around the clearing now seemed ominous and deadly.

"Gently, gently." Gracie tried to calm her. "We have time, we have time."

They reached the cottage doorway and Katelin collapsed through it. Gracie followed, lowering into place the leafy branch that hid them from view. The old lady helped Katelin across to a chair and laid her clothes beside her. "Dry yourself and get dressed."

"Who is it?" Katelin panted. "Who's coming?"

Gracie turned to gaze across the clearing outside. "We'll see," she said.

Katelin rubbed her arms, legs and hair with the towel, thinking herself in desperate need of sudden flight. Could she dress, mount Novita and escape in time? But her hands shook almost too much to put her clothes on straight. Her body was hot and shivering at the same time.

Katelin was not even half dressed when she saw Gracie hold up a hand. She thought the old lady was trying to calm her haste, but realised she was merely gaining her attention. For then she pointed a finger at the far side of the meadow.

Katelin ducked down and peered through the cottage wall of twigs and leaves. Her knee and arm protested, but she ignored the twinges of pain.

There was movement between the trees.

Katelin could only stare with a thrill of terror as a charcoal grey horse stepped out of the shadows of the forest. The man who rode it had close-cropped hair around an ugly bald pate. It was the same rider who'd stopped beneath the elm tree where she'd hidden.

Now others in the dark green and grey uniform of Baron Malgosy were appearing from under the trees. Katelin shrank back. At least a dozen men had entered the clearing, and before she could think to move they began to dismount and unbuckle their packs.

No! To see them so close and realise she had little defence was all her worst nightmares come true. How could she hope to avoid capture with a Malgosian camp on their doorstep? Katelin's panic made her scramble for her remaining clothes but Gracie's firm hand took hold of her shoulder. The old lady's brow was furrowed with concern, but her deep blue eyes were full of reassurance and calm. "They can't see us in here," she said.

"Shh," Katelin hissed. "They'll hear us."

Gracie shook her head, but lowered her voice a little. "Our words will be no more to them than the sigh of the wind through the trees. Our movements will be the rustle and creak of the forest."

"But … but they'll see the cottage, and find me."

Gracie's eyebrows rose. "Did you see the cottage when you first entered the clearing?"

"No, but there are a dozen of them, and if they camp here for the night, someone is bound to look in the right direction. By morning they're sure to have found us."

Gracie smiled.

Katelin couldn't believe it. She knew she should be reassured by the old lady's confidence, but it was clear that Gracie had no idea of the mortal peril she was in. After all, Katelin hadn't told the old lady who she was, or that the Malgosians were after her. She began to splutter a protest about needing to get away.

Gracie squeezed her shoulder to stop her. She helped Katelin upright and guided her back to a chair.

Katelin couldn't stop staring through the cottage wall to where the Malgosians were setting up camp. They were away from the cottage doorway, but had spread themselves out across the meadow. Her indignation rose at the way they trampled heedlessly over the wild flowers, and were even relieving themselves in the stream. Some were gathering dry wood for a fire.

Gracie sat down beside Katelin and laid a hand on her cheek, guiding her gaze away from the meadow to look into her deep blue eyes.

"The stream will wash everything away," she said. "They can't even see the flowers, and the grass will grow back over their fire."

"How can you be so sure they won't find the cottage?" Katelin demanded.

Gracie smiled again. "Because, my dear, I've learned not to underestimate what you call the magic of this place. Haven't you understood that there's something different and special about the Haven?"

Katelin stared at the old lady, and an inkling of how much she might not understand about the world dawned within her. Could there be powers and mysteries that would always be beyond her knowledge? Did the Divine give to her clerics, as well as healing powers and wisdom, the ability to protect and hide from danger?

Katelin drew the towel closer around her half-clothed body. And here was Gracie, who seemed to embody, or at least to understand, so much of that. Now was a chance to ask her.

"Well, yes, I can accept that this place is magical, but explain to me how I found it, then."

Gracie rested her hand on Katelin's knee. "You found it because you needed it. You needed a refuge, a haven, a safe place for rest and healing. And so, it was revealed to you. These Malgosians might want to find it, or to find you, but that's not the same thing. There's a world of difference between need and want."

Katelin opened her mouth to speak again but Gracie patted her knee. "Finish drying yourself and dressing, and come into the back. We can sit and talk in there if you'll feel more comfortable not having to watch those brutes."

She stood up and shuffled off towards the kitchen at the back of the cottage.

Katelin looked beyond the old lady's receding form, and out towards the meadow at the front where the Malgosians continued to arrange their camp in the late afternoon light.

Could she believe and trust Gracie? This kind and mysterious old lady, who lived in an invisible cottage in the middle of the forest? She'd been nothing but gentle and helpful, and there was no doubt about the magic of this place. Then again, did she have much choice? The only alternative might be to attempt a silent escape out of the back of the cottage with Novita in the dead of night. That didn't sound safe at all.

Katelin shrugged, finished dressing and rubbed her damp hair with the towel. One last glance out to the front revealed the Malgosian camp fire, where the flames glowed red off sharpened steel. Katelin shuddered, and eased herself back towards the cottage kitchen.

Gracie was working at a counter, chopping the core out of an apple. A platter on the table held hunks of bread and cheese and pots of butter and honey. A pitcher of water stood beside it, and a fruit bowl. Katelin struggled to contemplate sitting down to supper with a band of Malgosians only yards away. But she was hungry, and even if the night included a secret escape, she still needed to eat.

She lowered herself onto a stool and took a sip of water. The flavour this time was a hint of peach. She helped herself to some bread and began to butter it.

"You're sure we're safe here?" Katelin asked.

Gracie turned and held her gaze. "Even if all your enemies were camped surrounding this cottage, it would still be the safest place in the world for you. They can never find you or disturb us in here. And Novita too: they won't look behind the cottage, and he's clever enough not to show himself. Trust me. You're safe in here. I promise."

Katelin lifted the bread to her mouth, and then lowered it again. Gracie's words sounded for a moment as though she knew Katelin was Queen. That mention of "all her enemies". Her whole life, Katelin had been surrounded by those who would gladly and willingly give their lives for her. People for whom Katelin's life was more precious and valuable than their own. But it was ridiculous to hear that here. Gracie didn't know who Katelin was.

Outside, in the space behind the cottage, Novita shifted and stamped. Katelin was comforted to hear him there, to know that he was close at hand and safe from the Malgosians.

The old lady placed the chopped apple on the table and seated herself on the stool opposite. "Would you like to tell me why you think the Malgosians are looking for you?"

Katelin swallowed. Had she given that impression? Maybe she had, but she needed to disguise it now. She shrugged a half smile. "Well, I can't say it's me in particular, but I suppose they might be searching the forest for something. You know, bands of them combing through the trees for someone. Perhaps in my wanderings I've trespassed across somewhere without knowing it."

"Ah, I see." Gracie busied herself with the honey pot. "You don't need to tell me if you don't want to, but you definitely said, 'they'll find me'. That sounds as though you know they're searching for you."

Katelin looked down at her plate and chewed her bread slowly. Gracie had been sharp and perceptive, of course. She'd worked out Katelin's situation, and guessed at the cause of her panic and fear.

At once a weariness about secrets and deception stole over Katelin. Gracie could be trusted, couldn't she? She was some sort of cleric of the Divine, after all. She'd said so. Katelin needed to talk to someone about the Kingdom, and being Queen, and Aunt Sirika, and the Malgosians. She couldn't expect this old lady of the forest to understand about thrones or diplomacy or usurpers of power, but she was kind and wise, so what harm could it do? Was it easiest to tell her everything?

She swallowed her bread and then drew a deep breath. "Yes, it's me they're after," she said. She didn't look up to gauge Gracie's reaction until she'd said the next words. "I'm Queen Katelin of Anestra."

Again, she had the impression the old lady knew this already. But if so, Gracie masked her knowledge at once and feigned mild surprise. Her voice and eyebrows rose. "Really? Queen Katelin? Yes, of course. You're the right age, and now you say it, you look like her, too."

Katelin spoke slowly. "You live out here in the depths of the forest, and yet you know what the Queen of Anestra looks like. How would you know that?"

"Oh, I pop into Anestra from time to time," Gracie said airily. "Sometimes there are things I'd like which are easier to get in the city. I could have seen you at one of those royal occasions. But not up close like this."

Gracie smiled, and Katelin was sure those deep blue eyes held a twinkle. So the old lady had known it, but had allowed Katelin to keep her secret until she was willing and ready to share it. She might have guessed it from the start, from the moment she'd found a bleeding and wounded girl in the meadow. Gracie had been kind and helpful because she was Queen. Or—as a cleric, would she have tended to anyone?

Katelin sighed. She couldn't work that out, and didn't need to. She was the Queen, and Gracie had helped her, so what should she do now?

She gazed across the kitchen table at the old lady who was busy piling butter, cheese, honey and apple onto her hunk of bread. Gracie noticed Katelin's smile. "Have you tried them all together?" she enthused, waving her piece of bread. "They're great."

Katelin laughed, and set about copying Gracie's mound on top of the bread. As she added the final pieces of apple, she said, "I suppose I'd better tell you everything."

Gracie ate in silence as she listened to Katelin's tale, from the ambush on the road back from Mannismill, through to arriving at the wild flower meadow in front of the Haven. The old lady didn't interrupt, but nodded, murmured and raised her eyebrows at times. Katelin was relieved to tell someone, and Gracie had been right: her listening was as good as her bread.

The darkness of evening had crept into the cottage kitchen by the time Katelin finished. Gracie got up and lit a candle, reassuring her that this was also something the Malgosians wouldn't see.

The old lady placed the flickering flame on the table between them. "This Zane you speak about," she asked, "he's the young man you mentioned before?"

Katelin nodded, and picked a plum from the fruit bowl. Not that she was still hungry, but she wanted something to do with her hands while she waited for what Gracie would say. This old lady of the forest might have some wisdom to impart, though she didn't expect her to have the answers to all her problems.

"As well as falling in love," Gracie sighed, "you have the burden of a Kingdom on your young shoulders, Kat. My dear child, you have some important decisions to make."

"Yes, I know. But I'm at a loss about where to begin. Until recently, I thought I might need to choose between love and the Kingdom, between Zane and being Queen. I see now that it was childish, but I hoped I could have it all: both him and my destiny. But now it looks as though I can't or won't get either. Where does that leave me?" She said this with an angry sob rising in her throat. Putting it so starkly only confirmed to her the impossible situation she faced. She swallowed down the sob and looked across at Gracie, whose deep blue eyes were full of gentleness and compassion.

"When it comes to love," Gracie breathed, "I counselled you not to worry about what you can't change. Get on with your life and work, I said, and if he's still interested, let him come after you. Be yourself, let him see what you're like, and then you'll know if his love is true. I stand by that advice."

Gracie drew a deep breath and went on. "In the matter of the Kingdom, however, you don't have that luxury. I can't advise you to wait and see if the Kingdom comes chasing after you. There are too many others desperate to take your place and have your power to rule. Not only your Aunt Sirika and cousin Tajion, but also Baron Malgosy, the Duke of Lasseny, the Autarch of Unta, and countless others who would jump at half the chance."

Katelin frowned. How did this old lady of the forest know so much about the politics of the Western Coast?

But Gracie continued, "In this case, my child, it all comes back to you. The choice before you is this: how much do you want to be Queen?"

Katelin gulped down the mouthful of plum. Yes, it all came down to Gracie's question. How much did she want to be Queen? The two of them were alone in this old lady's cottage, and so maybe at last she was free to express what she really thought. She felt safe enough in this quiet candlelight to do her thinking aloud.

"Gracie," she said, heaving a breath, "I need to talk with someone about this, about being Queen, and what to do next. I have so much churning around inside my mind, and I hope that getting it out will help me to understand. I worry that I'm not thinking clearly, because the appearance of those Malgosians has unnerved me. You're the only person here, so it must be you. May I discuss my situation with you?"

Gracie smiled. "Of course, Kat, my dear. I love listening."

"And please don't just listen. Tell me what you're thinking in response. Don't worry about my feelings, because I need to try to be rational and objective about this. I value your opinions, so I'd like us both to be open and honest as I try to answer your question."

"It will be my pleasure. And I appreciate you trusting and confiding in me."

"Well," Katelin began with a sigh, "this last year as Queen has been just as difficult and daunting as I always dreaded it would be while I grew up. So that was unfair to begin with, because I didn't ask to be born a Princess, or to be an orphan as a child, or to become a Queen at such a young age. Where were my choices then, or has my whole life been subject to destiny and the whim of the gods?"

"No, none of us get to choose who we are as children, or when or where we're born," Gracie replied. "We can't choose who our parents are, or who else is in our family, or what sort of upbringing we receive. When we come of age, we can choose what to do with the start in life we've been given. So, at your age now, you face questions such as I've asked you this evening."

Katelin nodded. "As it's turned out, the responsibilities, expectations and conflicts of being Queen have been even worse than I feared. I suppose I could learn to put up with the ceremonies, the meetings and the paperwork, and share or delegate some of those tasks. But I know I'll struggle to like all those self-centred and self-important nobles of the Court, and I don't think they like or want me either. I could never have imagined that Aunt Sirika would continue to treat me with such implacable hatred."

"Something else we can't choose," Gracie pointed out, "is whether we have enemies or not. Sometimes opposition comes to us, whether or not we deserve it. In particular, when others decide to follow an evil path, and choose what is wrong, then it's up to all of us, whatever our station in life, to oppose them and try to keep doing what is right. And you've never faced that opposition alone."

"That's right," Katelin agreed. "I've had a lot of help from my friends along the way. From Hedger—King Edgaran—as an unexpected brother; from cousin Rashelin who is more like a sister to me; from Under-Father Ruis, and many others, such that I've never borne the burden of being Queen alone. But still it always seems to come down to me. So what about now? I've never felt more alone, or had so many enemies crowding round to oppose me. Can I keep up the fight, of being myself and of ruling how I wish, even against such determined opposition?"

"Yes, your role is key," Gracie said, "but I imagine you always knew that. This is what you were born to, so the Court will need to put up with you, whoever you are and whatever you're like. And you're a leader among your friends, Kat. From what you've said, and from what I've heard, you're a fighter. You have a fire within you, a strong spirit, and a keen sense of what is right."

"I appreciate your encouragement, Gracie, but to tell you the truth, I'm wilting at the prospect. What if the fight has become too hard? What if it requires more fire and spirit than I can muster right now?"

"This is what you need to decide," Gracie said. "There's no point in being hesitant or reluctant, half-hearted or dithering as the Queen, because it's a role that requires a whole-hearted commitment. And remember that you have access to the Divine's help through your sacred relic of the Crown of Anestra."

"But the Crown is locked up inside the Royal Treasury in Anestra Castle, so that can't help me now. Aunt Sirika and the Malgosians aren't going to let me tiptoe into the city and down into the Castle vaults to sneak the Crown out to guide and empower me."

Novita snorted outside, and Katelin became sure that her clever stallion was listening to their voices.

Katelin tapped the plum stone on the wooden table top. "Suppose that by now I've done all I can. What if I was only meant to be Queen of Anestra for this past year, and now my destiny is finished? Haven't I done as much as could be asked or expected of me?"

"I agree you've achieved much during your months as Queen," Gracie replied. "But one year is a short time when compared to a lifetime. I'm sure you have much more left you could offer and give."

"But what if I don't want to do this anymore? What if I really am 'unfit to rule'? What if it's true that these disasters of invasion and plague and the death of King Edgaran are somehow my fault? Maybe Aunt Sirika is right and the Divine really has abandoned my reign and wishes someone else to occupy my throne now."

Gracie sniffed. "You shouldn't believe that for one single moment."

"But maybe I don't have the best personality and temperament for being Queen, because I'm too impulsive and confrontational. Perhaps Rashelin could do a better job of it, if only we could get rid of her mother and the Baron. She's more popular with the Court, and has more patience and the necessary skills of diplomacy and tact."

"I'd say the best outcome would be the two of you working together, as Queen and Princess, each using your respective strengths for the benefit of the people."

Through the cottage's back wall of leaf and twig, the last glimmers of daylight were fading from the sky, but the single candle lent the kitchen a cosy warmth.

"But now we need to face the fact that I'm no use to anyone dead. Recounting my experiences of the last few days has made me realise that my life is precarious. Assassins are trying to kill me. I've fled from an ambush on the road.

I've climbed a tree to hide from a murderous Malgosian band. I've nearly been eaten by a bear, and had to ride through a battle even to escape with my life. Right now, there's a band of my enemies camped outside our door, such that if I show my face, I'm dead. What use is it whether I want to be Queen or not, if I'll only end up as a dead Queen?"

"Your life is precious, and valuable, and important. And not just for your own sake, but also for the Kingdom and for the whole Western Coast."

"So I need to try and stay alive," Katelin said. "I shouldn't endanger my life by plunging headlong into battle, or risk being caught by Malgosian bands. For everyone's sake, as well as my own, I need to be less reckless and a little more cautious. And yet going back to Anestra to face Sirika and Malgosy will involve precisely all of those risks."

"You are correct that all of life involves risk. All of us, every day, face unknown dangers and perils. We need to learn to assess and live with those risks. I grant that at the moment you face more of those risks than anyone else."

"But then it's not only about me, is it?" Katelin added. "I try not to be selfish and worry about only my own life, because I seem to bring death and anguish to those around me too. Some of Zane's people have died to protect me. For all I know, Zane and his band were all slaughtered during and after that battle, simply because I enlisted them as my bodyguards."

"I don't think that's true," Gracie countered. "From what you said, the Malgosians are only after you. Once you escaped from the fighting, your enemies had no reason to continue the battle with Zane's men. They'd have withdrawn at once rather than risk further casualties against them."

"But the Malgosians might have decided to wipe them out as punishment for hiding and protecting me. Who knows what goes through the minds of evil killers?"

"You're right to feel deep concern about the fate of your friends, Kat, for Zane and his people. But they consented to become your bodyguards, and chose to fight to protect their Queen, rather than to give you up. That was their decision, in the same way that you have your choices to face now."

"And what about Rashelin? I don't know whether she's still roaming free in this forest, or had a riding accident and in need of my help, or been caught by the Malgosians. Would the Baron's men kill or injure her, or take her back to Anestra, or Mannismill? What will her mother, the Lady Sirika, do with her? If Rashelin's still alive, then she's in deep trouble too. I've made her an enemy of her own mother, fracturing her family apart. And it's all because I'm Queen. I can't ask or expect anyone else to suffer like this for me."

Gracie's gaze remained kind and understanding. "Princess Rashelin made her own choices too, to be loyal to her Queen rather than to follow her mother into evil. She knew what she was doing, and accepted the consequences of those choices."

Katelin paused and gazed into the candle flame for a moment. "So now I come back to considering my present and my future again. About love and the Kingdom, and whether I might ever have either of them. Maybe I can never have them both, because being Queen is all about duty, and has already caused nothing but problems with Zane. Why can't I be free to choose my friends, and whom I love, without complications or fear of criticism?"

"Zane will make his own choices, to be with you or not, whether you're Queen or not. You can't make those decisions for him. And no friendship or love is without complication. Everyone risks rejection or criticism when they offer their friendship and love."

"That means *I'm* able to make choices about my friendships, too. I hate not knowing whether Rashelin and Zane are alive or dead. I need to know whether they're injured and in need of my help. And it's not only that I'm worried about them. They'll be worried about me too. They'll be distressed until they're sure I'm alive and uninjured and free."

"Yes, I'm sure they're worried about you. About you as their friend, and you as their Queen. The wellbeing of those dear to us is a natural concern, especially in such risky and turbulent times. And it's not only Rashelin and Zane, of course. All the citizens of Anestra will be worried about the fate of their young Queen."

Katelin raised her eyes from fiddling with the plum stone, and saw that Gracie watched her. The darkness outside the circle of their single candle wrapped the two of them like a warm blanket; the two of them could have been the only people in the entire forest, or even the whole world.

"Perhaps the best way to decide what I do next is to consider what's most important and urgent for me, and the order I give to my priorities. In which case, for all our sakes, I wonder whether I should place the welfare of my friends above my struggles over how to be Queen. I need to know they're all right, and let them know I'm all right. Right now, I could choose to regard my friends as my more important and pressing priority than the Kingdom."

A breath of evening breeze wafted through the Haven's kitchen walls of branch and leaf, causing the candle flame to gutter.

In that moment Katelin imagined Gracie as a younger woman. By a trick of the candlelight—or was this also magic?—Katelin pictured her straighter and slimmer, her old lady's wrinkles smoothed away, looking strong and vigorous again. The deep blue eyes were the same, but the silver hair was streaked with gold. She must have been a powerful cleric in her youth, more than anyone Katelin had ever known. Indeed, Gracie was powerful still. Perhaps as an older woman, she was closer to the Divine than ever.

In the candlelight, Gracie's eyes reminded Katelin of

dark blue silk, as a flag or cushion. And on it was a Crown of silver.

Gracie might have been reading her thoughts, for she broke the silence by saying, "So if you choose something else as a higher priority than being Queen, then who will rule Anestra?"

Her words ignited a spark deep inside Katelin. She didn't recognise it at first, but it began to burn, with love, and anger, and indignation. "You're right, of course, that Anestra is my home. I love both the place and the people. Can my love for them be enough? No, my choices are never that simple. Can I allow my precious people of Anestra to be misruled by another? They've suffered enough in recent years: from neglect through the Regency, then invasion and Plague. Isn't it time for the Western Coast to have justice and peace? Yes, it is, but am I the one who is supposed to give it to them?"

Katelin looked up, and Gracie's eyes were on her. "So yes, my main problem is where my choices leave cousin Rashelin and the rest of the people I love. I don't want to leave my friends and the Kingdom at the mercy of Aunt Sirika and Baron Malgosy. Not for ever. But how can I get rid of those two? I can't see how to do that at the moment. I'd like to rescue Rashelin at least, and any others who want to come with us, from those who want to oppress them. Not those fussy, annoying members of the Court, but the good, honest people of Anestra. I feel a duty to them, but I don't know if love and duty are enough. I hoped I could serve and care for the people entrusted to me during long years of peace, but I don't think now I'll ever get that chance. Maybe this one catastrophic year as Queen is all I'll get, and is all I'm meant to have."

Gracie's voice remained gentle. "The very best way you can help Rashelin, and Zane, and all your friends and your people, is by being their Queen."

Katelin looked up and met Gracie's gaze. "I understand

why you say that, but there are other things I want to do first. I want to discover the fate of Zane and his band. I'd like some news from Anestra city, of what is happening with Rashelin and the people. About what Aunt Sirika, Baron Malgosy and Prince Tajion are doing. Only then can I consider my longer-term future, and how to regain my throne."

"Time might not be on your side, my girl. You may miss your opportunity to wrestle the Kingdom of Anestra away from your aunt and cousin and Baron Malgosy. You have an army who are loyal to you."

"Is that it? Is the only answer to try to retake the Kingdom by force? Must there be fighting in the streets, Anestrans against Malgosians, to return me to power? Aunt Sirika and the Baron won't give up without a struggle. No, Anestra has suffered enough. I don't want any more deaths during my first year as Queen. Gracie, please allow me at least to consider what other choices I might have. There must be easier, quieter and safer options."

"Yes, of course there are," Gracie said, her voice gentle. "You've been through a lot, my dear. I understand. So, if you aren't ready to be Queen now, what else would you choose to do?"

"First of all, I need to confirm that Zane and Rashelin are alive and well. After that, if I really have a choice, I'd like to stay here with you at the Haven for a while, until everything calms down. In time, if there is a way to do it without bloodshed, I could try to return to Anestra and reclaim my throne. But I repeat that I don't want anyone else to die for the sake of me remaining as Queen."

Gracie's deep blue eyes were fixed on hers. "Your friends and people might consider your life and your reign to be worth dying for."

"They might, but I can't say I agree. If further bloodshed is unavoidable, then maybe I could be like you and hide out here, and live out my life in calm and peace. Or else I could keep going, travelling eastwards, deeper into the forest, or to distant lands. Maybe I could ask Zane, to see if he wants to come with me. You might call it running away, either alone or with him, but I can always make a new life for myself, unknown, safe and free."

"I'm sorry to say that for as long as you live, even if you're far away, you will always be considered a threat to anyone else who is ruling in Anestra. There's no getting away from you being the rightful Queen. Any successor will never stop sending assassins to target you, until they can be sure that you're dead."

Katelin stared at the woman perched on the stool opposite her. Gracie gave a deep sigh, and it was as though the powerful cleric in her youth had been laid aside, and she was wrinkled old Gracie again.

Katelin was tired too, and thought they'd covered all they needed to say. She laid her hands on the kitchen table. "Thank you for listening to me, Gracie, and for sharing your insights. I hoped I could be rational and objective about my situation, but I don't think I can be, because it involves my friends."

She gazed into the grain of the wood between her fingers, the candle's flickering shadows playing across it.

"How much do I want to be Queen? My narrow escapes from death in recent days convinced me something needed to change, but I couldn't think what. If you want my honest answer, then I feel that I value the wellbeing of my friends more highly than being Queen. They have remained faithful to me, and it's time I was loyal to them. Fighting over the rule of Anestra feels too much like the political manoeuvrings of the nobles and the Court, arguing over who wants power and influence. Even if I want to win back my Kingdom, where could I start with trying to get rid of Sirika, Malgosy and Tajion? No, I'd never forgive myself if Rashelin or Zane were killed in the middle of this. I'd rather die myself than ask or expect anyone else to die for me. So,

I consider I've lost this first battle for control, but hope that one day soon I might try to affect the outcome of this war of good against evil."

## 12

## DISTURBANCE

A silence followed, and Katelin wondered if she'd said too much. No, it was a relief to have unburdened herself, and told the truth. The conflict over her destiny seemed to burn inside, and she wondered if she'd ever feel settled about her decisions. It could be right, couldn't it, to seek out and help her friends first? But did she then have any hope of remaining as Queen? Well, one day she would see if she could find a way. She sighed and looked up at Gracie.

The old woman reached across and tapped her hand. "Thank you for your honesty, Kat, my dear. Although being Queen might seem too hard, you would always have allies in Princess Rashelin and the Under-Father, in Zane and many others in Anestra. You would also have that Crown of yours. You could use it more. But in the meantime, I suggest you sleep on this. You've wrestled with important decisions this evening, and what to do next can wait until the morning. Go to bed, get some rest, and we'll see what tomorrow brings us."

Gracie stood up, and Katelin got up too. Then she remembered the Malgosians camped outside. She dropped her voice. "Will I be safe in my bedroom? It's at the front, overlooking the Malgosians' camp."

Gracie leaned on the table and blew out the candle, plunging the kitchen into darkness. "Let your eyes adjust, Kat dear, and we'll find our way upstairs by starlight. And yes, you'll be quite safe." Katelin thought she saw Gracie smile. "Although I suggest you refrain from shouting at them, should the desire to do so come over you."

Katelin chuckled. "Thank you, Gracie," she breathed

into the dim kitchen air.

They picked their way to the stairs, and Katelin's eyes adjusted well to the half-light. She cringed at every creak of the wood, but then came an unmistakeable giggle from Gracie. "What is it?" she whispered.

The old lady seemed to be fighting hard not to burst out laughing. "Look at us," she gasped. "Creeping around our own cottage, when we're perfectly safe from anyone outside. It struck me as funny, that's all."

Gracie's giggle was infectious, and soon Katelin was trying hard not to laugh out loud as well. Feeling that she mustn't make a sound made the whole situation even funnier. They both stopped on the stairs, snorting into their hands, clutching the rail, shaking with their suppressed mirth.

When at last they calmed down, Gracie nudged Katelin's arm. "Look," the old woman breathed, and pointed upwards.

Katelin gasped. Above them the staircase ceiling was alive with stars. The two of them seemed to be outside, with the glories of the heavens arrayed above them.

"Glow-worms," Gracie whispered. "They light my way to bed."

"I love them," Katelin murmured, wishing that stars always lit her way to bed too. Then, "Good night, Gracie," she said, and escaped into her darkened bedroom.

She peered through the twigs and leaves of her front bedroom wall and sobered up at once. The Malgosians had lit a fire in the middle of the grass and two of them sat beside it. The other men were strewn across the meadow, trying to sleep. Their horses were tethered to one side, and none of them had weapons drawn ready for fighting.

Katelin gave a quiet snort of indignation. Of course not. Why should they be afraid? No one was hunting or pursuing *them* through the forest. The Malgosians gave off the casual arrogance of hunters, sure of their superiority and certain that they would catch their prey before long.

She was conscious of a strong temptation to stand at her window and loudly denounce her pursuers, and wondered how Gracie had known it. But she controlled the urge, tore her gaze away and lay down on her bed fully clothed. Now she became aware of low voices outside or the tread of footsteps, but forced herself to ignore them. She'd never get to sleep if she listened out for every whisper, rustle or creak.

Instead she made herself think about Gracie. Why was the old lady so confident they wouldn't be discovered? How could she find it funny to hide from dangerous men camped outside her door? Of course, the Malgosians weren't looking for Gracie, but Katelin was sure the Baron's men would kill her and burn down her cottage if they found her harbouring their prey.

And what about this place, the Haven? If the Malgosians departed in the morning without spotting it, then that confirmed the magic of the cottage's concealment. In which case, the power behind it came from Gracie herself. Or maybe the old lady had stumbled across the hidden cottage in the same way Katelin had, and decided to turn it into a home for herself. Katelin decided she would ask Gracie about it in the morning.

When Prince Tajion entered Sirika's study that evening, his mother wasn't there yet. But Baron Malgosy was sitting next to the desk, hunched over something on the table top. Tajion couldn't see what it was, but the Baron's dagger glinted in the lamplight.

"Hey, Tajion," Malgosy said. "Take a look at this. Have you ever seen a ladybird without wings?"

That was enough to pique the Prince's curiosity. He stepped closer, to where a covered glass bowl lay on the desk. The Baron was poking something with his dagger point.

Malgosy leaned back, and Tajion saw a small black insect

wriggling away across the desk. The Baron caught it in his fingers, lifted the cover and popped it back into the bowl.

"Let's do another," he said.

Tajion noticed that the glass bowl contained dozens of ladybirds, most with their familiar red and black wings, but a few as wingless black insects like the one the Baron had just added.

Malgosy reached in and picked out another ladybird, which obligingly clung to his fingertip. The tiny thing had no idea of the grisly fate that awaited it, holding with such trust to its torturer.

Prince Tajion licked his lips. As a boy, he'd dismembered insects himself, but hadn't come across adults who enjoyed it. The Baron could turn out to be fun.

Malgosy eased the ladybird onto the desktop and poked it with his dagger tip. By instinct the creature spread its wings to escape. In one deft move, the Baron's blade slipped under the wing and severed it against the hardness of the wood.

"Can I have a go?" Tajion asked.

Malgosy beamed, and handed over the dagger.

The half-dismembered ladybird was wriggling on the desk, and Tajion poked it as the Baron had done. The remaining wing opened and Tajion lunged. He wasn't as deft as the Baron, and in slicing off the wing he also severed the insect in half.

"Never mind," Malgosy said. "It takes practice to do it cleanly. Try again." He lifted the cover on the bowl and removed another ladybird.

"So once their wings are off," Tajion mused, "we won't need the cover on the bowl."

Malgosy looked at him with his pale blue eyes. "Yes, we will. They may not have wings, but they still have legs, and can crawl their way out. So, what's the answer to that?"

"Cut off their legs?" Tajion suggested.

Malgosy beamed. "That's the spirit. I see you're learning

well."

The ladybird on the desk was saved by the entrance of Sirika.

"What are you two doing?" she snapped. She approached the desk. "Put that away, whatever it is. We've important things to discuss."

The Baron lifted the bowl to a side table, with a wink at Tajion. He wiped his dagger on his trousers, and then began to use it to pick some meat from between his teeth.

Tajion went and slouched in a chair in the corner. More and more these days, Sirika—or 'Regent Sirika', as she'd now persuaded the Court to appoint her—allowed him to sit in on her meetings. He liked that. He wasn't interested in being part of the political manoeuvrings, but it was a fascinating show to watch.

This evening, they were planning their next move together. The Baron leaned back, one leg slung over the side of his chair.

"I can't hide that I'm disappointed," Sirika said. "You promised me that your men would have done the deed by now."

He waved his dagger in her direction. "You have no idea of the vastness of the Manniswood. Whatever else we think of her, we must concede that the girl excels at escaping and hiding. But it's only a matter of time."

"Is it?" Sirika spoke with her usual sharpness. "You still maintain that we'll get her before she causes any more nuisance? The last thing we need is for her to appear—"

"Relax," Malgosy interrupted. "My men are not only scouring the forest, they've also set up a cordon along this edge of it. There's no way the girl can escape from the trees and get herself back here unnoticed."

Sirika sniffed. "You had better be right. The longer this situation persists, the less I like it. We need to squash the people's sympathy for Katelin before it grows. Because I want to move on to the next stage."

She glanced across at Tajion, and the Baron also looked across to where he lounged in the corner. Sometimes Tajion thought they'd forgotten he was there, and that suited him fine. Whenever he was forced to speak or give an opinion, he balanced letting his mother think he'd go along with whatever she asked, against also keeping his lifestyle pampered and carefree.

He smiled at her with all the childlike innocence he could muster, and asked, "And what's the next stage, Mother?"

Sirika gave a humph. "Your sister, Rashelin. She continues to refuse to join our side or renounce her place in the line of succession."

"Torture?" suggested the Baron, now twiddling the dagger between his fingers.

"This is my daughter and a Princess of Anestra we're talking about," Sirika snorted. "We could never get away with that. Besides, her signature needs to be witnessed by Under-Father Ruis, and he will never countersign a Deed if he thinks it's being made under duress."

"So how else do we propose to break the Princess's will?" the Baron asked.

There was silence until Prince Tajion piped up. "I have a suggestion." The other two turned to face him. An idea had occurred to him, and he didn't know if it was reckless and foolish, but he decided to present it anyway. If it confirmed him as politically inept in his mother's eyes, it was no harm done. She thought that of him anyway.

"I think my dear, sweet sister is holding out because of loyalty to Queen Katelin," Tajion began. "She won't dare to decide anything while she thinks her cousin is still alive. So, I suggest we announce Katelin's death."

Sirika's eyebrows rose, and the Baron grinned.

"Risky," he chuckled. "I like it."

Tajion shrugged. "Yes, it's a gamble, but you said it's only a matter of time before your men get her. So, Katelin's as good as dead already. We know that Rashelin hates being up front, or having anyone oppose her, so once she thinks the Kingdom has passed to her I expect she'll crumble. She won't remain defiant once there's no point in remaining loyal to Katelin. What do you think?"

Sirika nodded. "I think you're right. She won't cope with the reality of the Kingdom in her lap, and all of us ranged against her. I believe Katelin thrives on that, but not my daughter." She glanced up at the Baron. "Very well, we can make the announcement. But I don't like being dependent on those men of yours finding and dispatching her. She slips through their hands too easily." Her bony finger was jabbing at the Baron.

Malgosy held up placating hands. "Don't worry, we'll get her. And that Royal Physician of yours has been detained at my castle and can't send any messages. We can bring the Queen's body back here all in good time once we've got it."

Tajion smiled to himself. This was an excellent game. His mother was pretending that her niece had died in an accident, while a whole Kingdom believed the lie of the Queen's death. His sister would crumble in grief at the supposed loss of her childhood friend. Meanwhile the Baron was ordering his men to accomplish the death that the whole Western Coast was mourning. But so long as he himself ended up as King, who cared?

Katelin awoke to the whinnying of horses. Her bedroom was dark, and she sat bolt upright in bed. Her first thought was for Novita, with a fear that the Malgosians had found him.

She scrambled to her feet, and that's when something felt wrong. At first, she thought her dizziness was the result of getting up too quickly, because the floor seemed to be tilting. She gripped the bedpost, but that was swaying too. Was the cottage falling down?

She staggered across to the window and steadied herself by grabbing a thick branch. The view to the front made her heart pound. It wasn't only the cottage. The whole clearing was moving. That's when her ears registered the deep, groaning rumble in the ground.

The Malgosian camp fire had burned low, but by its light Katelin saw figures tottering about. One or two clung to each other for support, or helped fallen men to their feet. The horses were snapping their tethers and bolting.

The meadow resembled the rippling of long grass in a strong wind. But the grass here wasn't that tall. It must be the earth underneath, rising and falling, undulating like the swell of ocean breakers. The thundering rose to deafen her. Trees at the clearing's edge swayed, thrashed and snapped, until one tore up its roots and crashed to the ground.

Katelin's tight grip on the bark of the branch began to hurt her hands, because the cottage was tossing her back and forth as well. She held on to stay upright for what seemed like minutes, watching the chaos below, until everything came to a sudden stop.

Maybe it had only been seconds. It was followed by the smell of damp earth and a stunned silence. Katelin didn't trust the cottage to stay still, solid or secure anymore. The Malgosians were clambering back to their feet, bracing against each other, as though waiting for the earth to move again. All seemed to fear being thrown down or sideways at any moment.

But the ground stayed still.

Katelin let go of the branch and rubbed her sore palms together. She looked up to the sky, where the first light of early dawn was spreading from the east behind her.

The Malgosian leader barked some orders. His men scrambled to gather weapons, to stuff their blankets into packs, and they moved off. Some were sent to find the horses and then, while Katelin watched, the Malgosians had gone. All that remained were bits of rubbish, trampled grass and the smouldering fire.

Katelin waited until the voices and sounds of movement

had faded into nothing and then drew some calming breaths. She looked around the bedroom, and noticed that some items had fallen over or slid to one side. It still felt strange to walk across a stable, level floor as she moved to set things back in place.

Gracie appeared at the doorway, holding a lighted candle. "I see your Malgosian friends have left," she said.

"Yes, they went off after their horses. Is Novita all right, or did he bolt too?"

"No, you've got a clever horse there, my girl. I watched him and he was rattled all right, but he stayed. He seems to understand that he needs to stay close and quiet."

Katelin chewed her lip, for she was still trembling. "Gracie, that was an earthquake, wasn't it? I've never felt anything like it."

Gracie nodded and frowned. "Yes, we've had a few tremors in recent days, but that was the strongest yet. The animals feel them before we do, but I don't think anyone could have missed that one."

Katelin stared at the old lady in alarm. "Do you think there will be others, then? Other tremors or quakes?"

Gracie held Katelin's eye. "I don't doubt it. An earthquake like that always has smaller tremors before and after it. But the more important question is this: was that the biggest quake we're going to get, or is it building up to an even greater one?"

Katelin felt the blood drain from her face. "An even greater one? Bigger than that? What sort of damage could that cause?"

Gracie moved to look out the front window and across the clearing. "I see we have one tree down, and there will be others like that across the forest, those with shallower roots. But a greater quake can level whole swathes of trees." She turned back to Katelin, and her voice was soft but grave. "My question to you, Kat, is this: what sort of damage would such an earthquake cause in your beloved city of Anestra?"

The old lady's words hit Katelin like a physical shock. The panic rose inside her. "It would … it would damage homes, and cause injuries. And a stronger quake might collapse buildings, and kill people." She was wringing her fingers. "Aunt Sirika and the Baron won't care about the people. I ought to be back there, to lead and comfort and look after them."

Gracie held up calming hands. "My dear girl, your devotion to your city and people does you much credit. Before you gallop off back to Anestra, we ought to think and plan. Come downstairs and you can eat while we talk."

The old lady left the room before Katelin could say any more. The urgency to try to help the people of Anestra seized her like a fever, and almost without thinking she was stowing her belongings in her pack. She was leaving the Haven this morning, and she knew it. She needed to find out what was happening in the city. Maybe they were her 'beloved people' after all.

Daylight was growing in the sky above her as Katelin left her pack, shortbow and quiver in the living room and sat at the kitchen table. Gracie had placed bread, cheese, honey and flavoured water before her.

"Will you try to head straight for the city?" Gracie asked over her shoulder. She was chopping up a pomegranate and some figs.

"I don't know," Katelin mumbled, through her first mouthful of bread. "There could be some damage, and they might need me."

Gracie turned back to the table, set the plate of fruit beside her and sat down. "This morning's tremor won't have caused too much damage to the city. The real danger would be if there's a stronger one to come. You could still have time to seek help before you try riding up to the city gates."

Katelin stopped chewing. "Whose help do you mean?"

Gracie shrugged. "Last night you decided to help your

friends as your first priority. Does that mean Rashelin and Anestra first, or Zane and his band? Would it slow you up too much to go to the city by way of his people? They could guide you safely though the forest, because I expect those Malgosians are still looking for you. You could apologise and be reconciled to that Zane friend of yours."

Katelin's heart twinged at the possibility of seeing him again soon. If she could set things straight between them, then they could ride back to Anestra together. Or set off for the east if there was no safe way back to the city. Or was this her romantic dreaming doing the planning?

She tried to think objectively as she ate. She didn't know where in the forest she was, let alone the best paths to Anestra. The wanderers could help her with that. They had also fought to protect her, and she might need to defend herself from bands of Malgosians on the way. She could move with stealth on her own, but then Zane's men were accomplished hunters and trackers themselves.

But what about Zane? Yes, she wanted the chance to apologise to him for her ill-judged words, as Gracie had suggested. The misunderstanding between them felt like a weight in her stomach that she was anxious to shift. When they met, she could marshal her feelings to consider him as no more than a good friend, couldn't she? She hoped so. And what was it Gracie had said? Be yourself, make your choices, live your own life and let him come after you if he's interested. You can't change how he feels about you, Katelin, so get on with your life and see what happens. She liked the sound of that.

"What? What is it?" Gracie's question broke into Katelin's thoughts.

She looked up.

"It's just that you're smiling," Gracie said, with a knowing twinkle in her deep blue eyes.

Katelin cleared her throat. "Yes, that sounds like a good plan. Zane's people. Guides through the forest, and all of that."

Gracie chuckled, and not for the first time Katelin wondered if the old lady could read her mind. "I sense it's important to you to discover whether that young man's love for you is real."

Katelin said nothing, but busied herself with her breakfast. At length she said, mostly to herself, "But how would I find him? I mean, find them. I can't search the whole forest. Where would we meet? Where might Zane wait for me, if he wanted to see me again? There's only one landmark I know, and that's Ryebald's Cleft. Do you know it?"

Gracie nodded. "Yes, it's in the foothills of the Eastern Range. But which way to direct you from here? You could follow the stream back up its course, but that would take you a long way around. You're best to strike off through the forest, away from the stream, and keep heading uphill. That way you're sure to emerge from the trees at some point and hit the paths that run along this side of the Range."

"And when I find the path, turn left," Katelin finished for her. "Yes, Novita and I can manage that. Are we both recovered enough for a long walk?"

The old lady's deep blue eyes flicked to Katelin's wounded knee. "I should think so, as long as you take it gently. Stop often for rests, and try to avoid running. I'll pray for your continued healing, and that the Malgosians don't find you."

Katelin finished the plate of chopped fruit and stood up, eager to be on her way. The fire of action smouldered deep in her spirit.

She went and took the old lady's hands. "You've been very kind and generous to me, Gracie, at a time when I desperately needed it. I'm very grateful, and I don't think I can ever repay you."

Gracie beamed. "You don't need to repay me, my dear, precious girl. Your thanks are enough. I'll always be happy to help you. Even if there are other things you need to do first, you're still my Queen."

This last word stunned Katelin. "Am I?" A warmth rose up her cheeks. "Am I your Queen? I mean, out here in the forest I'd say you owe allegiance to no one."

Gracie's voice was gentle, but sure. "If my allegiance lies anywhere, then it is with Anestra. You reign over that Kingdom now, so yes, you're my Queen."

"If I can ever win it back," Katelin muttered to herself, and then looked around. "It's such a wonderful place here, Gracie. May I come back someday once all of this is over, and see you again?"

"Oh yes, I'm sure we'll meet again. If you don't find your way back here, then I'll come and see you in Anestra." She guided Katelin through into the living room. "I'd like to see how you're getting on."

Katelin slung on her pack, quiver and shortbow, and gave the old lady a warm embrace. She peered through the doorway into the clearing, but there was neither sight nor sound of the Malgosians.

She stepped into the cool morning air and met Novita, who had come around the side of the cottage to wait for her. As though he'd known they were leaving this morning too. The white stallion came and pushed against her shoulder, his muzzle wet from cropping the dewy grass. This seemed his way of saying they'd hidden here long enough, and he was itching to stretch his legs among the trees again.

Katelin decided to walk, rather than ride, and stopped at the far edge of the clearing. She turned and saw Gracie watching from the Haven's doorway and gave her a last wave. The old lady waved back and then disappeared into the cottage.

Katelin wondered, once she left this clearing, whether the outlines of the cottage would merge back into the surrounding forest. Would this magical place become no more than trunks, branches, twigs and leaves around a grassy meadow?

Then she remembered she'd forgotten to ask Gracie over breakfast about her cleric powers and the magic of the Haven. The earth tremor had pushed those questions out of her mind. She wanted to get on her way, so it was too late to go back and ask about that now.

"Thank you again, Gracie," Katelin breathed, "and goodbye for now."

She turned and led Novita into the forest.

## 13

## MOUNTAINS

The morning air was still cool under the trees and Novita found a faint path to follow. Katelin let her horse go in front with no more than a simple direction to keep going uphill. She noticed with a smile that the stallion had lost his shyness about showing her his wounded rump, which had healed up well. Katelin was amazed that she felt no more than a slight twinge from her wounded knee, and thanked the Divine for Gracie's powers of healing the injured. Whatever the source of the old lady's magic, Katelin relished being free of pain.

Before long they were both sweating from the uphill climb. They followed Gracie's advice to stop and rest often, and the leaves shielded them from the heat of the sun.

At their first stop, Katelin was astonished to see a parcel of food and two bottles of flavoured water from Gracie in her pack. When had the old lady stowed these for her? Had it been during the night while she slept? But last night, before the earth tremor, she hadn't yet decided to leave. And she hadn't noticed the provisions when she packed this morning. Katelin couldn't work it out, so she shrugged, and was content to eat and drink the wonderful fare.

The forest seemed to go on for ever. They crossed other little streams and folds in the land, but always kept their direction upwards. Once or twice they came across fallen trees, their roots freshly uprooted, and the reminder of the morning's earth tremor spurred Katelin to keep moving.

They saw no sign of the Malgosians, nor sound of any other human movement. Perhaps Gracie's directions had been shrewd, sending them up towards the mountains, assuming the Baron's men would concentrate their search along the easier, flatter terrain of the Mannis River valley.

As they climbed on into the afternoon, Katelin's thoughts turned to Zane and his band of wanderers, and she began to doubt her chances of finding them. How many of them had survived the battle? What would they have done after fighting the Malgosians at Ryebald's Cleft? They wouldn't have stayed there, would they? They would have scattered and fled, rather than remaining where the Malgosians could attack them again.

But then once she was no longer with them, maybe Zane and his people could travel where they wished, avoiding and being avoided by the Baron's men as before. Would the Malgosians seek to punish them for harbouring and defending her?

Katelin sighed. She didn't know enough to work anything out. She plodded on, and by late afternoon found a hollow among the trees for the two of them to sleep in. The sun had gone in behind clouds and a wind had picked up, with a sense of coming rain. Her legs and feet ached, but at least this was from walking uphill and not from the wounds.

As she lay awake, Katelin thought about meeting Zane again and spent some time composing and rehearsing her little speech of apology to him.

She must have slept, because large drops of water from the leaves above woke her up. Incessant rain soaked through the trees and landed on her in large splashes. Katelin huddled into her hooded cloak but couldn't avoid the spreading damp. They couldn't move on in the dark, so she resigned herself to a wet and sleepless night.

The dawn was slow to arrive, under heavy clouds, and by then Katelin was soaked and shivering. The wet and cold had done nothing to ease her aching limbs, and the morning rain seemed heavier than ever. But at least in the daylight they could move, and the exertion of the upward path held the prospect of warming them up.

Novita cast Katelin a reproachful look from a sodden and glistening head before he set off through the trees. It was some hours before the warmth of climbing finally settled her shivering, but she couldn't stop coughing. She hated to think how she looked: soaked and bedraggled, face and clothes smeared with dirt, and with leaves and insects in her matted and knotted hair. Was this the condition in which she hoped to meet Zane? She had little choice about that.

The rain eased off at last, and was replaced by a dripping stillness. The wind had dropped, and Katelin removed her cloak as she tried to dry off. She couldn't tell which of her clothes were soaked with rain and which with her sweat. The sun came out above the treetops, and the trunks had begun to thin out on the rising ground. The elms and beeches of the river valley had given way to pines and firs as the mountainside began. Were they approaching the treeline at last, where the vastness of the Manniswood gave way to the towering Eastern Range?

Katelin came upon a gap between the trees where the noonday sun struck a patch of grass and decided it was time to dry off and warm up. She stripped off her wet clothes and hung them on branches, as much in the sun as possible. Novita stood and steamed. Katelin lay on the grass and closed her eyes, the sunshine warming her bare skin. It would be typical for the Malgosians to stumble upon her now, so she listened intently for sounds of movement.

She awoke feeling cold. A few hours must have passed because the sun had moved, leaving her in shadow. She berated herself for her lack of attention to the danger of being caught, but conceded that the wet night had robbed her of necessary sleep. She hurried to dress, her clothes having dried a little, though they were still damp.

She wanted to see where they were before the daylight faded, and she scrambled up between the thinning trees, ahead of Novita this time. A rocky outcrop rose higher than the surrounding trees, and so Katelin began to climb. Her aching muscles protested, but she heaved herself upwards to clamber onto its summit.

Her first sight was of the Eastern Range peaks that towered above her. Still capped in spring snow, they formed a jagged line to the north against the blue sky. They ranged to her right and left, east and west, an impenetrable barrier that could only be skirted.

The mountains descended in ridges and shoulders towards her, until the trees of the Manniswood began a short distance above her. She scanned the treetops to her left, into the lowering sun, towards where she assumed Ryebald's Cleft lay. Was that correct? Had she come up to the east of it? Yes, she thought so.

But now, which path to take? There was one above the treeline, running westwards, which must be the trail that passed the top of the Cleft. But it looked exposed, such that anyone from above or below could see movement along it if they looked hard enough. There must be another westward path under cover of the trees that reached the Cleft at ground level. Katelin couldn't see that, but supposed it ran below where the bare shoulders of the mountains plunged into the carpet of the forest.

Before she descended, Katelin carefully took her bearings, to know in which direction to head off from the foot of the rock-face. Behind her, the sweeping slopes of the Manniswood up through which she had climbed levelled out in the distance into the wide Mannis River valley. Malgosy Castle lay on the other side, and Katelin shuddered, glad she couldn't see it from here.

She slipped in her descent down the rock, cutting her hand. She swore, because it would make drawing her bow both awkward and painful. It was too much to hope that she wouldn't need to use it again soon. At the bottom of the outcrop she bandaged the cut with a cloth and set off with Novita towards Ryebald's Cleft.

The sun was sinking fast ahead of them as Katelin led her stallion between the trees, keeping the rising foothills to their right. Before long they came across a narrow track which led where they wished to go: where the forest clothed the mountains' feet. Too soon the slanting sunbeams disappeared altogether, leaving them to stumble through a shadowed evening hush. Gaps between the trees above the track allowed her to see the first glimmers of stars.

At intervals she stopped to listen for sounds of movement, remembering that this was where the Malgosians had attacked the camp. She hoped those rustlings were nocturnal animals emerging from their dens to hunt.

Keeping her dark-accustomed eyes wide, at last Katelin came across the place where the battle of Ryebald's Cleft had been fought. The grass was trampled, saplings and branches broken, there were gashes in tree trunks, a broken arrow, a discarded leather scabbard. She motioned Novita to wait and crept forwards to the opening of the Cleft. She unslung her shortbow and nocked an arrow to the string. Her cut hand stung.

No wanderer or Malgosian was on watch. Was that a good sign, or ominous?

With all the stealth she could muster, Katelin peered around the rocky cliff face and into the Cleft.

It was dark with shadows, but looked deserted.

She crept forward. There were signs of a camp here: the ashes of abandoned fires, firewood scattered across the ground. But it didn't look recent. How many days had it been since Katelin had fled for her life from here? She'd lost count. It could be that Zane's people had fled from here then, and not returned.

The back of her neck prickled. She had the sense of being watched. The sudden realisation hit her that of all places in the entire Manniswood this was the one most likely to be guarded. Wouldn't the Malgosians leave someone here in case of her return? She whirled around, raising her bow. She couldn't see or hear anyone, but now became fearfully suspicious of any rustle, creak or call of night bird.

She needed to escape the trap of the Cleft, and climb the path up the mountainside to where Zane had taken her before.

"Novita," she called in an urgent whisper.

It sounded dangerously loud in the night air. No response. She was about to whisper again when the fall of hooves sent a chill down her back.

Novita looked round the opening.

Katelin let out a long breath and beckoned him forward. He looked at her, and she held a finger to her lips. If she hadn't been so afraid, she would have laughed at the thought of him trying to tiptoe quietly across the grass. His hooves were too loud. And now even the starlight was too bright. It reflected with a shimmer off his white coat, making him an apparition, a ghostly beast.

She took his rein and led him as gently as she could towards the rear of the Cleft. No one jumped out at them, but Katelin was ready for them if they did. All the way, the sensation of being watched didn't leave her.

They reached the foot of the track which wound up the rock-face into the mountains. Katelin filled her lungs and began to climb, Novita clopping slowly behind her. Her leg muscles didn't thank her for more of this.

The night air was still and cool, and Katelin tried to keep her breathing shallow and silent. Halfway up the track, Novita snorted. Katelin turned and patted his nose, shushing him. The climb was not a problem for the stallion, but he was letting her know she was making him work. She stroked his flank and let out some rein, for him to go at his own pace.

Now that they were stopped, Katelin listened, and Novita also became still. Beyond the Cleft the night breeze sighed through the leaves of the Manniswood, but there was no sound of voice or footfall. A twig snapped, a night animal grunted, and then she heard a scurry through rustling leaves.

Katelin looked up. The stars crested the peaks of the Eastern Range, and moonlight washed the mountainsides in faint silver. She scanned the path that crossed above Ryebald's Cleft. It was too dark to see clearly, and she was at the wrong angle to see back into the crevices and hollows. She could see no movement along it. It was too late by now if someone was hiding up there, still, shadowed, watching her. What were the chances of Zane being there? The one she hoped to see. But did he wait for her, also hoping to meet her here?

Katelin breathed out with a silver mist and stepped forward. Novita followed at the same slow pace, and they didn't pause again until they neared the top of the track.

Katelin panted out her silent breaths through an open mouth, and stopped to steady her heart. She released Novita's rein and nocked an arrow to her shortbow again before cresting the ridge onto the path along the foothills.

Eyes wide, she scanned left and right. And froze. What was that? A darker shadow? She couldn't be sure, but was that a cloaked figure back against the mountainside?

She crept a step or two closer. The figure was alone, crouched. A glint of moonlight reflected off an eye. Katelin waited, not daring to speak. If he'd been watching, he couldn't have failed to see her enter, cross and climb up the Cleft.

The figure straightened up. Katelin drew back her bowstring and aimed. He raised two hands in surrender.

"Kat," he breathed.

She exhaled in relief. A cold thrill shivered down her back and she dropped the bow. Unable to stop herself she ran and threw her arms around him. "Zane."

He squeezed her in return. For some time, they stood and held each other, not speaking. Katelin hugged him as hard as she could, and allowed his body to warm her. How long had it been since she'd had the comfort of his embrace? It felt like too many days.

But he was here. Her mind raced. What did that mean? Had he been waiting here specifically for her, or was this simply a safe place for him to hide out? Keen and anxious though she was to know his feelings and intentions, she made the effort to hold off from asking him such probing questions.

She was also the first to slacken her grip and step back from him. She couldn't wipe the beaming grin from her face, though. "Zane, it's so great to see you. Are you all right?"

"I am now I've seen you." He was grinning back. "I saw you when you entered the Cleft, but I needed to be sure it was you."

"So I was right. I was being watched."

He was scanning her face. "Kat, where have you been?"

She decided to be vague. "Oh, hiding out in the forest. I don't really know where I was. What about your people? Where are the others?"

Zane shrugged. "After the battle, we scattered. Some have gone into Anestra. Others deeper into the forest. A few around the Eastern Range to Lake Timajet. Anything to get out of the way of those Malgosians."

She touched his arm. "Zane, you lost some of your friends in that battle, didn't you? I'm so sorry, because they were protecting me, allowing me to escape."

Zane swallowed and nodded. "Yes, some good people were killed and others injured. But defending you was the right thing to do, especially now I know you're safe. And the Malgosians lost more than we did. They divided their forces to try to trap you up here on the ridge, so we had the upper hand in the fighting outside the mouth of the Cleft. I don't think they'll risk attacking us here again. Have you seen more of them?"

"Yes, a band came searching for me, but I hid. I think I

was saved from them finding me by that shaking of the ground. Did you feel it?"

Zane nodded. "Yesterday morning. Caused some rockfalls up here."

Novita stepped up and nudged them, insisting on being noticed.

Zane chuckled. "Hello, Novita," he said. "I can't tell you how pleased I am to see you alive and well. Both you and your mistress here." He gave the stallion's neck a firm rub.

Katelin suppressed a gratified smile.

"What about food and water?" said Zane. "You must be starving and parched. Here, come and have something."

He stepped away, but Katelin didn't move. She paused, unsure what to tell him about Gracie.

He stopped, noticing she wasn't following.

"I've been fine, thank you," she said. "I have plenty of supplies."

Zane stared at her. "You've been on your own for days in the forest, and you tell me you're all right for food and drink?"

A smile twitched at the corners of Katelin's lips. "Hm-mm."

He narrowed his eyes, surveying her. "And what about your injuries? Don't tell me you've managed to arrange an excellent bandaging of your own wounds."

Katelin pulled up her sleeve to reveal Gracie's neat arm bandage. Now she couldn't stop a full-blown grin. She was enjoying this, and decided to keep him guessing and maintain her mystery a while longer. "And what about you? Are you hungry? Come, let me see to Novita and then we can sit and talk."

She left him standing there watching her, his lips parted in an intrigued half smile. She loosened the stallion's tack, and walked him over to the grass by the path. She unslung the pack from her back and joined Zane where he sat overlooking the Cleft.

As she removed Gracie's food parcel, she realised they were sitting close enough to where they'd sat the night before the battle. A warm flush of shame filled her cheeks, and she remembered to deal with that first. It was worth getting her apology out of the way so she could enjoy the rest of their time together.

She turned to face him. "First of all, I want to apologise properly for what I said to you here those nights ago." Zane opened his mouth to interrupt, but Katelin didn't let him. "We didn't get the chance to talk about it then, and it was thoughtless and selfish of me to let my imagination run away. I'm sorry if I embarrassed or upset you, because I don't want anything to spoil our friendship. So, do you forgive me?"

Zane was gazing at her, a lopsided smile on his face. He laid a hand on her arm. "Yes, Kat, of course I forgive you. But there's nothing to forgive. The upset was my fault, not yours. I'm over-sensitive when anyone makes assumptions about me, or tries to plan my future. Thank you for saying it, but to tell you the truth, I'd already forgiven you for that."

The twitch of Katelin's smile returned. "You mean I didn't need to pluck up my courage or rehearse my little speech? You might have told me. So, we're friends?" She held out a hand for him to shake.

He took it, but then pulled her towards him and kissed her cheek. Her blush was rising, but she decided she liked his token of reconciliation better than hers.

"Friends," he said. "All forgiven, but I'm not sure I'll let you forget altogether where your imagination was running off to."

Katelin gulped inside, but didn't show it. Despite her apology, or maybe because of it, Zane seemed more interested than ever. But she steeled herself not to focus on his feelings, because she couldn't control those. Before her blush grew out of control she changed the subject.

"You must try this bread," she said, offering Zane a

chunk of Gracie's loaf. "What do you think?"

His eyes widened as he bit and chewed. "This is fantastic," he mumbled with his mouth full. "And it's still soft and fresh. So, come on, Kat, tell me where you got it."

She gave him a sidelong glance. "What makes you assume I didn't bake it myself? And try this water."

She handed him a bottle of Gracie's peach-flavoured stream water and watched him lick his lips at the refreshing taste.

His dark eyes didn't leave her face. In fact, they seemed to glisten in the moonlight. "Something tells me," he murmured, "that you're starting off our renewed friendship by keeping a big secret from me."

Katelin sighed. "You're not going to rest until I tell you where I've been, are you?"

Zane shook his head.

"I met this old lady in the forest, by the name of Gracie. Do you know her?"

Zane frowned. "Nope."

"She lives in this hidden cottage, made out of trunks and branches, twigs and leaves. It's a most beautiful place, at the edge of a clearing by a stream. You should go there."

"I see. And where is it? How can I find it?"

Katelin shrugged. "No idea. It seemed to be deep in the forest, but I'm not even sure I could take you back there myself. The place had a sort of magical quality to it."

Zane's eyebrows rose and he broke into a roguish grin. "Ah, now I understand. There's this mysterious Gracie who lives in a secret, magical cottage by a most beautiful clearing and stream. I can see I'm not the only subject of your runaway imagination."

Katelin laughed. "You can scoff and doubt all you like. But it was Gracie who gave me this bread and water, and who bandaged my wounds. So there."

"Hmm. I grant that your supply of excellent food and drink, and your bandages, are hard to explain otherwise. So, if her cottage is a hidden one, how did you find it in the first place?"

"Aha," Katelin cried. "That's the magic of it, you see? Perhaps the Divine was looking after me, to send Gracie and her cottage along when I was in desperate need of a place of healing and refuge. But when a band of Malgosians entered the clearing and set up camp, they couldn't see the cottage at all."

Zane gaped at her. "You mean that you and this old lady, Gracie, were hiding out inside this magical cottage with a troop of Malgosians camped on your doorstep, and they didn't even notice you were there?"

Katelin beamed. "That's right. Then the earth shook and they all left, and I could depart safely. The stream there has the most wonderful pure water, so refreshing and healing to bathe in. I'm sure Gracie makes these drinks from it."

She was enjoying Zane's incredulous gaze, and relieved to have the firm evidence of the bread, water and bandages to confirm her story. Otherwise he'd think her an even more deluded, fanciful, day-dreaming girl.

He seemed lost for words, so she went on. "You asked where I've been, and where I got the food and drink, so now I've told you. But you can believe I ground my own grain and baked it in an oven to make this bread if you prefer."

"You're incredible," Zane said at last. "And by that, I mean unbelievable. But I don't know what else to think. I'll ask the others if they've ever met this Gracie, or found a hidden cottage by a clearing and stream."

A sudden thought occurred to Katelin. "Is it all right if we keep Gracie as a secret between the two of us? I don't mind you knowing, when you can see and taste the evidence for my tale in front of you. But anyone else might think I'm mad and talking nonsense. Would that be all right?"

Zane grinned. "Yes, of course, if you wish. Gracie can remain our little secret. It'll be just me who thinks you're mad and talking nonsense, then."

Katelin chuckled and said, "All right, I'll tell you what I think. Gracie admitted to being a cleric of the Divine, but she must be one of the wisest and most powerful I've ever known. She worked and prayed for my healing, and I feel so strengthened and refreshed after those few days with her. What do you think?"

Zane was nodding. "That makes sense. Clerics can heal, but it sounds as though she has some hiding and protecting powers as well. She's probably a nature cleric, or some sort of druid, to produce such food and drink out of the forest, not to mention growing a hidden cottage for herself out of the trees."

Katelin laughed. "Cleric, druid, or whatever she is, I liked her, and I owe her my life."

"To Gracie," Zane toasted, raising the bottle of peach-flavoured water in the air.

Katelin echoed him and they lapsed into silence. It was comfortable sitting there with him. The moon was riding high now, washing out the light of all but the brightest stars. The forest below them looked calm and still, for the breeze that had rustled the leaves had dropped.

Tiredness stole up on Katelin. It was late, and before she broke into cavernous yawns in front of him, she said, "We ought to get some sleep. I'd like to talk to you about what we do next, but let's leave that until the morning."

She stood up, and he did too. She reached and embraced him, and received another kiss on her cheek. She resisted the urge to kiss him back.

"Thank you for being here, Zane, and good night."

"I'll keep watch first, Kat, so sleep well."

She went and lay down on the grass, curled up in her cloak.

Zane was here. He'd been waiting for her. He'd forgiven her and they were friends again. These thoughts were so comforting that sleep came straight away.

## 14

## PLAN

The guards escorted Princess Rashelin along the Castle corridors, and she reflected that she never used to become nervous about seeing her mother. But now she folded her arms across her chest to stop herself from shaking.

Had it been an illusion before, that they'd been a happy family, able to get along? Or had her mother always been selfish and greedy for power? Had Rashelin been naïve to think that the Court of Anestra could be united, selfless, and servants of the people? Or had they always been incurably arrogant and self-seeking?

Two Mannismill guards were lounging outside Sirika's study door when Rashelin rounded the corner. They straightened at once when they saw her escort, for fear of being reported.

Rashelin entered the study, bracing herself for who would be here. And it was bound to be bad news. If any good news came—that Katelin was recovering, for example—then they wouldn't tell her, would they?

The room looked full, with Regent Sirika seated at her desk, flanked by Baron Malgosy and Prince Tajion standing one on either side. It was clear that they'd been watching the door, waiting for her. Rashelin's stomach tightened when she saw how pleased they looked.

"She's dead," Baron Malgosy blurted out, before anything else could be said. His face was plastered with a gloating grin.

Rashelin gasped, as though she'd been punched in the stomach. All her insides—lungs, heart, mind and soul—were suddenly emptied, and she couldn't think or breathe.

As though from a distance came Regent Sirika's voice. "Now, now, my good Lord Baron. We must break the news to her gently. The young lady was attached to her foolish cousin, and this will come as a shock."

Rashelin's mind clouded and her chest ached, so she forced her body to take a breath. And then another. She reached and steadied herself on the back of a chair. Then she lifted her gaze to regard her mother.

Sirika's cold, grey eyes were unflinching. "A messenger arrived from Malgosy Castle a short while ago. He informed us that Queen Katelin has died from her wounds. Of course, the Baron's men did all they could to save the young woman, but her injuries were extensive and she'd lost too much blood."

Rashelin was desperate not to believe it. She looked from one face to another—Sirika, Malgosy and Tajion—trying to detect signs of the lie, but she couldn't see any.

"I'm sorry, Rash," Prince Tajion said. "I know you liked her."

Rashelin looked away. She held up a hand to stop them from saying another word, and turned towards the window. She wasn't going to cry in front of them. What she needed was a minute to compose herself and think.

She straightened and stepped to the window. It was a sunny evening outside, too beautiful a scene for such news. The sparse clouds were fluffy and white, not grey and raining. The grass and leaves were green with life, not bare or stark or dead. The sun's setting rays bathed the city in a warm, comforting light, belying the grief that these three monsters would soon announce to it.

Closing her eyes, Rashelin prayed to the Divine to let her know if this news were true. Could she feel again that spark of hope, as Under-Father Ruis had taught her, the conviction that Katelin still lived?

No, her inner senses were in shock and turmoil, in too much distress to separate truth from lies. She couldn't distinguish her wishful thinking, and her heart's yearnings about Katelin's life, from the trauma of the tidings now delivered.

She needed to say something, to respond to her mother, brother and the Baron. She turned to face them.

"I need proof," she declared. "I need to see Katelin's body for myself. I want it brought back here and examined by the Royal Physician and the Under-Father to confirm the cause of death. Because otherwise I don't believe you. And I don't trust you, either."

Sirika's lips tightened and her eyes narrowed, although these might have been an attempt at a smile. She glanced sideways at the Baron. "Of course, we don't intend that the former Queen's body should remain at Malgosy Castle. It will be borne back here with all honour and respect, and buried at the Temple of the Divine. But your declarations of mistrust and disbelief are of great concern, coming from one who needs to consider her position as the next Queen of Anestra."

Sirika's words landed as a dead weight in Rashelin's stomach as the full force of the situation sank home. Of course. Katelin's death left Rashelin as Queen. This was why they had summoned her. All the previous threats and pressure now led up to this moment. What should she do? What would she decide?

"You have a choice to make, young lady," Sirika said. "There are two options open to you, and the Kingdom needs you to decide. You can become Queen and submit to our will." She indicated the three of them around the desk. "Or you can abdicate and leave the Kingdom forever. Which will it be?"

Rashelin bristled. "No, I have a third option too. I can become Queen and rule as I wish."

"You wouldn't last five minutes," Baron Malgosy breathed. "With the three of us and all the Court against you? And when accidents happen so easily?"

"Baron," Sirika warned, and Malgosy folded his arms in silence. This only served to flex his obvious muscles, to reinforce his threat that Rashelin could follow her cousin's fate.

Rashelin glanced at her younger brother. Prince Tajion appeared relaxed, shoulders slouched, hands in pockets. But he gave her the impression of a snake at rest, only too ready to coil, spring and strike with venomous fangs.

"You will grant me some time to think," Rashelin declared, and Sirika leaned back in her chair.

Rashelin turned back to gaze out of the Castle window, resting her hands on the sill. She wanted the chance to ponder, even though she'd been considering all her choices for days. Now that the moment had come, she wanted to be sure of her decisions.

One option was unacceptable at once. She would never submit to the will of Sirika, Malgosy and Tajion, and so had long discounted the 'acquiescent puppet' choice.

The course she had suggested was almost as futile. She knew she was not like Katelin. She didn't have her cousin's independence, or fire, or defiance to resist and oppose those ranged against her. She might have an ally in Under-Father Ruis, but who else? That option heralded a lifetime of struggle and conflict, and while Katelin might thrive on such things, Rashelin could not. She'd supported her cousin in the Queen's battle against Sirika, but now Katelin no longer had a side for Rashelin to take. On her own she would crumple in misery, and surrender to Sirika and the Baron sooner or later, simply to gain a quieter life.

So, what did that leave? Abdication and exile. But where to go and what to do?

There must be other places to live and other lives to lead than as a Princess. Perhaps she could go to the Manniswood first, to find Katelin's former outlaw friends, and journey onward from there. She was young, healthy and attractive enough, so there were other possibilities for life and happiness away from the traumas of Kingdoms and thrones.

It would leave Anestra at the mercy of Sirika and the Baron, but Rashelin saw no way to prevent this on her own. She could only entrust her people to the protection and compassion of the Divine.

In the meantime, she would return to her room and meditate for calmness. She needed to pray, for the Divine to show her clearly whether Katelin still lived, and for guidance over her own future.

But what to say now to her mother, brother and the Baron? Not to admit that they had won and defeated her, that was for sure. That would only encourage them, and she wasn't about to do that. It was time to muster her calmness, determination and dignity again.

She turned back to face her enemies in the study. "Once I have proof of Katelin's death—and only then—I will accept that I am the next Queen of Anestra. If and when that happens, and not before, your new Queen will inform you of her decisions. In the meantime, may the Divine have mercy on us all."

She didn't wait to register their responses before she marched to the study door and left.

Katelin stirred with the first light of a clear dawn across the mountainside. The air on her face was fresh and cold. She sat up and looked around, and saw Zane slumped against the rock-face, his stubbly chin resting on his chest, fast asleep.

Her first thought was indignation and annoyance that neither of them had kept watch for their safety. But then she softened, realising that Zane had chosen not to wake her in the night, to allow her some much-needed sleep. He'd persevered in watching over her, but had finally succumbed to slumber. Should she let him get away with sleeping on the job? Not on your life.

Katelin plucked a long blade of grass and tiptoed over to

where he sat. She knelt and tickled his ear with the grass. Zane shifted and mumbled at once, flailing a hand to swat away the imagined fly. But he was too deeply asleep.

So, Katelin did the same with the other ear, and then his nose, tormenting his dreams until he finally spluttered and lurched into wakefulness. Then there she was, inches away from his blinking, bleary face, his broad grin melting into a laugh.

Before he could even think of kissing her, she stood up. "Good morning, sleepyhead." She walked back to her blanket and rolled it up. "I can see I'll need to have stern words with my Captain of the night watchmen, to make sure no one falls asleep while they're supposed to be guarding me."

"But I hope you slept soundly, my Queen," Zane teased back, "warm, comfortable and undisturbed?"

"Oh yes, definitely undisturbed," Katelin replied, "so that I can rise refreshed for whatever today will bring." Then she softened her voice. "I'm touched you let me sleep, Zane: thank you."

He beamed. "So, we're both rested and no harm done. Can we have some more of your food and drink? I'll see to the horses and then we can talk while we eat."

Novita and Zane's chestnut mare Conker had wandered along the mountainside track in search of grazing. While Zane went to fetch them, Katelin got out her supplies of Gracie's bread, fruit and water.

"I know you want to discuss what to do next," Zane said, as he sat down beside her, "but there are things I need to tell you first. I didn't say them last night because I think they'll upset you, and you needed to sleep."

Katelin stopped chewing her hunk of bread and a finger of fear plucked at her insides. She stared at him. "What things? Tell me."

Zane sighed. "Yesterday afternoon, some hours before you arrived at the Cleft, Arch came past along this track.

You remember him, one of our band?" Katelin nodded. "Well, he was heading back east, further into the Manniswood. He'd come from Anestra city."

Katelin swallowed, both desperate and fearful to hear anything from Anestra. "He'd come from the city? Any news of Rashelin? And how are the people? What are Sirika and the Baron up to?"

"Kat, I'll tell you all I know if you'll let me explain. Princess Rashelin is unhurt and back in Anestra. After the battle with the Malgosians down here," Zane indicated the Cleft below them, "Arch thought he'd be safer staying with relatives in Anestra. But he only stayed there one night before returning to the forest. He didn't like what he saw or heard."

It was a relief to hear about Rashelin's safety, but Katelin was bursting with curiosity about her city and people. "Zane, tell me," she ordered.

"Okay, okay." He held up an apologetic hand. "First of all, there are Malgosians in Anestra. They're unmistakeable in their dark green and grey, and they aren't hiding their presence. They're at the city gates and Arch said he even saw them at the Castle gatehouse."

Katelin tore off another hunk of bread. "But they're banned from the city. Why was that allowed?"

"That's what Arch asked his cousin. Apparently, the decree of banishment only applies to Baron Malgosy himself, and not to his men. So, the Malgosians have every right to enter the city, as followers of a nobleman of the Old Kingdom. But it gets better."

"Better? I can't wait to hear it."

"The reports are that the Baron himself has come to the Castle."

Katelin choked and needed a drink to settle her throat.

"Arch's relatives said that our friend the Baron was brought into the Hall of the Court at the invitation of your Aunt Sirika herself."

"What?" Katelin spluttered. "Why did the Court allow that?"

Zane frowned. "I'm afraid this is the part you won't like. Baron Malgosy told them he had urgent and vital news concerning the future of the Kingdom. He said he had news about you."

"But he doesn't, does he?" Katelin scoffed. "The Baron doesn't know where I am or what I'm doing, other than roaming about in the Manniswood. And hang on a minute, how can Arch's relatives know what's going on in the Hall of the Court in Anestra Castle? Has the whole city been invited in to listen to the Baron?"

"No, Kat." Zane voice was soft. "Your Aunt Sirika has made sure that none of this is secret. In fact, she sends out regular reports to the people by way of the clerics." He caught and held her eye. "They're calling on everyone to pray to the Divine for your recovery."

"My recovery?" Katelin snorted. "What do you mean? There's nothing wrong with me."

Zane sighed. "That's not what the Baron told them. He reported to the Court that his men found your bleeding and wounded body deep in the forest, after what seemed to be a riding accident and then attack by wolves or a bear. The Court and people of Anestra believe you're lying mortally wounded in Malgosy Castle, and that your injuries might prove fatal."

Katelin stared at him. "They've reported that I'm dying?"

"Yes," said Zane, "and no one has a reason to disbelieve them. That's why I couldn't believe it when I saw you and Novita enter the Cleft last night. I thought I was hallucinating. I needed to see you face to face, and touch you, to believe you were here and still alive." He swallowed hard. "Kat, for a few hours yesterday, after Arch told me the news from Anestra, I thought you were dying. And I didn't like it." He shook his head. "Didn't like it at all. Those were the worst few hours of my life."

Katelin reached out and touched his arm. "I'm sorry, Zane. It wasn't true."

"Yes, I know that now. But that's why there's no question of us not being friends. To think you were dying, when we'd parted with such unfriendly words … well, let's just say that of course I'd forgiven you for all of that."

The threat of tears stung at Katelin's eyes. Before they leaked, she reached across and embraced him. But she still let go first. "For this alone, if not for everything else, then Aunt Sirika and Baron Malgosy will pay. To let everyone think I'm dying! Especially Rashelin. She'll remember leaving me in this forest and think she might have prevented my death." Katelin couldn't stay seated and jumped up. She paced back and forth, twisting some bread in her hands. "Because none of it's true. All I need to do is turn up at the gates of Anestra and everyone will see me and know it's a lie."

"That's why Malgosians guard the city gates. And why a line of Malgosian soldiers guards the edge of the forest leading towards Anestra. They didn't bother about Arch entering the forest, but anyone leaving it is stopped and searched. I guess their orders are to stop you from turning up at Anestra's gates at all costs."

"But their reports and actions don't match up. If they say I'm dying in Malgosy Castle, why do they expect me to slip out of the forest and back to the city? Anyway, they can't guard the whole length of the forest boundary, especially at night. Anyone could sneak through between them."

"I wouldn't be so sure." Zane shook his head again. "Arch said there are hundreds of them, patrolling back and forth. At night they light bonfires to keep watch between the mountains and the river. But, Kat, don't you see? Now that Sirika and the Baron have broadcast this news in Anestra, they'll stop at nothing to kill you. For them, everything depends on proving their reports true and producing your body as soon as possible. If you try to break or sneak through their line, they will shoot you dead first, and find out who you are later."

Katelin stopped in her pacing. "You said that Rashelin is unhurt. What's the news of her?"

Zane nodded. "Yes, she was escorted back to Anestra by the Malgosians. That was the first everyone saw of them. So I assume they captured her in the forest and took her back."

Katelin breathed out. "Then at least she's safe."

"Not exactly," Zane said, and Katelin looked at him sharply. "According to the rumours, she's under some sort of room arrest. You see, they're blaming her for your accident, or at least for abandoning you in the forest. Sirika's making it sound like Rashelin's fault if you die of your wounds."

Katelin's anger burned and she punched a fist into her palm. "But that's not fair! Rashelin tried to save me, and we only separated so we wouldn't both be caught. I need to go and sort this out."

She turned to go to Novita but Zane reached and caught her arm. "Kat, wait, stop. You can't go rushing back to Anestra. You need help. You need allies. Or at least you need a plan. What are you going to do and how are you going to do it?"

Katelin let him pull her back down to sit next to him. But she was tense, struggling with inaction when her fire of indignation demanded to gallop back to the city.

"I have allies," Katelin said. "The Anestran army, the soldiers and guards of the city will all be loyal to their Queen."

Zane nodded. "I would guess you're right. But you should know that Sirika has been poisoning the Court against you. She's been questioning in public whether you were ever the Divine's chosen for the throne. She points to the Lassenite invasion, the Ilbassi Plague, the death of King Edgaran, and now your accident, all within this last year or so, to question whether your reign isn't cursed. You know the people can be superstitious when they've suffered; it doesn't take much to persuade them something's wrong. Sirika is playing on their fears and giving them a scapegoat to blame."

Katelin sat in silence, not knowing what to say or think. Her anger at her aunt changed to wretchedness, and she began to feel small. She'd often doubted her destiny as Queen of Anestra, but now it was worse than ever. "Zane," she whispered at last. "Could it be true? Could it be my fault? Have I brought all this on Anestra, by my choices, or obstinacy, or selfishness?"

Zane reached an arm across her shoulders and squeezed. "No, Kat. Not at all. We've survived through all these things only because you're a great Queen."

"How can I make the Court and people believe that? I've tried to give them my best, but how can I prove the Divine's favour? The Crown?"

"Yes, Kat. That sounds like a good plan and a place to start. Everyone will believe the glory of the Divine through the Crown of Anestra, won't they?"

"They will, but that's locked up in the Castle Treasury. How am I supposed to get there without any Malgosians seeing or killing me?"

"Hmm. Let's consider the options. What about force? Do you have allies who could march here and protect you while you enter the city?"

Katelin sighed. "The Lassenites and the Untans are my vassals, but would take ages to get here. An army of them would make Anestran soldiers think they're being invaded, not liberated. The barbarians are unreliable and the Caldunate has little army to speak of, and anyway, I don't want anyone dying a violent death for me to be Queen. So, I don't see any option there."

"Okay, so that brings us to stealth," said Zane. "Which is probably the better starting point, seeing as it's just you and your faithful henchman bodyguard sitting here." He gave her one of his lopsided, roguish half-smiles that she couldn't resist.

She smiled back. "Yes, I'm grateful I've got you at least."

Zane grinned. "So, assuming we can get past or around the Malgosian line at the edge of the forest, how do we get into the city?"

"Hmm." Katelin shook her head. "There aren't many weaknesses, and I wouldn't like to try to scale the city walls at night. The walls are patrolled too, so the chances of meeting a Malgosian before I could get anywhere near the Castle are too high."

"Is there anyone inside the city who might be able to help us? To open the gates, smuggle you in, or anything like that, if we could get a message to them?"

"I once escaped from the city by sea, so we could try to enter the harbour from the Ocean side. But that would mean going somewhere like the Caldunate first to board a ship, and I'd still have the same problem of getting from the harbour to the Castle undetected."

Zane stayed silent, watching her, as her mind worked. Come on, Katelin, there must be a solution to this. How could she get into the city, to someone who would help and protect her? All to prove that the Divine still favoured her rule. She found herself missing Gracie's wisdom and counsel, because she felt sure the old cleric would have had some answer to suggest.

And then it all clicked. Katelin straightened and turned to face Zane, beaming.

"What?" he said. "What is it?"

"I've got it," Katelin replied. "Gracie. The Divine. The clerics. The Temple. It's outside the city walls, on the north-western side of the city. If I could get there, then Under-Father Ruis would be sure to hide me, with all the clerics as witnesses of my presence. He could even send for the Crown from the Treasury."

Zane was grinning too. "Sounds good. How do we get

to the Temple undetected?"

"That would need to be from the north. We must steer clear of the city itself. From here we could go around the Eastern Range to Timajet, and then from the Lake and monastery cut across the highway to the Coastal Range. Then we skirt back south to the Temple. Simple."

"Simple indeed. We can forget about the forest and the watching Malgosian line, and creep around these mountains to their northern side."

Katelin slapped her knees. "Are you ready?"

Zane laughed. "That's what I love about you, you know? All action and brilliant plans. Ready to gallop off to Anestra to save your people, but then, when you give yourself the chance, coming up with an excellent idea to accomplish it. No wonder the Divine made you our Queen." He stood up and went off to ready his mare.

Katelin sat stunned for a moment. Firstly, by the "that's what I love about you", and then by the rush of compliments that followed it. Had the Divine really equipped her with the skills to be an adequate Queen? She couldn't answer that, but remembered Gracie's advice. Was it time now to try to win back her Kingdom?

When their packs and horses were ready, Katelin asked, "Which way do we go? This path along the mountainside, or down and through the trees? I feel too visible up here."

"I suggest we stay up here. This path is quicker than weaving through the trees." Zane motioned Katelin westwards along the track, and they started walking. "Although it feels exposed, the canopy of leaves blocks us from the view of anyone down in the forest. They'd need to be at this edge of the trees to see us, and if they were, we'd meet them down there if we went that route anyway. But more importantly, we must avoid being seen by the Malgosians on the plain, so we can't risk emerging from the treeline down there. The path around the western end of the mountains runs at this foothills level, and we can wait until dark before venturing on to that. That's when this path does become visible to the watching Malgosians on the plain."

The rising sun was warm on their backs as they made their way along the path. Birds twittered in the treetops below them, and hawks and eagles circled above the mountain slopes above. The air was clean and fresh, the sky deepest blue, and the only clouds were wispy ones clustered along the horizon. It was impossible to believe there was anything wrong with the world, and Katelin found her hopes rising.

And she had Zane walking beside her. They chatted in low voices, in case their words carried across the forest. He told her everything she wanted to know about life in the Manniswood, how often they moved camp, where they found what they needed, and how they managed to cater for everyone who joined them. It sounded such an idyllic life that Katelin reminded herself that it might be harsher in reality.

They sat in the shade of a boulder by the track for a lunch of Gracie's dwindling supplies. They would both miss the exquisite taste of her food and drink when it was gone.

Afterwards they walked for a while further, until Zane stopped them. They'd reached a bend in the path where it curved around a massive shoulder of the mountains above. Zane cautioned that the other side of the shoulder was visible from the plain below. From around this corner they could look towards Anestra, and the Malgosians on watch might see their movement along the mountainside track.

Zane led Novita and Conker towards some grass, and Katelin sat on the edge of the path, looking out over the Manniswood below. They would wait for nightfall before moving on, but when they did so, she would miss being in this great forest that had been her home in recent days. She took a swig of Gracie's peach-flavoured water.

Without any warning, the horses bolted.

Katelin scrambled to her feet. Novita went with such

suddenness and force that Zane jumped back out of his way. Conker hesitated for a moment, and then galloped off after the stallion, along the path and around the mountain's shoulder.

No! They might be seen from below.

And then Katelin heard it. A deep rumble, as if far away, or down in the ground.

She looked at her boots. And felt it too.

Before she could move, the edge of the path where she stood gave way.

## 15

## QUAKE

Katelin had no time to think about Zane or the horses, for she was falling.

At first it felt as though her feet had slipped, and the small patch of grass had come loose. She twisted and grabbed the edge of the path behind her, only to discover that it too was moving. She was face down on a slide of grass and soil, and she kicked her legs to slow or stop herself. But there was nothing firm or solid with which to connect.

The mountain slope gave an almighty heave. With a deafening roar, the ground threw Katelin up into the air. She was nothing more than a plaything, a discarded toy among the forces of nature around her. She flailed her arms and legs, trying to stay up and away from the sliding earth, but nothing could slow her crashing back to the maelstrom of soil and gravel that used to be the mountainside.

The landslide gave a sickening lurch, as though a yawning chasm had opened in the depths of the earth, and Katelin dropped. She screamed. She sank into an open pit of suffocating soil, kicking and beating the ground with her arms.

The earth churned around her, buffeting her body as the slope rolled inexorably downwards. Helplessness overwhelmed her, and desperation to get out and away from this slide that had the power to snap her spine in a moment. All she could think was to swim.

With an enormous effort, she flexed her arms and legs as though the rolling soil was the surface of the Western Ocean. For a moment it worked. Her face and shoulders broke through the waves of the earth. She needed to get on top. She must ride it like the ocean breakers.

She struck out, and kicked, and thrashed, and pulled, and rolled onto her back. She was riding the landslide, when a sharp pain scored her cheek. Another hit the back of her head, then her shoulder, and she buried her head in her arms. Gravel was shooting down the slope at lethal speed. But cocooning her head meant abandoning any control over riding on top of the earth.

The ground heaved again, tossing her over, and she gasped. Her mouth filled with soil and dust, and she choked. She cupped hands over her mouth and nose, trying to breathe.

Please, please, please, make it stop. Was the earth still quaking? Or was this only the landslide it had started?

She couldn't look up or around, for the air was filled with dust and flying gravel. A stone smashed into her arm and bounced away.

Katelin's boot hit a branch. It jerked her leg upwards, but the force of the impact broke the branch. At once the sinking realisation dawned: the landslide was colliding with the forest.

Was this her chance to grab something solid? Her body could be smashed to pulp against a tree trunk, or her head or limbs severed by a passing branch. But she needed to try. A tree might hold, firmly rooted against the sliding earth.

Divine, help me now. You must save me from this.

She peered through her arms that cradled her head, cracking open her stinging, dust-encrusted eyes. Out of the dust, a tree flew past at terrifying speed. An outlier of the forest, up the slope from the rest, and Katelin heard it snap off like a twig. She was moving too fast.

Without warning another tree flew past on her right, and she grabbed for it. Her reactions were too slow, and her trailing fingers slapped the bark. The next came on her left, closer to her, and she flung her arms towards it. She couldn't hold on, her arms almost wrenching from their sockets. But the grab slowed her, swinging her round below the tree, but even so it disappeared above her as she was carried down, down by the landslide.

The air between the trees seemed clearer, so perhaps the leaves were catching the dust. But still the soil, gravel and pebbles churned and roiled beneath her legs.

And then she saw it.

A large tree stood directly in her path, and she was flying towards it.

She tried to heave herself upwards from the landslide and braced her arms forward for the impact. Her body smashed squarely into the trunk, and her face buried itself in the bark. The crash forced all the breath from her body, but by instinct she wrapped her arms and legs around it.

She couldn't breathe. Her muscles locked. She clung with all her might to the solid tree, rough and hard against her face and chest.

A pebble thudded into her back, and it felt like an arrow wound. More gravel pelted into her body, and this alone made her gasp for breath. It was like being stoned.

She didn't dare release her grip on the tree for fear of being swept away again. But then it too began to move.

No, no, no, please, no more.

The trunk lifted. Had it been uprooted, or was the earthquake still shaking the ground?

The tree dropped again, and she felt, rather than heard, the roots snap. The thunderous rumble of sliding earth and rock was joined by the sharp cracks of branches, roots and trunks giving way.

The tree tilted over, falling with Katelin on top of it, and she had no choice but to hold on. Her arm and leg muscles had lost all feeling and no longer responded to her commands.

Katelin felt as though she fell off the edge of the world as the tree sent her forwards, and then down. This would be her end: falling into a pit of the earth, into the depths of a crushing, suffocating death.

The branches above her crashed together, and the tree stopped. She twisted her face, tearing her cheek on the bark, and dared to open her eyes. Her tree had fallen, to lean at an angle against another.

A piece of gravel stung behind her ear, and she buried her head against the stoning. She could do nothing but endure the pummelling of her legs and back.

Divine, no, make it stop. This is going to kill me, and I want to live.

For too long Katelin wept as a whimpering wreck, clinging to her fallen tree, as around her the side of the Eastern Range collapsed into the Manniswood. But at last the roaring in her ears began to subside. The firing of gravel into her back seemed to lessen. She had almost begun to hope it was all over, when a boulder crashed down the mountainside to her left and pulverised the remaining trees in its path.

Katelin sobbed into the bark of the trunk, and prayed for life, until the only sounds became the rattle of stones down the slope above her, and a thundering boom echoing off into a distant silence.

She tried a deep breath, but the air was filled with dust. Her lungs went into spasm, and she vomited. She retched and retched into the trunk until the wracking of her body reduced her to a limp ruin.

She must have blacked out, because she came to with stabbing pains in her arms and legs. She couldn't move. Her muscles had seized, but they were aching and screaming at her to let go of the tree.

With enormous effort she commanded her thumbs to move, and they flexed, lifting themselves away from the trunk. Then one by one her fingers, her palms, her wrists followed. As soon as she loosened an elbow, she began to slide around the trunk, falling to its lower side, but she had neither the strength nor the energy to stop it.

Her hips and knees twisted with the rotation, and she needed to let go. And she was falling again.

The blow of landing on her back winded her, but it hadn't been too far. The ground was not hard, but a broken mixture of soil, gravel and rock.

Katelin lay on the ground and tried to wipe her face. But everywhere was caked in dust. Parts of her face were wet, from tears, vomit and blood.

But she was alive. She had survived. But for how long?

She was too exhausted to move and tried to locate the sharpest pains. Was anything broken? The wealth of bruises and cuts could be borne, so long as her bones and organs were intact.

She flexed each joint and limb, felt down her chest, all over her head. Cracked bones here and there without doubt, but there didn't seem to be any full breaks. Maybe bleeding inside. And she was so tired. More than anything she wanted to lie here and rest until the terror and exhaustion passed. Something told her she shouldn't sleep, because her body had suffered so many shocks, but it was too tempting to resist.

And then she remembered.

Zane.

He'd been up on the path when it started. Had he come down the slope too, or was he buried somewhere up on the mountainside?

With sickening dread in her stomach, Katelin tried to move. It was too painful at first, but she moved each limb, gritted her teeth, and gasped to regain her breath after each effort. She needed to know what had become of Zane. He might need her help. He might be dying ... or dead—no, she couldn't contemplate that.

At last she rolled over onto her front. She grabbed a nearby broken branch from out of the soil and used it to lever herself onto her knees.

And now she looked around.

She was surrounded by broken trees, ruined statues amid the swirls of dust. The ground had risen, by how many feet Katelin couldn't guess, but those trees that still stood seemed half-buried in a tide of rock and earth. Mighty branches, which should have been way above her head, now grew out of the ground at Katelin's level. Stones still trickled down the slope.

She looked up. Through the dust, the Eastern Range still towered above her, but the side had been gouged out, a bare wound of rock lying open to the air. There was no way to see from here where their path had been.

She needed to get back up the slope. She must find Zane. How could she do that?

To her left, the shoulder of the Eastern Range still stood. It was the one that had shielded them from view from the plain before the quake, before the valley on this side of the ridge had collapsed into the forest. If she could make her way across the landslide to that shoulder, she might find firmer ground for the climb. But was her body in any condition for such an ascent?

Divine, you need to help me. Hedger. Gracie. Anyone. If I'm ever supposed to be Queen of Anestra, then I must get out of this.

She remembered that clerics of the Divine had the power to heal. Did any of that power lie in her, in her Divine blood? She needed to try.

"White Goddess, our Life Weaver," she breathed. "You see our condition, our need. Send your compassion and strength to help us. If there is any cleric power within me, the ability to heal, then by your blood that is in me, let me use it now. I need to live, to escape this disaster, and to help others. Please."

She heard some clicks, as though of knuckles cracking. Katelin turned her head, as they seemed to come from behind her. But then looked down. No, they'd been inside her. Had that been the sound of fractured bones closing up?

She placed a hand on her chest and stomach. "Divine, any injuries inside me, please heal them enough for me to move, to last long enough for what I need to do. Thank you."

A white glow shone from her hands—or was it a glimmer of sunlight through the dust?—and a warmth rose inside her. Was it all in her mind, that the sharpness of pain lessened? Had the Divine knitted her together inside, sealing up any bleeding and damage? She flexed her arms and back. Yes, those moved more easily now.

She drew some deep breaths, and then leaned on the broken branch to lever herself to her feet. She stumbled a couple of steps to collapse against a snapped-off tree trunk, panting and gasping, but she was still upright. Her whole body ached with stiffness, and she shuddered to think of the extent of her bruises and cuts, but she needed to move.

Katelin looked up. Yes, there was a route across the landslide to her left that she could cross to firmer ground. She breathed hard, resting her weight on the branch, and took the first few steps.

Her boots sank into the soft soil and gravel. This would be heavy going, even if she weren't so exhausted and sore. She planted the branch deep into the soft ground and used it as an anchor to progress. It was reassuring when a tree trunk came within reach, in case she needed to collapse, but these became fewer as she crossed the slope.

Sweat trickled down her back with the effort. Her muscles complained at every move, but she was getting there. She couldn't estimate how long it took, but at last the solid earth seemed within reach.

Then the branch broke.

It had been cracking for the last few steps, but the repeated planting and uprooting defeated it. Katelin sprawled on the ground, her mouth filled with earth and gravel again.

She sighed, resting for a moment. She forced Zane's face

into her mind to stir her into trying again. Could she crawl the rest of the way? She needed to, for there was nothing else within reach to lever herself up. She flexed her elbows, bent her knees, and began.

The ground kept sinking beneath her, sliding off down the slope, and she scrabbled at the loose surface. A large boulder lay ahead of her on the near side of the ridge, and she squirmed her way towards it. With her hand, her arm, her shoulder wrapped across it, she finally felt able to rest, in exhilaration at having escaped the landslide.

Katelin rolled over, lying on her back, gazing up at the clear blue sky. Her desperate urge to sleep remained, but she knew she needed to go on, to find what had become of Zane and the horses. Were they even alive? The chill of dread forced Katelin to roll onto her knees and manoeuvre herself up.

It took some moments to steady herself against the rock, breathing hard. Then she made herself look up. And quailed.

The slope of the ridge stretched up out of sight. Had she fallen and slid so far? It looked impossible, in her weakened state, to climb back up to where the path had been. But Zane might be lying trapped up there, in need of her help. The thought of him lying crushed under a rock-pile was too hard to bear. She needed to move.

She heaved herself away from the rock and took a first step. Then another. She stopped, leaning her hands on her knees for breath. Then she levered the next footstep upwards.

This was in danger of taking all afternoon. She couldn't afford to take that long, not if Zane lay injured somewhere up the slope. She straightened her back, wincing at the pain, but making herself upright enough to manage the uphill walk.

And she began. In no time she was panting, but she kept up the pace. The pounding of her legs against the solid earth made a rhythm with the heaving of her breaths. She could do this. It was energy, and strength, and determination that she needed, and surely the Divine could supply her with these. She thought of Zane, of Novita and Conker, of Gracie, of Rashelin, of Anestra, and willed these thoughts to keep her going.

She shoved aside the aching pains of bones and joints, and stumbled on. Her breaths became ragged, rasping, but she staggered up the ridge.

She paused to steady her breathing, gasping the air into her lungs. She rubbed her face, wiped her eyes and looked about.

Dust lay heavy in the air. It formed a thick mist, blanketing the mountainside, with no breeze to disturb it. It covered the land in a shroud of death.

Katelin shivered. Below her, rock and earth had ploughed large swathes into the forest. She turned towards the plain, in sudden fear of being visible to Malgosian watchers. But the air was too thick for her to see anything of them, or for them to see her.

She trudged on. After what might have been an hour or more, head down to concentrate on the tramp of her feet, Katelin stopped. Her upward trek had come to a sudden levelling out. Was this their path? If so, then Zane was somewhere on her right.

Katelin edged forwards, conscious of the fragility of the fissured ground. Large sections of the path had subsided, and other parts were deeply cracked, or strewn with boulders. Near to the cliff face above her, there was a way along.

Did she dare cry out? She risked it. "Zane?" It was a croak. She licked her lips, swallowed, and tried again. "Zane, where are you?"

Silence.

She picked her way further, clambering around boulders, stepping over the wider cracks. At times her boots sank into softer, fallen soil, and at others she sent rocks and gravel spinning off down the landslide.

"Zane!"

She listened hard. Had that been a murmur in reply?

Then she saw him. She was near enough to see through the hanging dust to where Zane lay half-buried in a rock-fall.

"Zane, can you hear me?" She scrambled over loose rocks towards him, and his eyes flickered open. But only his top half was visible. Dirt and stones covered him from the waist down.

She grabbed his hand and touched his face, willing his eyes to focus on hers. "Zane, I'm here. It's me, Katelin. Look at me." She knelt beside him, wishing she had water to give him, for his face and hands were dusty and bloody, his lips parched.

"Kat," he sighed. "The mountain fell on me."

"Yes, I know. I was swept down a landslide." Already she was removing the stones that were crushing his legs. "Talk to me, Zane. Tell me what happened, while I get you out of this."

He drew a deep breath and winced. "When the quake began, I was over by this rock-face. Stones started falling, so I saw no choice but to cower against it, underneath it. The rock-face held firm, it didn't crack or collapse. But stones came over it from above and buried me. I tried to get out, but I couldn't."

By now Katelin had cleared enough stones to reveal Zane's legs. His left one was bent at an alarming angle. "Zane, can you feel your legs?"

He tried to move them, tensing the muscles, flexing them. Then he cried out, sweat breaking onto his face, screwing up his eyes. "The right one's not too bad," he panted. "But I couldn't feel the left, until I tried to move it." He was gritting his teeth.

"Okay, hold still," Katelin said. "I need to straighten and

set your left leg." She reached and felt for the broken bones, causing more cries from Zane. She stopped, and they clutched each other's hands.

Their eyes met. And in that moment, Katelin saw his mortal fear. The desperation of their situation almost overwhelmed her. She swallowed. "Listen, Zane. We need to get away from here. There could be another earthquake at any moment, bringing more of the mountainside down. We need to get down to the safety of the plain."

Zane was shaking his head. "I agree with you, Kat, but I can't move."

Katelin swallowed her doubts. "I believe in Divine healing, Zane. The White Goddess helped me to get back up here from the bottom of the landslide. It may be that she needs me to help the people of Anestra right now. I've seen clerics heal people. I've felt their healing touch myself. We need to trust that she's able to heal you now. Pray with me."

Zane was staring at her. She saw him gulp before she turned her gaze back to his broken leg. She placed her hands either side of the broken bones. Zane was whimpering, hissing through his teeth, clutching at his thigh.

"White Goddess, Divine, Life Weaver, I don't know how to do this," Katelin began. "I need your help. Zane needs your help, your healing." She closed her eyes. "Relieve his pain. Knit these bones back together. Enable him to stand, to walk. If you need me now, for Anestra, for anything, then I'd like him with me. I can't do what you ask of me alone. I want Zane by my side. So, heal him. Now. Please."

She stopped, because her hands tingled and her skin prickled with sweat. She must have been gripping Zane's leg too tightly, because he'd fallen silent. She opened her eyes to the sound of an unmistakeable click, and saw a fading white glow. She let go of his leg and looked up into his face, expecting him to be unconscious from the pain.

But he was staring at her, an inane grin spreading across his face.

"What?" she said.

"How did you do that?" he exploded.

"Do what? Has something happened?"

Zane didn't say a word. Instead, he shifted himself, bent both his legs, and clambered out of the rocks to stand on his feet. Katelin held out hands to restrain and steady him, but he didn't need her help.

Zane spread his hands. "How did you do this?"

Katelin stood up too. She had caught Zane's grin. "Me? I didn't do that. Must have been the Divine." She shrugged. "She does that sometimes."

Zane gripped her shoulders, forcing her to gaze close into his eyes. It was intoxicating.

"Kat, my Katelin, my Queen. Don't you realise what this means? You have the power to heal! You can mend broken bones."

Katelin chewed her lower lip, tried to step back, but Zane's grip was firm.

"I don't know how I did that. Other than asking the Divine to do it. But I get the feeling it means we're supposed to do something. We've been healed for a reason. And first, we need to get out of here."

Zane looked around him, at the devastation of the mountainside, his face grim. "Agreed. We'll talk about this later, then. Where are the horses, have you found them?"

Katelin shook her head. "When the quake started, they bolted along the path around the end of the mountains. That's where we need to go, anyway. And we need water and food."

"The supplies were in the saddlebags. Another reason to find Novita and Conker. Let's go."

They started picking their way through the debris of rock and soil along what had once been the path. Katelin scanned the ground for hoofmarks, but there was too much damage. She and Zane looked out over the plain as they rounded a shoulder of the mountains. Here, a breeze from the north had cleared away much of the dust in the air, and they could see into the distance.

The plain had been ripped up like a ploughed field. Vast furrows of bare earth were striped across it, with mounds and gullies strewn at random. Lifting her eyes, Katelin saw Anestra city, and her breath caught. Was that dust, or smoke, or both, rising from it?

Zane touched her arm. "There." He was pointing to the slope below them, down the great shoulder stretching from the mountain range to the plain. Katelin saw him too: the white glimmer of her stallion, Novita. He was stamping and pawing the ground, pacing back and forth, clearly distressed.

"I don't see Conker," Katelin said, "although she's better camouflaged. Let's get to Novita."

They started off gingerly down the slope, and the stallion saw them. He began a steady walk up the incline to join them, his head bowed. Katelin was thrilled to see her horse alive, and seemingly uninjured, but she knew at once that something was wrong.

Novita seemed surer of his footing than they were, because he made better progress upwards than they did down, and they met not far below the level of the path.

"What is it, Novita?" Katelin asked, stroking his muzzle. The stallion tossed his head, indicating back down the slope.

Zane gripped Katelin's arm, and pointed. At first, she couldn't see it. Then she saw Conker, a smudge of chestnut amid the broken ground where Novita had been pacing. The mare was unmoving, and seemed to lie twisted, broken. It couldn't be clearer: Conker had fallen, or been crushed or thrown, and broken her legs and neck.

They didn't need to go down to check. Conker was dead. Without a word, Katelin and Zane turned into each other's arms and held one another for a while.

Katelin didn't dare ask him how long Conker had been his horse. The mere thought of losing Novita was unbearable, and overwhelmed her with grief. What could they do now? Could Novita carry them both? Zane shook in her arms, and she squeezed him tighter. She let him cry on her shoulder, and didn't let go, in case he didn't want her to see his tears.

It was Zane who patted her on the back, for them to release each other. She looked down while he wiped his face, and said, "I'm so sorry, Zane."

As she raised her head again he nodded. "I'd better get my stuff from her saddlebags," he said in a choked voice.

Katelin turned to fetch the water bottle that was tied to Novita's saddle, but Zane said, "Kat!"

His tone made her spin around, for it was one of alarm.

"What is *that?*" asked Zane, pointing towards the west.

Katelin squinted westwards, shading her eyes against the lowering sun. The air was clearing of dust all the time as the breeze from the north blew it away across the forest and the Mannis River. Anestra city was becoming more visible in the distance.

It was too far away for any detail, but the dust or smoke still swirled over it as she'd seen from the ridge. The Castle at least still stood, surviving all the shaking of the earthquake, with its solid stone walls and deep foundations on the hill of rock.

"What is it? What's the matter—"

Katelin stopped before she could finish the sentence. Something didn't look right about Anestra, and it took her brain some moments to process what it was.

An icy lance stabbed up her spine and straight into her heart.

From their raised position they could see across the city and into the Bay beyond.

It was the Ocean that had changed.

The water level in the harbour and the Bay was too low. It was as though the entire Western Ocean had receded. But how could that be?

And then Katelin saw what Zane had seen. The horizon

was too high.

The smooth surface of the Ocean curved upwards, instead of down and out of sight. The seawater had gathered together on the horizon, drawing back from the city and the Bay.

Katelin could do nothing but watch, her heart pounding, her cheeks cold with fear, as the colossal ridge of water approached. It was a wall of water—no, a whole mountain range of it—stretching as far as her eyes could see from north to south, racing towards the shore.

With terrifying speed, this greatest of all waves overshadowed the Bay with deepest darkness, blocking out the rays of the setting sun. The top of it crested white, and then toppled, to break with full force upon the city of Anestra.

## 16

## WAVE

The earthquake had flattened the street. Rish ran his hands through his curly blond hair and surveyed what had been the houses of Spring Channel. At the shaking of the ground, the terraced buildings had collapsed like so many paper boxes in a gale. Parts of walls still stood, some as high as the ground floor windows, especially where the bricks joined at the corners of houses. But the rest was all rubble. Ceilings and upper storeys had collapsed, crushing unknown numbers of people underneath.

Rish sighed. At least his cousin Marla had got her children out in time. At the first sounds of rumbling, they'd all rushed into the street to see what was happening, only for their home to crumble into rubble behind them. He looked across at them now, to where Marla was trying to comfort Jen and Cal. What a thing to happen when you're only eight and six.

Jen was trying to be a brave girl, her arm around her little brother. But Cal was sobbing, clutching a dusty square of blanket they'd pulled from the rubble. Marla was going between them and the ruins of their home, trying to pick through the damage, to find anything of use. They needed water, shelter, food, warmer clothing—anything to survive the coming days. Until what? Until help came, from where?

Rish shook his head. He stepped across to the stream that gave Spring Channel its name. This fresh water from the spring by Anestra Castle should have satisfied one of their needs. But it was muddied. The quake had fractured the channel, and churned up the soil beneath, so was it safe to drink? They needed some water, and this was all there was.

Marla had retrieved a leather bottle from the rubble, so Rish washed the dust off it first and then dipped it into the flow. He placed his fingers across the opening to try to reduce the silt entering the bottle, but some got in anyway. This was the best he could do.

He stood up, holding the bottle to let mud sink to the bottom, and took a sip. He grimaced. It tasted gritty, but they all needed the liquid. He took it across to the children.

"I'm sorry the stream water's muddy," Rish said, "but we need to drink. Jen, Cal, please have some."

Jen took the bottle and tried a little, and then helped her brother do the same. It broke Rish's heart to see their shocked, staring little faces screw up in distaste at the best he could offer.

"What did you find at the Castle?" Marla asked.

Rish swore, and wished he hadn't, because of the children. "Locked up like a fortress," he added quickly. "One of the few buildings left intact, and they won't help us. I bet it's that Regent Sirika and Baron Malgosy's order. Looking after only themselves and all they've got. The gates are bolted and barred, and there's an angry crowd camped in Crown Square. No one's got homes, so what else are we to do?"

"We might fare better at the Temple," Marla said. "We'll be better off in the care of the clerics than trying to storm the Castle."

"I agree," said Rish.

"What about Uncle Arch?" asked Jen. "Do you think he's all right?"

Rish knelt beside the children. "Yes, Arch went back to the forest. He'll have felt the earthquake there, but there aren't any buildings to fall down. He'll be able to find food and water there, too." He looked up and caught Marla's eye. "In fact, I think that might be a good idea for all of us. What do you think, Jen and Cal, would you like to come with me and camp out in the forest for a while?"

Their little faces brightened. But Marla was wringing her hands, and she turned away to survey the ruins of her home. Rish saw her nod, her back still turned, and then she said, "I need to find my ring and bracelet. I took them off to do the vegetables."

Marla picked her way through the rubble, back into the ruins, searching among the dust and broken bricks for her jewellery. Rish turned back to the children.

"Listen, Jen, Cal, I know this is hard. The earthquake has destroyed everything, but we can come back and rebuild your home. We'll go and spend tonight with the clerics at the Temple of the Divine, and then in the morning set off for the Manniswood—"

Someone screamed. Rish broke off at the sound of a shout: "Wave!" People were running.

He jerked his head to look down Spring Channel. At once he saw the wall of water in the Bay, tossing up ships as though they were toys.

He scooped up Jen and Cal, one under each arm. "Wave!" he yelled at Marla, but she was at the back of the ruined house. Their eyes met for half a second before Rish turned and ran.

If the street had been clear he might have made it. But there were people and rubble all the way up Spring Channel and he dodged and weaved.

The children were squirming in his arms, so he yelled at them to keep still. "No, even better, hold on to me. We need to get higher."

Others were jostling, pushing, screaming, clamouring up the street to get away from the impending deluge. Rish was nearing the top of the road when the water hit his back.

In an explosion of foam and spray he was lifted off his feet and thrown forward. His arm muscles locked around Jen and Cal, who clung to him, all of them instantly drenched and tumbling like corks in a whirlpool.

They were sucked down, Rish's mouth filling with sea

water. Then they slammed into a wall. The force of the impact blew all the water and air from Rish's body, but his feet hit solid ground. He pushed upwards, with one other thought: Left. Left. We need to go left.

But the surge of water was going right, dividing at the top of Spring Channel, with most of it flooding downwards to South Side.

Rish struck out left. "Hold on," he yelled to the children, and let go of them. He swung powerful strokes to get them into the flow going upwards and left.

Jen was still at his side, but Cal was slipping. Rish grabbed him and waded into the now shallower water surging up to Princes' Park. The flood was carrying them, but getting deeper and stronger all the time.

They needed to anchor themselves, and Rish saw their chance in the trees of the Park. The earthquake had uprooted some, but others still stood, the floodwaters already surging around their trunks.

"Grab a tree," Rish yelled above the roaring of the water, and Jen seemed to understand. She reached for the first, but the waters swept them past it too quickly.

With one arm still around Cal, Rish tried to steer them towards a towering oak that lay right in their path. The rising floodwater had lifted them to the height of the lower branches, but threatened to take them round the trunk.

At the last moment, Rish flung Cal onto a branch, and threw his other arm around it too. But Jen had only one hand on it and was being swung past it by the torrent.

"Hold on," Rish yelled at Cal, and dived for Jen's wrist just as she let go. But their hands and arms were wet and slippery, and she was sliding through his fingers. He gripped her hand with both of his, so hard he was in danger of crushing her bones.

But they held. He stopped her momentum and pulled her back against the raging flow.

"Climb," Rish shouted at Cal. "The water's still rising, we

need to get higher."

He hauled Jen onto their refuge and pushed Cal's bottom upwards towards the next branch. The children understood and scrambled ever higher through twigs and leaves.

Rish followed, but the water was rising too. When would it stop?

Then Jen asked the question that Rish couldn't think about.

"What about Mummy?"

Rish paused long enough to look back through the leaves towards the lower parts of the city. The Ocean had invaded. All the streets leading up from the harbour were fully submerged, with no trace of roofs, walls or homes above the surging tide. Debris and people tossed about on the surface, but the Ocean still sloped upwards to the horizon. There was yet more floodwater coming.

He caught Jen's stricken eye, because she'd looked at the same scene. "We'll meet up with Mummy afterwards," he said. "Marla's a good swimmer."

But he couldn't hold the girl's gaze. Because strength at swimming was nothing compared with the Ocean's fury unleashed against them.

"Up," Rish said to Jen and Cal. "We need to keep climbing. The water's still rising."

But the children were shaking. They seemed frozen with shock and fear at the unspeakable horror around them. Rish reached and lifted them, and they held on when he placed them on a branch.

But the flood rose faster than they could climb. All their muscles ached from holding and climbing, and the waves broke over their legs and backs.

Then a surge took Jen. She was swept off a branch before Rish could even reach out to grab her. For one agonising moment, Rish debated what to do. He looked back and saw that the Ocean would cover the whole height of their tree.

He grabbed Cal and let go of the branch. Better to stay

together, he prayed, as he swam after Jen's receding figure.

The flow was so fast that in a moment they were crossing Crown Square in a flood of many feet deep. Only the walls of Anestra Castle, buttressed like a cliff, stood firm against the roar of spray and wave around it.

Then they were falling, as the floodwaters passed over the top of Anestra hill and fell in rapids down the other side.

Trying to keep his and Cal's head above the water, Rish saw they were heading for the city's East Gate, through which the Ocean was flooding. He thought he spotted Jen's body floundering through the gate in front of them, as the seawater began to fill up the fields beyond.

Zane touched Katelin's shoulder. "There's nothing we can do," he said.

Katelin shook herself out of her horror and turned to him. "We need to go," she said. "I should be there."

Zane was gripping her shoulder now. "No, Kat, listen to me. There's nothing we can do except get swept away ourselves."

She batted his hand away from her shoulder and glared at him. "How can you say that? How do we know if we can help until we get there?"

"But Kat, you need to stay hidden and safe. Your aunt and the Malgosians are after you, and they'll kill you on sight."

Katelin's anger rose. It was unfair to take it out on Zane, but she couldn't control herself. "I don't care about getting caught. I care about my people, and they're suffering right now. I'm their Queen, and whatever they're going through, I should be with them. And don't you dare try to stop me." She turned away towards Novita.

Zane held up his hands in a gesture of surrender. "I understand, Kat. You're their Queen, and I don't know what that's like. But how will we get there? Can Novita carry us both, or will you ride off alone?"

Katelin stopped, and turned back to him, biting her lip. It was stupid to get angry with Zane, because she wanted him with her. It seemed she also needed his clear head to think straight. She softened her voice. "Yes, I'd like you to come with me, if you will. You're right. I shouldn't ride off and do this on my own. We can see whether Novita manages with both of us."

Zane nodded. "All right. Let me get my things and …" he swallowed "… say goodbye to Conker. I'll meet you down the hillside. But I suggest we stay out of sight of the plain by riding down the north side of this ridge. No point in being seen if we don't have to."

Zane stepped away and sidled down the slope towards the body of his horse. Katelin watched him go. Perhaps she needed Zane's experience to temper her own rash desire for action. She couldn't help thinking that they made a good team. But she marvelled at him, masking his grief at the death of Conker. To lose Novita would be unthinkable.

As if he'd read her thoughts, the stallion nudged her shoulder.

She turned to look at him, stroking his neck. "Novita, we need to ride in haste and secrecy to Anestra. You see that Zane has lost Conker, so could you carry us both?"

Novita tossed his head and seemed to look down the slope towards Zane. Was he assessing the man's weight, to gauge the burden of them both?

Katelin added, "We'll walk down the slope, and only ride across the flat of the plain."

Novita seemed to nod, and Katelin wondered again at how much of her speech this remarkable horse understood.

She took one last look towards the plain, where the dust of the earthquake was settling, and felt pleased to be out of sight of the Malgosians. She longed to put them also out of her mind, but knew that she now faced the test of reaching Anestra unchallenged.

She turned and led Novita along the remains of the path,

picking their way between fallen boulders and loose ground. The cool afternoon breeze from the north struck her cheeks as she rounded the bend at the end of the Eastern Range and began the descent to where Zane knelt by the fallen mare.

The going was slow, but Katelin recognised Zane's wisdom in descending a valley, whereas she would have galloped down the ridge in full view of everyone, heedless of danger in her rush to the city. A few times she and Novita each slid on loose gravel and other debris from landslides, but they reached Zane without falling.

She didn't want to intrude on his grief, but Zane stood up as they approached. He was strapping on his sword and lifting the saddlebags clear of Conker's broken and twisted form.

Katelin didn't know what to say, but wanted to say something. "I'm very, very sorry, Zane, for your loss of Conker."

Zane held her eye. There was grief and anguish there, but also self-control. He sighed. "I will make time later to grieve for Conker," he said. "But we cannot afford that time now, for we have things we must do. Let's get going."

He moved off further down the slope, and Katelin gave the chestnut mare a last, lingering look, before following him.

Zane preceded them all the way down to the plain, setting an urgent pace. Maybe the task of finding a safe route was a welcome distraction for him. Out of the breeze, the dust still hung in the air, and the wreckage of earthquake was everywhere: boulders, uprooted trees and bushes, gashes of bare soil in the earth. Would the land ever recover from this disaster?

He waited for them at a gully where a rise to their south kept them out of sight of the plain in front of the Manniswood. This was the end of the Eastern Range of mountains, where the heights gave way to the coastal plain that stretched as far as Anestra Bay. Here they mounted Novita, Katelin in front, and the stallion adjusted himself to the unaccustomed weight.

In any other circumstances, Katelin would have relished Zane's closeness, as he rode with an arm around her waist. His body was warm at her back.

As they set off, Zane urged Katelin to keep her shortbow ready in case of stray or watching Malgosians, so she tried to do so as they took turns with the reins. Novita soon picked up the pace and seemed to enjoy the challenge to his speed and strength. They settled into a breath-taking rhythm, as the stallion's hooves thundered in a sure course across the damaged fields.

More than once they saw Malgosians and veered away or sent an arrow in their direction. But the Baron's men were not mounted for pursuit: their horses seemed all to have bolted in the quake. Novita made short work of leaving pursuers, even those who tried to run, far behind. Katelin conceded that amid all this destruction, the earthquake and wave had left the Malgosians in too much disarray to intercept her.

She began to see others in the fields, not wearing the dark green and grey of Malgosy. These were farm workers, coming to see, drawn to observe the unfolding disaster in a paralysis of horror. Then they passed people stumbling away from Anestra: soaked, bedraggled, their faces carved in terror at what they had experienced. Katelin called out to them, but the survivors looked too numb to respond.

They reached the water.

Novita's hooves began to splash in puddles as they made their gradual descent towards the city. He slowed, not liking the softer ground, and needing to pick his way for a footing. Everywhere the water was moving, flowing further inland or drawing back to the Ocean as the lie of the land dictated. The smell of salt was in the air.

Katelin intended to approach the North Gate, as less

likely to be manned by Malgosians, who would watch the South and East Gates the most. But as they drew nearer, the highway from Lasseny was an impassable route into the city. The rivers of retreating seawater had pooled into an expansive lake in front of the gate. Its depth could only be guessed by the knots of people wading their way through its edges, and she wasn't going to force Novita to enter the city that way.

She lifted her eyes towards the setting sun and the Temple of the Divine. And gasped. Although situated on a hill, the Temple had borne the first onslaught of the Ocean's fury. Some of the white marble columns had broken, whether through earthquake or flood Katelin didn't know, and one end of the roof had collapsed to the ground. Clerics and survivors milled around it in confusion. Her heart ached to go and help them, but knew she needed first to make her appearance at the Castle.

They veered left towards the East Gate, which stood at a higher elevation.

"Zane!"

Katelin reined in Novita at the call and swung around. They peered at the man who had spoken. Here was another drenched survivor, holding the hands of a forlorn-looking boy and girl.

Zane choked behind her. "Rish?" he asked.

The man stepped forward, and now Katelin recognised the curly-blond-haired wanderer. He looked wretched. The children at his sides were shivering.

"Rish, you're alive," Zane gasped. "You should get to the forest. You know how to survive there."

Rish frowned. It seemed an effort for him to think or speak. "We're heading for the Temple," he mumbled. "We thought the clerics might help us."

Katelin shook her head. "No, Rish, the Temple roof has collapsed. I doubt you'll find much help there. Zane's right: your best bet is the forest."

Rish squinted at her. "Kat, is that you? They said you were dead."

"No, I'm not dead. I'm trying to help my people. Head to the forest."

"But we need to find Jen and Cal's mother," Rish said, indicating the children beside him. "We need to know what happened to Marla when the wave came."

Katelin pressed her fingers to her eyes to stem the tears that smarted there. Zane squeezed her shoulder.

"Listen to me, Rish," he said. "It isn't safe here. There could be more quakes and waves, and buildings might collapse. It will be a while before help can be organised or order restored. You need to save yourself and the children, and you can do that in the forest."

He paused, and Katelin looked up. The two men were staring at each other. Then Zane added, "You can meet up with Marla again later. Once all of this is over."

Rish swallowed hard. He looked down at the children, and Katelin's heart was breaking with pain and sorrow for them. How could anyone tell the youngsters that their mummy had probably drowned and been swept away by the flood?

Zane was unbuckling Novita's saddlebags. "Here, Rish, take our blankets and food. You need to look after Jen and Cal for the moment, so take them to the forest."

Katelin was desperate to say something to comfort and reassure them, but all she could manage was, "As soon as we can, Zane and I will come and find you, and see how we can help." She tried to force out an encouraging smile, but it wouldn't come.

Rish took the saddlebags as the little boy, Cal, asked, "Are we going to the forest now, Uncle Rish?"

He let out a sigh and then lifted his face towards Katelin and Zane. "Go on, you two. You have more important things to worry about than the three of us. We'll be all right." Then Rish knelt on the wet ground to speak with Jen and Cal.

"We'll see you soon," Katelin said, but her voice failed, and she didn't think Rish or the children heard her.

Zane shook Novita's reins so that the stallion walked on. He leaned forward and said into Katelin's ear, "The survivors are the reason we need you in charge of Anestra, Kat."

She tried to draw a steely resolve from his words, but struggled to calm her grief and trembling.

As they approached the East Gate, picking their way through the debris of sodden clothing and furniture, Katelin eyed the guards there. Some wore the dark blue and silver of Anestra, but others were in dark green and grey. She nocked an arrow to her shortbow and made a point of heading for the Anestrans.

As Katelin and Zane rode up, a female sergeant of the Anestran city guard waved her arms at them. "No, miss, sir, you don't want to come in here. It's terrible."

They stopped in front of her. "This is our city, sergeant," Katelin said. "We've come here to help. But first, I need you to protect me from these Malgosians."

The woman's eyes widened as she stared at Katelin's face, then her shortbow, and the white stallion. "Are you …?"

From the corner of her eye, Katelin saw the nearby Malgosians notice her.

"Yes, I am," Katelin declared. "Spread the word: your Queen is alive and has returned." She turned on the Malgosians, aiming her shortbow. "And as for you," she spat, "get out of my sight and back south of the river."

The look of terror on the Malgosian faces was almost worth it. They scrambled to get themselves away from Katelin's aim, all of them breaking into a run towards the south-east at once.

"Queen Katelin is alive! She's here!" the sergeant was shouting, and her fellow guards took up the call.

They entered the East Gate. Sea water still flowed down the sides of the street and gushed out of the ruined doorways of fallen houses. Citizens clung to their rubble and tried to stop their possessions from washing away into the fields. It was a wretched, heart-breaking scene, and Katelin nerved herself to ride on. Getting herself to Crown Square and the Castle gate was the best help she could give them.

Before they reached the Square, Katelin heard shouts and the screaming of a great crowd. She was glad to have the city guards who now went before her.

Queen Katelin rode into Crown Square as the last light of the setting sun shone in from the Western Ocean. The people of the city were pounding on the closed Castle gates, pleading for help, some of them using a doorpost as a battering ram.

A silence spread outwards from her, as the city guards shouted of her return, followed by the wondering murmurs and calls of: "Queen Katelin, she's alive, she's here."

Then a woman screamed.

A moment later, from the back of Novita, Katelin saw it too.

For the sun had set. But it had been too sudden.

Above the devastated houses towards the harbour, the waters of the Bay were receding. In the distant Ocean, the horizon curved upwards with the wall of water that formed the second wave.

## 17

## THRONE

For one moment, Katelin sat on Novita's back, transfixed with horror. This time she wouldn't be watching it from the distance of the mountains. This time she was in the middle of it, directly under the Ocean wave's path.

She shook herself and rode Novita to stop in front of the Castle gates.

"Open these gates!" she screamed. "In the name of the Queen, the Divine and the Crown, open up the Castle!"

A voice shouted down from the gatehouse battlements. "The Queen is dead. And the Divine has forsaken us."

The fury of frustration boiled up inside Katelin's belly. "I don't speak for the Divine," she shouted back, "but I do as your Queen. For I tell you that I am Katelin of Anestra, and you will open up my Castle, for me and my people. Now!"

A head appeared at the battlements, staring down, followed by others.

"A second wave is coming," Katelin shouted. "And we are going to save these people's lives."

Then came the call: "Open the gates!"

Katelin steered Novita to the side, out of the way of the crush, as the bars of the gates were lifted. She called, feeling she needed to, but doubting its effect: "Keep calm, go in order, make for the grass in the grounds. There's plenty of room, all will get inside, no need to push or rush."

But there was danger of a stampede, as those at the front shoved the gates open and pushed back the guards. Katelin kept glancing over her shoulder at the oncoming wave as the crowd surged through the gatehouse.

Zane gripped her shoulder. "We need to get you in there too."

Katelin shook her head. "I go in last."

People were running across Crown Square to join the back of the crowd, some of them slipping and falling on the wet cobbles. But with each second, citizens were saving their lives within the protection of the Castle's high stone walls.

The thunderous roar of the Ocean wave breaking on the remains of the harbour wall made Katelin jump. Novita started forwards, and she never knew whether it was Novita's decision, or a spur from Zane to his flanks, but the stallion joined the press through the gatehouse. The crowd shrank back from the horse, and no sooner were they through than the two of them leapt down from the stallion's back.

Outside the walls, the Ocean was pounding its way over the rubble of the lower streets and through the fallen trees of Princes' Park. Looking back through the gates, Katelin saw the tide enter the Square, catching the stragglers, overtaking those running, the surge racing towards the Castle with greedy intent.

She held off as long as she could before giving the call, "Close the gates!"

They were almost too late. It took all the guards, Zane, herself and some of the survivors to push closed the great wooden doors against the pressure and inflow of the Ocean. As it was, a torrent of seawater made it through the breach before the bars of the gate were in place.

The survivors on the grass screamed and cowered at the approaching deadly flow, but the waters trickled aside into drains, gullies and the grass without reaching any depth. The spray catapulted over the walls as the wave broke against the Castle walls.

But the gates and walls held.

Katelin let out her breath. She heard a scuffle behind her

and whirled around to see three Castle guards wrestling two Malgosians to the ground. The Baron's men had swords out and had been coming for her. A crossbow bolt whistled past her ear and she dived to the flagstones as Zane leaped in front of her. She looked up to see those in Anestran colours overpower and disarm those who wore dark green and grey in the Castle courtyard.

She rose to her feet, reaching out a trembling hand, to stand beside Zane. His two-handed sword was out, and Katelin unslung her bow.

"We need bodyguards for the Queen," Zane called, and a dozen Castle guards bustled forward.

The others were restraining the Malgosians. "Take those to the dungeons for now," Katelin ordered.

The Baron's men were dragged off, not without curses and threats that their lord would pay her back for this.

Katelin turned to where Novita stood watching her. She needed to leave him now and enter the Hall, but was aware that he'd been her near constant companion through her recent days. She hugged his neck. "Thank you for seeing me safely through my travels," she breathed. She let go and met his eye. "And for saving my life more times than I can count."

Novita tossed his head, giving a great whinny of satisfaction and pride. Katelin handed his reins to one of the grooms who waited there, and watched her stallion walk off towards the stables.

"Time to face the Court," Katelin said, turning to Zane. "Bodyguards, with me, and disarm any Malgosian."

She marched towards the doors of the Keep, Zane at her side, soldiers of the Castle flanking her at front, side and back.

Katelin was shaking inside, her stomach churning, but she couldn't let it show. This was the confrontation she'd been anticipating for days, and she needed to be strong. In fact, it might be the final battle in the war of wills with her

Aunt Sirika that had lasted most of her life.

Divine, help me. I need your strength.

The entrance hall was crowded with people, all taking refuge from the earthquake and flood. Katelin was appalled at the sudden sense of normality inside, compared with the devastation in the rest of the city. In here the Castle still stood, stone walls built on a deep foundation of rock, while outside its ramparts lay only rubble and flood. The earthquake might have cracked and shifted the stone blocks and ceilings, but nothing was in danger of imminent collapse. The Court of Anestra might well seek refuge in here, but it was the fate of the citizens outside that incensed Katelin.

There were Malgosians here, and Katelin saw her bodyguards move to restrain them before weapons could be drawn.

Her boots echoed loudly off the flagstones as Zane and the guards called out, "Make way for the Queen."

The crowd parted, with exclamations and murmurs, and Katelin caught sight of the silver-haired Yardles, the Royal Steward, at the double doors to the Hall.

His expression mirrored that of the others: shock, as he thought he saw a ghost, but then joy as he recognised that she was alive.

"Announce me?" Katelin asked.

Yardles fumbled for his staff and indicated to the door-wardens to open up. He banged his staff three times on the threshold and called: "Her Majesty, the Queen Katelin of the Old Kingdom of Anestra and the Western Coast."

And Katelin marched into the Hall.

The place was packed, and there were immediate shouts and cries of disbelief and consternation. Katelin had never been so aware of every eye fixed upon her as she strode between the parting ranks of courtiers. She became aware of how she must look: covered from hair to boot with dirt, bruises and blood from the landslide, but that was the least of her concerns. She heard Zane a couple of steps behind her, and the guards were fanning out to keep back the throng of nobles and officials.

It was a long walk up the length of the Hall, and all the way Katelin kept her gaze fixed upon the dais at the end. As she went, she was aware of the cries falling away to mutters and murmurs, and then finally to silence, except for the tramp of their boots.

On the dais, the chairs for the Royal Family were occupied. To one side sat Princess Rashelin, her eyes and face shining to see her Queen alive, and it was balm to Katelin's soul. Beside her sat Under-Father Ruis, who must have been summoned to the Court either after the earthquake or since the first wave damaged the Temple. On the other side of the centre sat Prince Tajion, mouth half-open, eyes wide at seeing her.

In pride of place, and on Katelin's carved wooden throne, sat Aunt Sirika, self-styled Regent of the Kingdom, and at her shoulder, the Baron Malgosy.

At Katelin's approach, the Baron stepped forward, his polished black leathers gleaming in the light of the lamps, and she saw him flick a dagger from his belt.

At once, Zane leaped in front of her and up the steps of the dais, his two-handed sword raised to quiver in front of Malgosy's neck. "Drop your weapon," Zane hissed.

There was a gasp from the Hall, as the Baron's dagger clattered to the dais, and he stepped back. Zane moved aside too, his sword still poised at the Baron's chest.

Aunt Sirika hadn't moved. She watched her niece with cold, calculating grey eyes. Katelin guessed the old woman was thinking fast at this unexpected turn of events.

With slow and deliberate movements, Katelin raised her shortbow and pulled an arrow from her quiver. She nocked it to the string and drew back, aiming for Sirika's heart.

"Get out of my chair."

Sirika refused to hurry. She stood up from the throne but

instead of stepping back she came forward, passing Katelin, to address the Court.

"You see that the false Queen resorts to threats of physical violence to assert her right to rule? That she aims an arrow at your Regent's heart, and uses the sword of a vagabond to intimidate a noble lord of the Kingdom?"

Katelin relaxed her bow and seated herself on the red velvet cushion of her throne.

"Lady Sirika, sister-in-law of my noble father, the King Etharan of Anestra, you have no leave to speak. Sit down."

But Katelin was trembling. How could she command the respect and obedience of the Court, while her aunt showed flagrant disobedience and contempt? And Sirika was a canny operator. She had a lifetime of experience and relationships in the Hall of the Court, while Katelin was made to feel an upstart, a newcomer. She knew she was young and inexperienced. Was her title and position as Queen enough to sway the mood and opinion in her favour, or had Sirika already sowed too many seeds of doubt and suspicion over her fitness to rule?

"She orders me to be quiet," Sirika was saying to the Hall. "In this noble Court, with its long tradition of open discourse and debate, is your Regent to be silenced? Am I to be allowed no opportunity to present an account of my deeds to safeguard the rule of the Kingdom?"

Katelin seized on this, if only to interrupt Sirika's speech. "Yes, let us examine your decisions and deeds, Lady Sirika, and how they have damaged the future of this Kingdom. How dare you, in this time of earthquake and flood, bar the gates of this Castle against the people of Anestra in their hour of greatest need? While you swan around in here, in your finery and thrones, the people whom you are meant to serve are *dying* out there."

Sirika rounded on her. "And what would you have us do, O wishful-thinking but gravely misguided Queen? Throw open the gates to those very floodwaters? Allow inside this

Castle every last citizen of the city? We have neither rooms nor beds, clothes nor blankets, food nor drink to accommodate a whole city!"

A few around the Hall laughed and nodded their agreement.

Katelin leapt to her feet. She tried to restrain the years of resentment she'd bottled up against her aunt, but struggled to stop her anger from overflowing in public. "That is exactly what I expect you to do. And you don't need to agonise over whether to do it or not, because I've already done it." She pointed to the Hall's double doors. "Outside in the courtyard are some of the survivors of our great city of Anestra. They have escaped from the rubble of their ruined homes and the floodwaters of the giant waves to seek refuge in this Castle. And that is precisely what we will give them: shelter, refuge, safety. We will open our rooms and stores, to give them blankets, dry clothes, food and water until they have somewhere else to go."

There were gasps from the nobles and courtiers, and nervous glances towards the doors, as though at any moment an angry rabble would come bursting through. Katelin felt hot with indignation, but was aware that she was failing to win over the Hall.

Sirika was quick to take up the outrage of the Court. "You have done *what*? You expect us to take commoners into our chambers and allow them to sit at our tables?"

"Yes, I do," Katelin shouted. "For they have no chambers or tables left to them." She tried to lower her voice. "Listen, I know this is difficult, for it is a time of trial for us all. In case you haven't seen it, the whole city has been flattened by earthquake and flood, and the only way we will get through this is by helping one another. I'm sorry for the inconvenience, but our people are homeless, starving and desperate, and this is the right thing to do."

As Katelin expected, Sirika looked unimpressed by her appeal, and so did most of the Court. Sirika now addressed them in a confident, victorious voice.

"And so we reach the root cause of all our problems. Not only do we have a pretender as Queen, who makes the wrong decisions in times of crisis, but it is also clear that she is the one who brings these disasters upon us. In little more than a year, as if invasion, plague and the death of King Edgaran were not enough, she now brings earthquake and flood to our doors. Is any further evidence needed that her reign, far from being blessed by the Divine, is in fact blighted and cursed instead? I am no seer or prophet, but the signs are hardly difficult to read."

Katelin found herself stammering. How could she answer that? "I … I did not cause or bring any of these things. The Lassenites invaded and Ilbassi sent his Plague. King Edgaran sacrificed his life to save us. How can you suggest I have the power to shake the earth or make the Ocean rise?"

Sirika was shaking her head. "You simple-witted girl. No one here is suggesting that you can click your impetuous little fingers to bring invasion, plague or destruction. But we all know that our White Goddess, the Divine, oversees all things, and has allowed them to happen during your short and tragic reign. If we allow you to occupy this throne for much longer, then none of us will be left alive for you to rule."

Katelin seized her chance to appeal to the one thing she'd been hoping for all along. "Very well then. Send for Quevelle, the Royal Treasurer, and the Crown of Anestra. Let our sacred relic show us once and for all whom the Divine wishes to rule."

A satisfying shadow of doubt and fear crossed Sirika's face. The glory of the Crown was outside the Regent's control. "There is no need for the Crown," Sirika said at once. "The evidence of Divine abandonment is all around us and abundantly clear."

"What's the matter, Sirika?" Katelin snapped. "Afraid

that the Crown will show everyone that I'm the Divine's true Queen?"

For the first time since entering the Hall, Katelin sensed the majority in the Court were with her. The murmurs and nods were for the Crown: "Yes, send for it, let's see." Many courtiers would be keen to see Divine glory shine from it again, or merely curious to see how this shouting match would turn out. The radiance of the Crown was an added spectacle for the show.

Sirika and Baron Malgosy exchanged a worried glance, and Katelin knew she had them. The Crown would confirm the Divine favour upon her, and no argument, however heated, could contradict the evidence of the miracle of her glory.

Sirika was back-tracking already. "No matter what the Crown shows, we can only agree that the ill-fated reign of Queen Katelin needs to come to an end …"

Katelin spoke over her, calling to Yardles at the far end of the Hall. "Royal Steward, is the Treasurer summoned?"

"Your Majesty," Yardles answered, "we have already sent Quevelle to fetch the Crown."

Well done, Yardles, Katelin thought. As soon as she'd mentioned it, her faithful Royal Steward had seen the Crown as the way to end this argument and persuade the Court onto his Queen's side. Katelin turned and seated herself back on her throne.

"While we are waiting," Katelin went on, "you will all be pleased to learn that you have been lied to by my Aunt Sirika and the Baron Malgosy. As you can see, I am neither dead nor gravely injured, greatly though they desired to accomplish this."

It was Sirika's turn to be outraged. "How dare you? To suggest I might wish to harm my niece! All I have done has been for the welfare of this Kingdom."

"Oh no, you wouldn't dare to lay your own bony fingers on me. That is why you employed this thug from Malgosy to perform all your dirty work for you." Katelin turned towards the Court. "Bands of Malgosians have roamed the Manniswood, searching for me, with orders to kill. My aunt's intention all along has been to remove me from this throne and place one of her own children here instead. And that, as we are all aware, is treason. As soon as the Crown confirms that the Divine wishes me to rule, then Lady Sirika, the self-styled Regent, will be locked in the dungeons. Baron Malgosy will join her there while we decide whether banishment beyond the Mannis is too lenient for him."

Anestran Castle guards stepped forward at Katelin's words, already poised to seize Sirika and the Baron at their Queen's command.

"The Royal Treasurer, Quevelle, and the Crown of Anestra," Yardles announced, and the doors swung open. A wave of murmurs and whispers rushed through the Hall, with much craning of necks to see.

Quevelle processed forward in her neat blue suit, her brown hair in a tight bun. In white cotton gloves she held a dark blue silk cushion upon which sat the Crown of Anestra. It was silver, ornate, jewelled, ancient, and glowing with the brightness of an inner light. Every light in the Hall seemed to reflect off it and enhance its inner radiance.

Katelin took a moment to glance at Princess Rashelin and Under-Father Ruis to one side of the dais. She smiled at them, and they returned it.

As she turned back to watch Quevelle's approach, Katelin thought she saw an old woman among the courtiers, silver-haired and with deep blue eyes. Gracie? But the dear old cleric couldn't possibly be here in the Hall. It must have been someone who looked like her.

Quevelle reached the dais. Katelin stood and walked forward. No doubt it was supposed to be the Treasurer or Under-Father who did this, but Katelin was determined to perform this act herself.

There was a scuffle to her left, and it seemed that the

Baron had tried to reach for, or throw, a weapon, but had been restrained by Zane and the Castle guards.

The sooner she did this, the better. The Royal Treasurer held up the cushion, and Katelin reached for her Crown with both hands.

She always expected the Crown to be cold metal, but it wasn't. It was warm and alive to her touch. Nor was it heavy, but light and smooth under her fingers. Katelin's heart always leapt in its presence, and today was no exception. Yes, this was hers, and she belonged to it, whatever anyone else might say.

But most of all, and as expected, the silverwork of the Crown brightened at her touch. The colours of a thousand rainbows burst forth, flooding the Hall with a glory that melded into a purest white light. This was what she needed. This proved to herself, and to everyone present, that there was no mistake. Katelin was Queen, and was meant to be so, with Divine blessing on her reign, whatever tragedies and disasters might come to Anestra.

From the corner of her eye, Katelin saw Aunt Sirika and Baron Malgosy slump in defeat.

Katelin lifted the Crown towards her head …

… and something changed.

At first, she couldn't understand what, but the Crown seemed heavier, colder, duller. She paused and looked up.

In that moment the Divine glory seemed to circle the Crown twice and then roll up. It reduced to a single point, lifted from the Crown's highest pinnacle, and then shot away upwards, disappearing through the Hall's roof.

To Katelin the message couldn't have been clearer. The Divine's blessing on her reign had been there, but was now taken away.

## 18

## TRIAL

Katelin couldn't believe it. She stared at the dull, lifeless thing in her hands. She shook the sacred relic of the Crown of Anestra, as though to make it work. She placed it on her head, then snatched it off again. Still nothing.

She kept touching the silverwork with her hands, willing the glory to come. But from the wretched thing there was no longer even the slightest glimmer or spark.

She became aware that everyone in the Court had also gasped. The message seemed clear to them too. The shouts and cries were rising.

Regent Sirika rose triumphant above them all. "You see! You see? What did I tell you? The Divine has abandoned her reign!"

Katelin almost threw the Crown away from her to smash on the Hall's flag-stoned floor. But Princess Rashelin, coming to her side, caught her arm, and the Treasurer Quevelle dived to catch the relic as it slipped from Katelin's fingers.

Rashelin squeezed her arm, and Zane came across to her other side. But Katelin couldn't meet their eyes. She could only stare at the flagstones. What was happening?

Katelin became dimly aware that her aunt was speaking again.

"Royal Treasurer," Sirika said, "bring me our sacred relic of the Crown. Now the Divine has clearly demonstrated she does not wish Katelin to rule, we must test her successors for Divine glory."

Katelin paid little attention as the Crown was brought and placed on Princess Rashelin's head. Nothing happened. Sirika seemed to swell even further with relief and satisfaction, as she then passed the relic to her son. No Divine radiance appeared for Prince Tajion either, at which Sirika looked less pleased.

Katelin struggled to understand. The Divine had turned silent and absent today. No glory, no guidance, no endorsement of anyone's right to rule. Not even a hint or clue of what the White Goddess wished. What was the Life Weaver doing?

"Thank you, Quevelle," Sirika was saying. "Take our sacred Crown of Anestra back to the Royal Treasury. Keep it safe there until we need it for a new coronation."

Katelin could have been boiling with rage at this. But she hadn't the energy. All the breath and fight had been sucked out of her, following the Divine glory out through the roof. How could the Divine have abandoned her reign?

Zane pulled at her arm and Katelin looked up. He was indicating that they should go, leave the Hall.

Katelin had never agreed with him more. She wanted to get out of this place. Away from the Court and the Hall, from Aunt Sirika and the Crown, and leave it all behind.

She gripped Zane's hand and together they stepped off the dais. But Princess Rashelin caught her, hugged and squeezed her in a tight embrace. Katelin couldn't bring herself to look at Rashelin's tears, the dismay and horror on her face. She embraced her back and then stepped away, looking towards the doors.

A line of Malgosians—the Baron's retinue, Katelin realised—blocked their way. Katelin hated their dark green and grey with a sick loathing. She looked down. Zane still held his sword, and she had her shortbow. Could they fight their way out of here?

From behind her came Sirika's voice, "Stand back, soldiers of Anestra. Katelin is no longer your Queen, as the departure of Divine glory has shown us. We must all abide by the clear decision of our White Goddess and take time to think and pray what this means for our future. We must remain calm. I will continue as Regent of the Kingdom, as this Court has previously appointed me."

It crossed Katelin's mind to order the Castle guards to fight for her. But how could she? Could she command their obedience without Divine blessing? Could she expect them to shed their blood for her, when she was no longer anyone of consequence? She was no longer Queen, not Princess, not ruler, not anything. No, there would be no more bloodshed on her account. No one else was to die for her.

Sirika went on, "In this time of uncertainty and distress, we need to keep our former Queen safe. There are crowds in the courtyard, so the safest place in the Castle will be under guard in her rooms. The Castle guards and our friends, the Baron's men, will conduct Katelin and her outlaw companion upstairs. We would hate anything foolish or dangerous to happen."

Katelin's spirit and life seemed to ebb away, and yet she hated that in victory Sirika still sounded gracious and measured. If they took her away, what did it matter where they guarded her? Her royal apartments, the dungeons, or anywhere else in the Castle—the only difference was in the surroundings, and those didn't matter. It was over. She had tried. And she had lost.

Anestran guards came and took Zane's sword, and Katelin handed them her dagger, quiver and shortbow. She would surrender her weapons to them, but not to the Malgosians.

Katelin kept her gaze down towards the flagstones as they led her out of the Hall. She shut out the looks and murmurings of the courtiers, because she couldn't face them.

At the entrance to the Keep, Katelin glanced out through the doors. The crowds were milling around in the grounds in the fresh evening air, too preoccupied with their own distresses to notice hers. The only consoling thought Katelin could summon was that at least she'd saved their lives from the second wave.

She was tired. No, more than that, she was weary to her bones. She'd been through too much today: earthquake, flood, and now this. Being marched up the steps to her rooms. No, not hers anymore, but Sirika's, or whoever would come after. She couldn't think about that.

Poor Zane, she thought, as the guards separated them into different rooms. She'd brought him all this way, into such danger, and this might prove his downfall too. She mustered the courage to glance at him, and he was looking at her, of course.

"I'm sorry," was all she could mutter.

Zane didn't look angry. Just confused, concerned, resigned. He nodded and entered his room.

Katelin stepped into hers, and the heavy door slammed shut behind her. The lamplight flickered across the plastered walls as the key clicked in the lock.

She lowered herself into a chair, hugged her knees, and rested her head on her arms. How small, how insignificant could she make herself? Was it too much to ask to stay here, unnoticed, forgotten? Then perhaps she could curl up and die in peace.

Prince Tajion had never seen his mother so happy. If it hadn't been inappropriate for her exalted station, he thought Regent Sirika might even have skipped and danced her way along the corridor to her study. As it was, the light in her eyes, her clasping of the Baron's hand, the twitching of her lips, told the Prince one thing.

They had won.

Tajion allowed himself a satisfied smile, a lifting of the heart, a filling of the lungs with a victorious breath. He could soon be King. With no Divine glory for any of them from their sacred relic of the Crown, Sirika could continue as Regent. It was only a matter of time before Katelin and Rashelin officially stepped aside, and he would ascend to the royal throne. He would get the best of both worlds: the prestige and respect for being King, without needing to do any of the work. He would leave the actual running of the Kingdom to his mother and the Baron and live however he wished. Yes, this was going to be good.

The study door had barely closed behind the three of them before Sirika exploded with joy. "Did you see that? I could never have imagined it would be so clear. Divine glory taken away from that wretched girl in front of the whole Court. Wonderful!"

Tajion made sure he was first to congratulate his mother. "I always knew the Divine was on your side, Mother. Now we know it's true. All those years you put up with raising my useless cousin, and now you reap your reward. Our faith in the Divine is vindicated, and she will see us through to the end."

Baron Malgosy seemed keen to bring their self-congratulation to an end. "So, what happens now? Katelin is locked in her rooms, but we can't keep her there forever."

Sirika nodded. "You're right. She needs to die. We can't allow her to live, even if she consents to abdication and exile. That worthless girl has too much fight in her, too great a sense of her own Divine calling and destiny. Even if she agreed to our terms now—which I doubt—she would always be a spear at our backs."

"I agree," said Malgosy. "But we can't kill her in the Castle. An accident in the forest is one thing, but dying in her rooms, while under our care and protection, and after her accusations in the Hall, would look damning."

"Can we accuse her of treason?" Tajion suggested. "People can be executed for that."

Sirika and Malgosy looked at each other, and then his mother shook her head. "That wouldn't work. There's too much residual affection for the young woman, and respect for her former position. The Court would never agree to execute her without a cast-iron case. The nobles would give her the benefit of the doubt, that she's done everything in good faith, thinking it the best for the Kingdom and without malicious intent. No, they wouldn't sentence her to anything worse than abdication and exile."

"So, we need something else," Malgosy said. "Something legal and public for getting rid of her. Isn't there anything in your history or traditions we can use?"

They fell silent. Their victory celebration was muted by the need for further planning. To Tajion, the throne seemed tantalisingly close, but he couldn't quite seat himself upon it yet. They needed to think of a way through this.

He still marvelled that the Divine had revealed herself to be on their side. Now even Under-Father Ruis and the clerics would side with the three of them against Katelin.

Thinking of the clerics reminded Tajion of what Malgosy had asked. Was there something in their history or traditions that they could use? As a Royal Prince, Tajion endured regular lessons with cleric tutors. A memory of something he'd read flitted across the edges of his mind. Then he had it.

Tajion looked up. Regent Sirika sat at her desk, head bowed in thought. Baron Malgosy watched her, waiting for the next masterstroke that she would produce. Tajion felt a quiet satisfaction that this time *he* might be the one to solve their problems.

"Mother, Baron," he said slowly. They looked at him. "I have a suggestion. Why not use the Trial by Poison?"

Sirika frowned. "Trial by Poison? I haven't heard of that. What is it?"

Tajion's delight grew as he realised this was something unknown to his mother. "It's something I read about in one of my history lessons. When I study the Tome, I make my cleric tutors find the most interesting parts of the Book of Histories for me. You know, the passages that include death, torture, cruelty, assassinations, those sorts of thing. The clerics don't like it, but I insist."

Baron Malgosy's stare at him broke into a smile, and Tajion recognised a kindred spirit.

"Anyway," Tajion went on, "I remember reading about something from long, long ago, during a civil war over the succession to the throne. The Crown wouldn't shine for either the existing King or his rivals, so they devised the Trial by Poison to end the war."

"What is it, then?" Sirika demanded. "Go on, Tajion, explain."

Tajion tried to remember the details. "We can look it up in the Tome to get the right poison and procedure. The Temple Library or the Royal Physician will have it. The gist is that all the rivals drank a deadly poison and left the Divine to sort it out. They made the White Goddess intervene to save some from the poison and leave others to die from it. I forget the outcome back in that civil war, but you get the idea."

Baron Malgosy slapped his thigh. "I like it. Katelin drinks a fatal poison, and it's all backed up by a precedent in your history. That will do it."

"Wait a minute," Sirika interrupted. "I'm all for pouring poison down that wretched girl's throat, but you said all the rivals drank it too. Does that mean some of us would need to take the poison as well?"

"That's no problem," Malgosy boasted. "I know my poisons and have worked up resistance to most of them."

Tajion frowned. "Yes, there were definitely a few of them who drank. Not just the King, but also his challengers and those who were next in the line of royal succession. But don't you see, Mother, this is the beauty of the idea." He was keen to press the brilliance of his plan. "It doesn't matter who or how many need to drink, because the issue is resolved by the Divine herself. I'm impressed by your poison resistance, Baron, but for all three of us, given the strength of this poison, we need the will of the White Goddess to be on our side."

Baron Malgosy nodded, and the Prince pressed on.

"I wouldn't suggest this if we hadn't just had a clear indication of the Divine will here. The Life Weaver is on our side, Mother, and against Katelin, so we have nothing to fear. Our White Goddess will save the three of us from the poison, and let my cousin die from it. I'm sure of it. And think of the prize. When this works out, we'll have done it. Katelin will be dead. Rashelin will be convinced to get herself out of our way too. And everything will be ours at last: the throne, the Crown, the Kingdom, and the rule of the whole Western Coast."

Sleep must have come, for when she stirred, Katelin was curled up in the chair, her muscles stiff. The room was dim, with only the flicker of a single oil lamp. In the low light, Katelin saw Princess Rashelin lying on a couch across the room, watching her. Katelin stretched and yawned.

Rashelin looked dreadful. Her gown was crumpled, her blonde hair dishevelled. Her normally glowing cheeks looked sunken, and her blue eyes were red-rimmed and dark. She was twisting her fingers together.

"Are you a prisoner of your mother too?" Katelin asked, her voice croaky.

Rashelin nodded. "Yes, in a way. I asked if I could visit you. I'm allowed back to my room if I wish, but I'm also under guard."

"What time is it?"

"The early hours, sometime before dawn."

"What's happening down there?" Katelin thought her voice sounded small and lifeless, but she needed to distract herself by asking about the rest of the world.

Rashelin sighed. "Sirika and the Baron ordered the Malgosians to evict all the Anestran citizens from the Castle grounds. Some of the people resisted, and there was fighting and bloodshed. But the courtyard is clear now, so our people must be trying to survive in the rubble and ruins of their homes."

"Has the Ocean receded?"

"Yes, the wave passed and has drained away for the most part. There haven't been any further tremors or waves. Yet."

Katelin shifted her position but couldn't get comfortable. She'd become as numb on the outside as she was on the inside. She was acutely aware, in the silence that followed, that she and her cousin were avoiding talking about the one thing that really mattered.

Then Rashelin whispered it. "Katelin, I'm so, so sorry."

"Don't apologise, Rashelin. You've been loyal to me throughout and helped me when you could. You overheard Sirika and Tajion at Mannismill at the start."

Rashelin nodded and gave a weak smile. "But I feel responsible, that somehow I should have exposed Mother's and the Baron's plans to the Court."

"None of this is your fault. If anything, it's mine, because of how I behaved, being proud and wilful and alienating Aunt Sirika and the Court."

The memory of her night-time conversation with Gracie in the Haven's kitchen came back to her, saying that her friends might be a higher priority than being Queen, anyway. Was that still true? Zane and Rashelin were here and safe for now, but the future for her people remained to be decided.

Katelin shrugged. "As for the Crown, what can we do? The Divine bestows her favours where she wills. Perhaps neither of us is at fault. We're just caught up in the middle of it."

Rashelin was frowning. "But over the last year, while you've been Queen, have you ever had a sense that the Divine is displeased with you?"

Katelin considered that. "No. In fact, only yesterday afternoon, after the earthquake, the Divine sent her power to heal Zane and me. I assumed that was so we could get back here in time. But clearly not."

"In which case, why would the Divine do that for you in the afternoon, only to remove her glory from your Crown last night?"

"Don't ask me. I've never understood the Divine, and even less so now. You were always the one who was better at that."

Rashelin furrowed her brow. "We need to start by recognising that the Divine loves us. She wants the best for us, for Anestra and for the Western Coast."

Katelin couldn't suppress a snort. Rashelin looked up.

"Forgive me, Rashelin, but it doesn't feel like the Divine loves me right now. Not after what she's just done to me. Maybe your mother's right, and all these disasters of invasion, plague, earthquake, flood and death are my fault, and the sooner I'm out of the way, the better."

Rashelin was pointing a finger. "Now don't start thinking or talking like that. My mother is wrong and a liar, and all she wants is power for herself. There's no way she's following the Divine will for Anestra."

"What is it, then, Rashelin?" Katelin's voice was calm now, but quiet. "Explain it to me. What is the Divine doing? What's going on?"

She could tell her cousin was casting about for something to say, for some way of understanding the inexplicable.

"Well, maybe there are other things going on here that we can't see or understand yet. There must be some bigger picture, or higher purpose, beyond who rules this city and Kingdom. Or something like that."

Rashelin trailed off, and Katelin knew she hadn't even convinced herself. They were quiet for a while.

Then Rashelin asked, "Katelin, what are you going to do?"

"Don't you mean, what is your mother going to let me do?"

"No, I don't mean that. Yes, she wants to get rid of you, but she wouldn't dare to kill you here in your rooms, not now everyone in the Court has seen you alive and well. She could get away with tales of a riding accident or wild animal attack in the forest, while you were out of sight of them all. But not now."

"What do the people think of me, Rashelin? I don't mean the nobles and ministers of the Court, but the citizens of Anestra. Have I been a good Queen to them?"

"Yes, you have." Rashelin's answer was firm and immediate. "They love you, Katelin. You're their champion against the rich and the nobles, against anyone who might try to oppress or exploit them. They were devastated when they thought you'd been hurt or killed. You saved many of their lives yesterday evening. Now that they've learned how my mother and the Baron lied to them, they'll be even more on your side."

Katelin nodded. It was good to hear. But it only made her next words even more difficult. "Then they'll be sorry to see me leave. Because, Rashelin, it seems my only option is to go away from here."

Rashelin was staring at her.

"Your mother will never let me stay around here, and she can't keep me locked up in my rooms forever. It will be only a matter of time before she finds some other way to do away with me. So, I'll go back to the forest, and then keep going, further and further east, until I find somewhere else. Somewhere that has never heard of Anestra or the Western Coast, and doesn't care about Princesses or Queens, where I can start a new life. It will be banishment and exile, I suppose, but I can't see that I have any other choice." A tear sprang to her eye, and she was surprised that her numbness could manage that much.

Rashelin's hand was over her mouth, and she swallowed hard. "On your own? Will you go alone?"

Katelin shrugged again. "I guess that's up to others. I'll ask Zane if he'd like to come with me, or any of his band. You can come too, if you'd like." She tried a weak smile, but

Rashelin was in anguish.

"But you can't leave here for ever. Oh, Katelin, please don't make me choose between never seeing you or Anestra ever again."

Katelin crawled across the rug to sit next to her cousin. They wrapped arms around each other and clasped hands.

"But Rashelin, don't you see? Maybe this is what is meant to be. Perhaps this is that bigger picture or higher purpose you mentioned. Maybe I was meant to be Queen of Anestra for this one year only, to get everyone through these difficult times, and then go on to something else. Now that Anestra city is ruined, perhaps we're not supposed to rebuild all the homes and workshops, and the Temple, but to start anew somewhere else. We could see if any citizens of Anestra want to come with us. We could start off in the Manniswood, in the way Zane's people have done, and then either stay or move on as we wish. Maybe I'm meant to lead a new community, a new people, and leave your mother and the Baron, the nobles, the ministers and the Court behind. We could leave them to rule over their own little Castle, and start the New Kingdom elsewhere. What do you think?"

The words came flowing out of Katelin's mouth almost before she had the chance to think them. Was this an idea that could excite her, or was it all too fanciful again, another childish dream? She could tell that Rashelin was doubtful. Was it too much change to ask of her cousin, the Princess, the tactful reconciler, the Court diplomat?

She went on, "Or would you rather stay here, Rashelin? Because after me, you're next in line for the throne. It comes down to you, or otherwise Tajion, to rule Anestra. But it will be with your mother and Baron Malgosy behind your back. Could you do that?"

Rashelin gulped, and Katelin felt her cousin's trembling. At last she said, "No, I couldn't do that. Not on my own." She lifted tear-filled eyes and said, "I'm sorry, Katelin, but I'm not like you. I don't have your fight or your strength. I couldn't stand up to my mother, and the Baron, and Tajion, and all of the Court on my own for the rest of my life."

"Come away with me, then," Katelin said, but Rashelin began to cry. So Katelin held her until her own tears came and they could weep together.

By the time the light of dawn filtered through the curtains and across the floor, Rashelin had left and returned to sleep in her room.

Katelin didn't think she'd slept further, but was grateful for her cousin's visit. Talking with Rashelin had helped her see that her future might lie away from Anestra city and be a new and freer life.

Her enthusiastic dreams were short-lived, as her door was unlocked and a Malgosian soldier appeared. "Come with me," he grunted. Katelin swallowed her indignation and rose to follow him out. Another Malgosian opened the door to Zane's room, and ordered the two of them to come with them to the Hall.

As they were marched away, Katelin had a brief moment in which to find Zane's hand and speak with him. "If we get the chance," she said, "will you come away with me?"

Zane forced a grim smile. "Of course, my lady. Anywhere is better than this." He indicated the locked room he'd vacated. "But where could you go?"

Katelin shrugged. "I don't know. The forest, further east. Just away."

Zane managed a nod before the Malgosians forced them apart and down to the Keep entrance.

Katelin turned to look out through the doors and into the daylight of the Castle courtyard. The cobbles were wet and smelled of sea water, and the prints of many boots marked the grassy grounds. Katelin sighed at the absence of her people, who now fended for themselves among the rubble and ruin of the city. But were they still her people?

The Malgosians marched them towards the Hall, and

Katelin steeled herself for whatever might happen now. She would act like a Queen even if the Divine had abandoned her reign. She straightened her back and flicked her hands to dismiss the Malgosian guards beside her. She motioned to Zane to accompany her and made her entrance into the packed Anestran Hall of the Court.

At the doorway, she passed the silver-haired Royal Steward, Yardles. Unbidden, he knocked his staff thrice on the threshold and called, "Her Majesty, the Queen Katelin of Anestra and the Old Kingdom of the Western Coast."

At once, cries of "No" and murmurs came from some courtiers within the Hall. From the corner of her eye, Katelin saw nobles and ministers shaking their heads at her, but she ignored them. It crossed her mind to wonder what her title was now: former Queen, Princess again, or no title at all? Yardles had announced her as a sign of his support, in the midst of all the opposition from the Court, and she appreciated his loyalty and confidence.

If anything, the Hall was even fuller than the evening before. No wonder the courtyard had been silent and empty, as anyone who had an excuse was here: ladies and lords, ministers of the Kingdom, even lowly officials, had abandoned their duties to be present. She couldn't blame them. Why be in your study, room or tower when you could be here in the Hall to witness the fate of your former Queen?

And what was that to be?

Katelin kept her shoulders back and her head high as she paraded the length of the Hall. She heard Zane's boots close behind her, and almost smiled at the memory of his complaint about needing to spend his life two steps behind her. Well, here they were together after all.

The royal dais held Princess Rashelin and Under-Father Ruis on one side, and Prince Tajion on the other. As Katelin expected, Aunt Sirika occupied pride of place on the royal throne in the centre as Regent of the Kingdom. But unlike last night, when Baron Malgosy had stood at her shoulder, this morning he lounged in a companion throne beside her. They looked for all the world like a King and Queen, husband and wife, and a chilling thought stabbed at Katelin's heart. What if these two were to marry? They might suit each other well, with their cruel viciousness and lust for power, but what an unstoppable partnership they would make. How could she leave the people of Anestra in the hands of these two?

Katelin decided to distract herself. She would speak before she reached the dais, to seize the initiative and forestall whatever plans her aunt and the Baron might have.

"I have decided," she called, as she closed the gap before the dais, and the murmurs in the Hall subsided to nothing. "I have decided," she repeated over the sound of her boots on the flagstones, "to go away. No one regrets more than I do that the Divine has chosen to withdraw her support for my reign, but I accept the clear will of the White Goddess, our Life Weaver."

She reached a stop in front of the dais and turned her back on Sirika and the Baron. Zane moved beside her as she addressed the Court. "It seems my life must take on a new direction from this morning, and so I will leave Anestra city at once. You may rest assured that you will never see me here again. I consider myself banished forthwith from this city and Kingdom, and therefore I will travel far away, wherever my steps might take me."

Regent Sirika's voice interrupted her from behind her on the dais, and Katelin gritted her teeth.

"Noble words, my young former Queen, but hollow ones. You make the appearance of 'regrets' and 'consider myself banished', but in truth you merely seek to do what you have always done: to have your own way. This offer of yours never to return is no more than an excuse to embark on your latest adventure. And when you tire of it, or feel yourself in need of a warm bath, a soft bed or a good cooked meal, you will turn up again at our gates. So no, you foolish girl, we don't believe you."

Katelin bristled and turned to face her aunt, raising her voice for all the Court to hear. "Whether you believe me or not is of no consequence. I am prepared to swear by the Divine and the Crown that I will never return."

Sirika gave a slow shake of her head. "Not good enough. Are we to accept that your oath, taken in the name of our White Goddess who has so clearly and completely abandoned you, should hold any lasting power over your heart, mind and will? No, you will renege on your oath just as quickly as you threw off the yoke of anyone who tried to discipline you. You were the same all those years growing up, and you've not changed now. You are impossible to tame."

"You are wrong. I have changed. I have met with Ilbassi and the Divine herself. On more than one occasion I have given every last ounce of my strength and courage to save these good people of Anestra. For I am no longer the foolish little girl you tried and failed to bring up. No, Aunt Sirika, I have grown up. I am a woman, and a Queen, and although my reign has been short, I have seen our people through the most trying times of our history."

Sirika's face twisted in disdain and contempt. "Hear the arrogance of the girl. She seeks to defend and justify her crimes and mistakes. But let me ask you this, O noble, grown-up, former Queen. Would you go into exile on your own, or would you take anyone with you?"

Katelin shrugged. "That is for them to decide. I have friends here, and they must choose whether they wish to remain here in Anestra under your rule, or else accompany me on an uncertain journey to somewhere faraway and unknown. Neither of us can determine where others might choose to travel or to live."

"Aha!" Sirika cried. "Now we get to the truth of it. Hear the words of this young, innocent, former Queen as she seeks to sow the seeds of a following. 'Any may accompany me if they wish,' she says, and so invites our people to oppose my rule and go over to her side. Do you think I am stupid, or as foolish as you? How can I fulfil my duties as Regent of the Kingdom and allow a renegade, deposed Queen to live at large beyond our borders, building her army? No, that would merely prepare the ground for civil war."

Katelin stared at her aunt. "Civil war? That is a ridiculous suggestion, and I promise you that the thought never entered my mind. I would never do that to the good and loyal people of Anestra. I love them too much." But even as she said these words, Katelin understood how much Aunt Sirika feared her. Allowing a former Queen to live and escape would be a constant threat, a splinter in the Regent's flesh, a sword resting on her neck.

"You love them, do you, these good people of Anestra? Enough to lay down your life and die for them?"

"Of course," Katelin snapped. "And so should you."

"It is well that you say this," Sirika gloated, and her voice rose. "We have heard enough of your juvenile fancies and dreams, and it is time that we came to the solution of the matter. You see, it is not what *you* have decided that matters here, but what *I* have decided. In this time of uncertainty, with no Divinely appointed ruler, the supreme authority in the Kingdom rests with the Regent. With me. And therefore, to resolve the matter of the future of the Crown, we invoke the Trial by Poison."

## 19

## POISON

Katelin frowned. She hadn't heard of this. But it didn't sound good. If Aunt Sirika suggested it, then it must be designed to kill her.

At the same time, the assembled multitudes in the Hall gasped and descended into shocked discussion. Katelin scanned the faces of those on the dais.

Aunt Sirika, Baron Malgosy and Prince Tajion wore broad grins. On the other side, Princess Rashelin sat watching her with hands clasped, shoulders slumped, eyes shining with tears. Under-Father Ruis stood nearby, head bowed, gaze downcast to the floor. Katelin glanced at Zane, and he stared at her, the muscles in his jaw tightening, swallowing hard.

She looked around the Hall. Among the earnest discussions and shaking of heads, Katelin thought again she saw the deep blue of cleric Gracie's eyes among the courtiers, but when she looked again they were gone.

Then she noticed the side table. Near to Under-Father Ruis stood a low table on which lay a tray with an old bottle and some cups. Trial by Poison. What on earth could that involve? She thought she knew, but the dread of that knowledge was too awful to contemplate.

She cleared her throat. "Trial by Poison?" she called, and the commotion subsided. "I'm not familiar with it. What does that involve?"

Sirika's voice was a sneer. "Not familiar with it? Of course, my rebel niece failed to study her history. It was the young and noble Prince Tajion here who suggested our solution." The Prince acknowledged his mother with a bow of his head. "We're grateful to him for his knowledge of the more … um … colourful episodes in our past."

Katelin folded her arms. "Go on, then. Trial by Poison. What is it?"

"Another way to discern the will of the Divine," Sirika declared. "At various times in our past, when the Crown failed to shine as expected, the Court of Anestra devised a new way of testing disputed claims to the throne. The clerics reported that royal blood is supposed to be stronger than others, and able to resist poisons. So they prayed to the Divine, for our White Goddess to reveal her will by saving those she wished to survive the poison. The Divine has withdrawn her glory from your Crown, so we're going to test your claim now."

Under-Father Ruis stepped forward and spoke up, interrupting Regent Sirika. "It is a primitive and barbaric practice, and I now make public my opposition to using it. Trial by Poison sets a trap for the Divine. We try to kill ourselves and force her to intervene to save the one she wants to rule the Kingdom. But as your aunt says, your Majesty, the supreme authority here rests with her, and not with anyone else, so she has overruled me."

Katelin planted her hands on her hips. "In which case, I say no. I refuse. I won't take any part in this Trial by Poison."

Sirika's eyes lit up, almost with glee, as though she'd been hoping Katelin would say this. "You defy my orders? You resist the will of the one whom this Court has appointed as Regent of the Kingdom? That is treason, my girl. You can be executed for that. So, do you choose to persist in that course, or will you submit to the Trial by Poison?"

Katelin folded her arms. She looked back around the Hall and noticed now the prevalence of dark green and grey among the guards. Of course, Aunt Sirika and Baron Malgosy had been careful to fill the Hall of the Court with his Malgosian soldiers, far outnumbering any Anestran Castle guards. She couldn't count on enough of the lords or nobles, the ministers or officials, to fight to prevent her execution for treason on the spot. Sirika, Malgosy, and Tajion too for all Katelin knew, itched to do away with her. They would seize any excuse or pretence for her death, so what else could she do?

"Let me be clear," Katelin said. "What happens in this Trial by Poison? I drink a cup of it and then we all see what happens? Whether the Divine saves me or allows me to die?"

Under-Father Ruis answered her. "Yes, you will drink a measure of the poison, my lady, but you will not be alone. When this barbaric custom was devised in the past, certain rules for it were established. They couldn't have it invoked at will, with anyone's minor grievance against the King or Queen. So, the challengers must also drink. And to avoid those next in line for the throne attempting to assassinate the current ruler, two of those in the royal succession must also drink."

"So, who are the challengers? Who else will drink the poison with me?"

"I am," Aunt Sirika declared. "And the noble Baron Malgosy. On this occasion, five of us will drink the poison: you, me, the Baron, Rashelin and Tajion."

Katelin stared at her, at Under-Father Ruis, and then at the others. Her gaze came to rest on her cousin, the Princess Rashelin. "But this could kill you," she blurted out. "Rashelin, I can't have you drink poison for this."

Rashelin shook her head. "We don't have any choice, Katelin, my Queen," she said. "I'm next in line. I must drink. Mother insists on it."

Katelin's mind raced. If they all drank, then maybe the poison would kill Sirika and the Baron as well as her. But what about Rashelin and Tajion—Sirika was risking the lives of her two eldest children as well. How much did they know about the strength of royal blood? That theirs was in fact Divine blood, given by descent since the White Goddess gave birth to their ancestors?

She needed to think. Katelin, Rashelin and Tajion were of royal birth, born as cousins in her family. But Sirika and Malgosy were not. Aunt Sirika and the Baron were of noble birth, but not royal. Was that enough of a difference?

She became aware that everyone watched her. "So, if I agree to this Trial by Poison," she said, "then the five of us each drink a cup of it, and we wait for the Divine to sort it out?"

Aunt Sirika was smirking, and Katelin didn't like the look of it. There must be some cheat, some deception, a trick up the Regent's sleeve to be sure of winning this contest. And Katelin was right.

"There is one small detail that perhaps we ought to mention," Sirika answered, not restraining the triumph in her voice. "The Baron and I, my daughter and son, we are required to take a smaller measure of the poison than you. You see, we must compensate for the legendary strength of Anestran royal blood, the rumour that our Kings and Queens are born with steel in their veins. So the volumes in the cups are prescribed. Why, the four of us take no more than a sip." Her voice became an undisguised snarl of vicious cruelty. "While you, my foolish, useless niece, you wayward, rebellious girl, you deposed, former Queen, you must drain the whole goblet."

A punch of dread landed in Katelin's stomach, and she almost staggered. Zane's hand on her arm steadied her. A whole goblet of poison? That wasn't fair. They should drink equal amounts. But Katelin knew she couldn't complain. Whether by treason or poison, Aunt Sirika now held all the power, and was determined to kill her.

So, was this it? Was this where she would die? Here, in the Hall of the Court in Anestra Castle, as a public spectacle, with the nobles of the Western Coast all watching? Would they laugh and point as she writhed and screamed, as the poison dragged her away to oblivion?

There was no chance, then, for Queen Katelin the Great to live a long, full or contented life. To die in her bed as an old lady, satisfied and at peace, surrounded by her loving children and grandchildren. But what of her destiny to be a great Queen of Anestra? Had that been a lie, or had she done that already? Had her efforts this last year been enough to make her a great Queen?

No chance either for her dreams of escape, for the New Kingdom of her people in the forest, or of travelling to discover and explore strange and distant lands. No, this was the end. This was *her* end.

She looked up and managed to say, "Aunt Sirika, you will give me one moment. I will speak with Rashelin, Ruis and Zane before I decide."

Katelin turned her back on the thrones of Regent Sirika and Baron Malgosy. The Princess, Under-Father and former outlaw came to her side. She laid a hand on Rashelin's and Zane's arms. "I don't see we have any other choice but to accept this, do you?"

Zane glanced around the Hall. "Your aunt and the Baron have secured the Hall with their Malgosian men. We have no chance of fighting our way out or escaping."

"No, I don't see any other options, my Queen," added Ruis. "I've tried to dissuade the Regent and Baron from this course, but to no avail. They are determined to see this through."

"Yes, Katelin," Rashelin murmured, "I fear the time for diplomacy or negotiation has passed. We must trust the Divine to spare and save you."

Katelin squeezed her cousin's shoulder. "But Rashelin, you need to drink this too. Is your royal blood strong enough to fight it?"

The Princess swallowed hard, her eyes shining with tears. "We shall see."

A dreadful thought clutched at Katelin. "Under-Father Ruis, is this poison painful? Please say that it's a slow, gentle drift into a dreamless sleep."

The Under-Father pursed his lips and then sighed. "I'm so sorry, your Majesty, your Highness. I'm afraid not. The substance prescribed is called Fireblood, and the clue is in the name."

Rashelin clutched at Katelin's arm, and she clasped her cousin's hand back. "We will fight it, Rashelin, we must. There is something of the Divine in our blood, and she is stronger than any poison. We need to trust her, and you've always been so good at that. Don't stop believing in her now."

Rashelin looked to the timbered ceiling of the Hall and drew in a deep breath. As she nodded, a single tear rolled down her cheek.

Katelin had to look away, or tears would start from her own eyes too. "But why, Under-Father Ruis? Why will Aunt Sirika and Baron Malgosy put themselves through this, the pain, the risk?"

Ruis shrugged and said, "The survivors get to rule. Whoever lives after the Trial by Poison can claim Divine authority over the Kingdom. They need to get rid of you, and then trust their own blood and physical strength to survive the ordeal. Since the glory was withdrawn from your Crown, they think the Divine has abandoned you and sided with them. They see little risk. They will never get to rule without this, and their thirst for power seems to have blinded them to all else."

They were all silent until Katelin nodded. "Very well. Under-Father Ruis, please finish your preparations for the Trial by Poison."

Ruis bowed to her and clasped her hands. "Queen Katelin, your Majesty, in the event this doesn't turn out as we all hope, it has been an honour to know you. You have been, and always will be, my Queen."

Katelin's throat constricted with emotion as the Under-Father turned away.

She gave her cousin a tight embrace. Rashelin whispered, "This could be goodbye, Katelin. My dear cousin, my best friend, my sister, my Queen."

Katelin couldn't deny the possibility. She forced out a smile. "Didn't we burn brightly during the years we've had? My nineteen, your twenty-one. Did we make a difference?"

"Yes, we did," Rashelin said at once. "We worked hard, we tried and gave our best, we did what was right. We trusted the Divine, and we won't stop now."

"Maybe the Divine is calling us home," Katelin breathed. The Princess gulped, nodded, let go and stepped away.

That left Zane. Katelin wished they weren't standing in the middle of the Hall of the Court with a host of people watching. Why couldn't this happen in some quiet forest glade, with dappled sunlight on their backs, and a breeze and birdsong in the trees?

His strong arms drew her into a hug, and Katelin closed her eyes and imagined the forest. Katelin threw all her strength into her arms to squeeze him, to press her body to his.

Zane whispered in her ear. "I'm sorry I never got to build you that cabin in the forest, my lady Kat." Then his voice broke. "Or to share a life with you there."

She clung to him for one moment more, and then they pulled apart.

Zane's teeth were clenched, and he was swallowing hard. But she could see the tears in his warm, dark eyes, and she lifted a hand to touch his stubbled cheek and chin.

"I love you, Kat," Zane breathed.

Katelin stared at him, and Gracie's words in that hidden cottage in the Manniswood came back to her. "Don't you follow after him. Let him prove whether his love for you is real and true." Well, Gracie, too late for that, Katelin thought. He's chased and caught me after all.

"I love you too, Zane," she said.

She meant to turn away before her tears could overflow,

but Zane held her head and drew near for a kiss. He paused before their lips met, and Katelin was sure she saw his twitch into a smile. She smiled too. And then they kissed.

For that long moment there was no one else in the Hall. There were no thrones or Kingdoms, no Crowns or usurpers, no Queen or destiny. There was only one young woman and one young man discovering they loved each other. And so they could have been deep in the forest or on the other side of the world, for all that Katelin knew or cared.

But the moment passed. The kiss ended and they broke apart.

Their faces were still close, but Zane's smile had gone. His brows lowered into a frown. "You must survive this, Kat," he breathed.

Katelin looked deep into his eyes. She swallowed hard. "I'll fight it as hard as I can," she whispered. "You know I will. But I'm scared."

Zane's jaw clenched and he looked down. His voice trembled as he said, "Our courage in the face of death says as much about us as our courage in life. Be strong, my Queen."

Katelin swallowed hard. "Whatever happens, Zane, my love, good night, and I'll see you in the morning."

Zane stared at her, nodding slowly.

"Stay with me?"

Zane tried to break into one of his lopsided smiles. "I don't think the Baron's men will let me wander off anywhere."

Katelin linked her fingers between his and turned away, drawing him with her towards the dais.

The Hall came back to her. With it came all the nobles and courtiers who watched her, but she no longer cared whether they regarded her with distaste, disapproval or concern. She would carry out what she now must do and accept the verdict of the Divine.

"I am ready," Katelin declared to the silent and waiting Hall.

Had she done enough as Queen? Had she tried her best to do what was right, or could she have offered more? The nagging doubt and worry persisted: the withdrawal of glory from her Crown.

Rashelin's words of days ago came back to her: 'You don't want it to appear as though in rejecting her Crown you are rejecting the Divine herself.' Was that what she'd done, rejected both the Divine and her Crown? Was the Divine displeased with her, such that she wouldn't now be saved? If she was no longer Queen, was her blood no longer strong enough? The best she could hope and pray for was to trust the Divine enough to go and rest with her forever.

Attendants had moved the low table with the bottle and cups to in front of the thrones. Under-Father Ruis lifted the old bottle from the table and uncorked it. "In the absence of the Royal Physician," he said, "the task of administering the Trial by Poison falls to me. And during any incapacity of the Regent, Queen, or successors to the throne, the authority to rule the Kingdom also rests with me. Is that understood?"

A murmur of assent circulated around the Hall, and those on the dais nodded.

As Katelin stepped forward, Ruis began to pour liquid into the cups. Four of them were no larger than a thimble, but the last was a jewelled goblet. Its silver interior sparkled as the crimson liquid splashed into it.

"I found the necessary bottle and equipment among the Royal Physician's supplies," Ruis was saying. "The poison in question is called Fireblood. It is slow to act at first, but in normal circumstances is fatal in any quantity. The challengers and the successors to the throne will step forward to join the Queen."

Aunt Sirika and Baron Malgosy seemed to object that he still called Katelin Queen, but they levered themselves out of their thrones and paraded down the steps of the dais to stand on the flagstones of the Hall. Princess Rashelin and Prince Tajion moved to join them around the table.

Katelin sensed everyone in the Hall now leaning forward and craning their necks to watch. It was as though they hadn't experienced such enjoyable entertainment for years. She resolved to ignore them all, and focus her attention solely on the Under-Father, and Zane, and on the five of them who would drink.

Ruis handed out the full cups. Katelin released Zane's hand to take her goblet, but felt him move to rest it on her back. The others held their thimbles between forefinger and thumb, while Katelin needed both hands to cup the weight of her silver, jewel-encrusted goblet and the fatal liquid it contained.

"Let us pray," the Under-Father called to the assembly in the Hall, and even the rustle of clothes and shuffle of feet ceased.

"O Divine, our White Goddess, our Life Weaver," Ruis prayed, "you created all things, and you care for your world and people. Forgive our arrogance in testing you today. We need your wisdom and power. We ask you to touch and heal those whom you wish to save. Let this Trial by Poison show to your people who it is you wish to rule over them. Have mercy on us all. Our lives are in your hands."

"Our lives are in your hands," came the response from around the Hall, and from across the table.

"My life is in your hand," Katelin mouthed to herself, and meant it.

"The challengers drink first," Ruis instructed.

Baron Malgosy tipped his thimble back at once, and plonked the drained cup back on the table, licking his lips.

Aunt Sirika glared at Katelin, her cold, grey eyes piercing her to the core with fury and loathing. But there was a look of triumph on the Regent's face as she lifted the thimble to her thin lips and emptied it.

Ruis checked the cups were indeed drained, and then said, "The successors."

Prince Tajion looked paler than usual, as though an unaccustomed seriousness gripped him. But he made to copy the Baron's swagger and drained his small cup with a flourish.

Princess Rashelin's hand shook as she lifted it, so she gripped it with the other. Katelin watched her force herself into the action, to raise and tip the cup. But then Rashelin too had taken the poison.

Under-Father Ruis received the cups back from Tajion and Rashelin, and then turned to Katelin. "And your Majesty."

She looked at him, and anguish lined his face. He couldn't even manage to give her a reassuring smile.

"We trust the Divine," Katelin whispered, and the Under-Father nodded.

She looked down into the goblet and was mesmerised by the soft interplay of crimson liquid against the silver cup in the soft light of the lamps. It looked so innocent, almost beautiful.

She raised it to her lips and drank it all down in successive gulps until the goblet was empty.

## 20

## FIRE

The poison tasted bitter and smoky as it went down, but not as awful as Katelin had anticipated. She handed the goblet back to Ruis and wiped her fingers across her mouth.

Across the table from her, Sirika clutched her stomach and stumbled backwards. She retreated to the edge of the dais and sat down on the lower steps. Baron Malgosy went to sit with her, rubbing a hand up and down his chest. Prince Tajion seemed to have decided the best place was to lie flat on the Hall floor. Princess Rashelin lowered herself to her knees and then slid sideways to the flagstones. Under-Father Ruis clicked his fingers and healer clerics hurried forward to attend to each of the poison drinkers.

A fiery aftertaste grew in Katelin's mouth, burning her tongue and throat. She drew in deep breaths to try to cool them down, but this only seemed to fan the flames.

She fumbled for Zane's hand and gripped it hard. He enfolded her in his arms and said into her ear, "See you soon."

Katelin hardly heard him because the fire was trickling down inside her chest. She pushed him away, because she needed cool air, not his warmth, around her. But she clung to his hand, squeezing it as hard as she could. He loves me, she thought, so he won't mind if I break his fingers.

She wanted to look at him, but now she couldn't stand still. She tried to pace back and forth, but her steps seemed more of a stagger. To her ears came shouts, and cries, and screams, but she couldn't focus her thoughts to see what was happening to anyone else.

For the fire had settled in her stomach. It seemed to be gathering there, growing, brewing, trickling together before it launched its fatal assault. Heat washed through Katelin's body, and she tingled and sweated all over.

She screwed her eyes shut to focus on the furnace inside. Dizziness tilted her head, and she thought she might have fallen, or been caught by Zane on the way down. But she could no longer pay attention to anything outside her own body.

She curled over, cradling and massaging her stomach, as though by doing so she might smother or quench the flames. But nothing helped, nothing eased the burning.

She still had her mind, and before she lost it, Katelin repeated to herself: We trust the Divine. See you soon. You must survive this, Kat. I love you too, Zane. I'll fight it as hard as I can. My life is in your hand.

But the words began to jumble, and Katelin feared she was gibbering, the nonsense of madness taking hold.

And then the poison struck. As if on command, the fire oozed out of her stomach and into the neighbouring blood channels. At once her traitorous heart began pumping it to every part of her body. Katelin shouted at her chest to stop, or to slow, but it was no use. With every moment and heartbeat, the fire was spreading down her legs and up to her shoulders.

Katelin tensed her muscles to fight, to resist, but this was no external enemy to battle. Her body itself had become the battleground.

She thrashed and screamed, heaving air into her lungs to vent the frustration and agony in any way she could. But the flames continued their relentless course, towards her feet, down her arms, until there was no part of her that was not on fire.

Katelin whimpered with the pain. This was one enemy from which there was no escape, no way to flee or run, for it came with her, closer than her skin, contained within her thrashing torso and limbs.

She needed to let it out.

She began to scratch and claw at her thighs and arms and stomach. If she could open her body up, the fire would have somewhere to escape. She could let it go, to burn elsewhere, to consume anything else.

But her nails weren't strong or sharp enough. She needed claws, or talons, to rip apart her own flesh and release the flames to the air.

A moment of clarity surfaced. No, no, she would bleed. The poison was Fireblood. It had bonded to the very life flow that circulated inside her, and she could never be free of it and live.

Her blood. It was strong. The strongest, they said. Or it used to be. How could she get her blood to fight the poison?

It was too late. Already the fire was consuming her hands and her feet. They were burning and dying. But she needed them! How could she live with charred, smoking, ashen stumps at the ends of her limbs?

How could she live? I must survive this. We trust the Divine. My life is in your hand.

Something shifted.

She was dizzy, disorientated, for she seemed to have become detached from her head, to be outside her body.

Was this an effect of the poison? A madness? Or a first sign of approaching death?

No, because another moment of understanding came with it.

Her mind, her soul, her spirit had separated from the agony of her body to be able to fight.

She re-entered her skull and drifted down from her head to her neck. Then into her chest, relieved to detach from the torment of agony and terror that besieged her brain. Her mind, her functions, were shutting down, but now she was—not free—but separate from them, able to view them from a close distance.

At once she was running through the tunnels and chambers of her own body down towards her stomach. This was where the battle of blood against fire raged, and she needed to join the fight.

The searing heat of flame scorched her face and front, but she seemed to have nothing more than a small blade in her hand. A dagger, which shone with a white and silver light. Was this the steel in her blood? But how could metal fight fire?

She lunged at a flame, and it seemed to recede, as though doused with water.

Water!

Now she recognised the white and silver light. It wasn't metal, silver or steel. It was the churning of water, of froth and foam, of ocean spray and breaker, of sunlight on the waves.

She lunged again and again, and each time the flames retreated. But her dagger was too small. And this was only one place, while everywhere else in her body the fire was advancing.

"Divine, I need a river!" Katelin yelled. "A torrent, a flood!"

At her words, a trickle of water flowed past her feet. From behind her, a stream was running towards the flames. The fire abated, but then roared back to life. The heat was too intense, and the stream water boiled and steamed away around Katelin.

"More, more," she screamed, stamping her feet, but somehow she knew this was all there was. This was the flow of Divine water she possessed.

And it was flowing too widely. It spread out to all parts of her body, thinner and fainter in each place, unable to keep back the walls of flames, to hold the fire of poison at bay.

Fall back, fall back, she thought. Find the spring and make my last stand there.

She took one last, desperate lunge at the flames with her dagger, and then turned and fled. Behind her, the fire roared and galloped after her like a ravenous, blood-crazed beast.

Through passages and chambers Katelin sprinted upwards towards where she knew the spring must be. Her heart.

She careered into the vast, echoing caverns of her own heart, the walls pulsing and thundering with each beat of her life. She splashed and waded into the pool of water that lay there, the bubbles of a spring rising in its midst. She plunged into its coolness and knew that for the moment she was safe.

But the fire had pursued her up the tunnels from her stomach. Even now it roared and spat at the entrances to her heart, the flames licking at the edges of her pool of life.

And elsewhere? Her arms and legs were lost. The flames had consumed them and moved on. The fire now burned up her stomach and would come with all its heat and fury to here.

Her head and neck remained, and Katelin ordered the stream of water to flow that way to keep her mind and memories from burning. But even as the waters moved at her bidding, Katelin knew that her spring was insufficient to guard all she needed to.

The fires were gathering, like a pack of hunters cornering their prey. Those from her arms moved from her shoulders to assault the waters defending her neck. Those from her legs and stomach joined to encircle her chest and heart. Already the edges of her pool were evaporating, as the heat boiled her life force into nothing.

Katelin looked down at her hand. She still held the silver dagger, but it glimmered with only a pale light, reflecting the crimson fury of the flames. What more could she do in this battle of fire against water, poison against steel, crimson against white?

The defences in her neck were failing. The fires were closing like pincers, like jaws to sever the waters that protected her head. Soon her mind would be lost, her memories too, and all that she had been.

A sadness filled her, at the loss and waste, of too short a

life that would never achieve all she'd hoped. But maybe this was her destiny, to go now and be with the Divine, and rest from all her struggles. There was courage too in facing the end with calmness and peace.

Katelin stood astride the life-spring of her heart and placed her dagger deep into its bubbling waters. The pool glowed white in answer, asserting its stillness and purity over the raging fury that surrounded it.

For the flames were assaulting Katelin's heart, prowling and circling and spitting at her. Her head and neck were breached, burning up under the crimson fury of the implacable poison. This was her last stand, as already the pool at her feet diminished.

Yet Katelin knew a surprising peace. Yes, I burned brightly during the nineteen years I lived. Yes, I achieved much, saved some people's lives, made a difference.

The flames that licked closer held no terror for her. They were merely the passage to the Divine, the way by which she could finally be free and at peace, and rest for ever.

Then the waters were gone. The spring had bubbled dry under the intense heat of the poison's fire. Katelin lay down and curled herself into a ball around the parched wellspring of her life, and prayed.

I trust the Divine. My life is in your hand.

But I'm sorry, Zane, I'm sorry.

The crimson flames roared up and over her, consuming all in their path.

Around her, the pulsing thunder of her heart faltered, and then died.

And the chamber burned away into cold, dark ash.

## 21

## WAKING

First, there was birdsong. It twittered in the distance, and chirruped nearby, as it rose and fell in its timeless melody.

Underneath was the sound of the stream, as it rippled and burbled across rounded pebbles in its passage from the mountains to the Ocean.

Above it all was the breeze, rustling the leaves and sighing through the trees in its restful, joyful whispers of creation.

Katelin didn't open her eyes. She'd be content to lie here forever, listening to the sounds of the forest, for they were beautiful enough not to want anything else.

She filled her lungs and smelled the wildflowers in the meadow outside. The air couldn't have been purer or sweeter. The bed was comfortable and soft, the blanket warm. The linen had been freshly laundered in the stream, and then dried in this clean forest air.

At last she sighed. The sights would be wonderful too, so she opened her eyes to drink them in.

The shadows of leaves danced across her blanket as though playing a game. The sunbeams gave a green, filtered light as they came to rest inside the woodland cottage of the Haven.

The Haven!

Katelin jolted awake in shock. How did she get here? What happened to the Hall of the Court, the Castle, the city? What about the Trial by Poison, the dying consumed by fire?

An awful thought occurred. Was this death? The afterlife? Wherever souls went when they died? Had her spirit conjured an image from her memory to create an illusion of still living?

But if this cottage was the Haven, was that Gracie the cleric humming downstairs?

Katelin sat up in the bed. For she could do so without pain. She felt a little sore and weak, and her arms were pale, but without signs of poison or burning. Or death.

She cleared her throat, coughed, and then called, "Gracie?"

"Coming," came the reply.

Katelin stared at the opening to the bedroom. Could this be real? Was it a dream? She didn't think you could talk like this to people in dreams, not in the way she'd just called out to Gracie.

Or it crossed her mind that the last few days could all have been a dream: meeting up with Zane, the earthquake, the flooding of Anestra, her Crown losing its Divine glory, and the Trial by Poison. Or more of a nightmare than a dream. Had she imagined it all in her sleep, and been here in the Haven all along?

Gracie was stumping up the stairs. There was one way to find out the truth, and that was to ask the old woman what she knew of it.

Gracie backed into the bedroom carrying a tray. She beamed to see Katelin awake, and laid the tray down on the bedside table. There was a pitcher of juice and a cup, a loaf of Gracie's wonderful bread, and a bowl of sliced fruits.

"How are you feeling, my dear?" She poured Katelin a drink and handed it to her.

Katelin took a sip of the cool, refreshing apricot flavour, while Gracie seated herself on the chair by the bed. "Better than I thought I'd be, thank you. Gracie, can you tell me what's been happening over the last few days?"

There was a twinkle in the old lady's eye as she smiled. "You're wondering if all this is real, aren't you? Well, I can tell you that you left here a few days ago, off to meet that young man of yours, Zane. Then there was that terrible earthquake, much worse than the tremor we felt while you were last here. The city of Anestra was flooded by Ocean waves, and you've just been through the Trial by Poison."

Katelin stared at her. The last few days must have been real, not dreamed, if Gracie knew about them. "But how could you know about all of that, if you've been here in the forest all this time?"

Gracie regarded her, a twitch to her lips, as though waiting for Katelin to work something out. "I was there, too. I was in the Hall of the Court in Anestra Castle, and I believe you saw me."

Katelin took another drink while she tried to remember. "Yes, I thought I saw you there. But I can't see how you travelled there so quickly, especially with the earthquake and flood. Did you bring me back here to the forest by yourself? How long did it take you to carry me all the way from Anestra?"

"Yes, I brought you here from Anestra. The Trial by Poison ended about half an hour ago."

Katelin's mouth dropped open, and she was glad she wasn't in the middle of eating or drinking. "Half an hour?" she spluttered. Then one of the other possibilities re-surfaced, the one she dreaded the most. "Am I dead, then? Is this the afterlife? Are you a cleric here to guide me into the arms of the Divine?"

Gracie's smile faded a little, and she sighed. "Yes, my dear young Katelin, you've died. But you still have one last choice before you."

Katelin's mind reeled. She'd never imagined death to be like this. But the old woman's comment intrigued her. "What choice?"

"You can still decide the outcome of the Trial by Poison."

Katelin frowned. "What do you mean? I can't decide the ending of the Trial. The poison killed me."

Gracie drew a deep breath. "Yes, it did. I'm very proud of you, Katelin. You fought so bravely and so well. No one else could hope to survive a goblet full of Fireblood."

Katelin's frown deepened. "How can that poison have killed me, and yet now I feel fine? I don't understand. Is this what death is like? You're talking to me in riddles, Gracie. Explain everything to me, please."

The old woman looked at her. Katelin noticed a reflection of sunlight in the cleric's deep blue eyes. It reminded her again of the flag of Anestra, of the radiant silver Crown on its dark blue background or cushion.

"Have you worked it out yet, Katelin?"

A chill washed through her body, followed closely by a thrill of delight. It couldn't be, could it? Katelin stared and stared, unable to grasp what she was thinking, what had just occurred to her. She swallowed hard.

"Are you … the Divine?"

Gracie beamed. "Am I all that the Divine is? All that she ever has been and will be? I can't see that one little old cleric woman can lay claim to all of that. But yes, Katelin, my dear, I can tell you that the Divine and I have the closest of relationships." She chuckled to herself again.

Katelin looked away. Her mind couldn't grasp the shock of sitting here, chatting with the Divine. Yes, you went to meet with the White Goddess after death, but this was Gracie, the old cleric who had helped her in the forest days ago.

For something to do, she grabbed the loaf of bread, tore off a hunk and took a bite. She wanted to be sure she understood this.

"You're the Divine," she said. "The White Goddess, the Life Weaver. You've come down to the Western Coast to meet with me and help me."

Gracie smiled at her. "If you like to think of me in this way, then I accept it."

Katelin waved her hunk of bread at the woodland

bedroom around her. "Then what is this place, the Haven? Where is it and how did I find it?"

"This is where I live," Gracie said in a soft voice. "You noticed yourself that it has a magic to it. It can stay hidden from unwelcome eyes, like those Malgosians. It is always ready to provide a refuge for those who need it. I keep it as close as possible to anyone who calls. Some stumble on this Haven in their hopes and dreams, but others think of it by another name. They call it heaven."

Katelin stopped chewing. No, she hadn't made the connection between Haven and heaven, but what did this mean? A bitter taste had entered her mouth again, and it wasn't from the bread. She forced herself to chew and swallow to finish the mouthful. Gracie waited and watched her.

Katelin stared at the bedclothes. "You said that I'm dead. So, it's all over. This is the afterlife. I'm with the Divine, and I'm here in heaven. I can't see that I get any more choices or decisions now."

Gracie's voice was firm but gentle. "I'm giving you this one last choice, Katelin. I said that the poison killed you, and that is true. I told you that you still have a choice to determine the outcome of the Trial. And this is your choice: do you wish to stay here with me, or to return to Anestra?"

Katelin moved her gaze away from the old woman's face. "I don't understand. Are you offering me life or death?"

Gracie tilted her head to one side. "I wouldn't put it like that. After all, everyone lives and everyone dies. It's simply a matter of timing. You live for a while on the Western Coast, and then you come to rest with us. Your lives are longer or shorter, but however long you live in the world, your rest with us is eternal. So, which would you like, Katelin? Do you choose to begin your everlasting rest now, or would you prefer to live out the remainder of your life in Anestra first?"

Katelin looked away. Her eyes turned to the window, to

where the meadow of wildflowers danced in the morning sun, next to the clear, bubbling stream that meandered its way through the forest. Yes, it would be so wonderful to stay here, to rest.

"Gracie, is the rest of heaven as glorious and as beautiful as the Haven?"

The old lady snorted with laughter. "As beautiful as this? Certainly not. The rest of heaven is much, much better. The Haven is merely a sort of waiting room, a front porch, if you like. This is where I like to meet those in need and the new arrivals, to give them somewhere a little more familiar, more like your world."

"And where is everyone?" Katelin asked. "I always thought heaven would be full of people, like my brother and my parents, so where are they all?"

Gracie's eyes twinkled. "You will meet them, if you decide to stay. Or if you return to Anestra, you will meet them here when the rest of your life is over."

"I could meet my parents? And Hedger again?" Katelin almost jumped out of bed at the prospect, so that Gracie laughed.

"Yes, of course," she said. "But think carefully. They will always be here, and they're more than happy to watch over your life on the Western Coast, and to welcome you back here in the end."

"So even if I choose to go back to Anestra, I can still return here, even as an old woman, and see you again, and meet the rest of them too?"

"Yes, of course you can," Gracie said. "I promise."

Katelin lay back on her pillows. It was a good choice. Either she could begin her rest and reward now, or else enjoy a longer life in Anestra and come here in the end anyway.

She chewed her lip. The thought of her life in Anestra brought back too many other memories. Like being Queen.

"Gracie, what would be waiting for me in Anestra if I

choose to return there?"

The old lady's face became serious. She gave a heavy sigh and then looked Katelin in the eye. "My dear, I owe you an explanation. I followed your wishes, but I know you're upset about what we've done."

Katelin frowned. "What do you mean? Upset about what?"

"The Crown," Gracie said, and Katelin remembered. The Divine had withdrawn her glory and her blessing from Katelin's reign. So why was Gracie being so kind and nice to her now, if the Divine was so disappointed in her time as Queen?

"Katelin, you're the child of my heart as well as my blood," Gracie went on. "I could never be disappointed in you. You're my daughter, and I love you dearly. It broke my heart to see you in doubt and distress for a while. But I hope you'll be able to overcome your uncertainty when you know and understand the truth."

"What truth is that?" she asked, still not quite able to meet Gracie's eye.

"The truth that I listen to you, and respect to the utmost your wishes and requests. A few days ago, you sat downstairs in this cottage and said you had higher priorities than being Queen. Your role was causing death and distress to those around you. You wanted to save your friends, and I accept that. So, I healed you to let you save Zane. I helped you to get back to Anestra and Rashelin. And then I set you free. I could never force or lock you into a destiny you don't want. I withdrew the glory from your Crown to allow you to be anything else you wish. But that couldn't stop your enemies from still wanting to take your life. If you wish it to be so, then your reign has ended, and you've come here to be with me for ever."

A finger of dread traced its icy way down Katelin's spine. If her reign had ended, then she needed to know what the Fireblood had done to the others. Gracie could tell her that, so she swallowed hard and cleared her throat. "What happened to Rashelin, then? And to Sirika, Malgosy and Tajion? Have they all died too?"

Gracie held Katelin's gaze. "No, they didn't all die. Rashelin and Tajion survived. They have royal blood, of course, my blood, and that's strong enough for them to survive their sip of the poison. Their blood isn't as strong as yours, Katelin, but it's strong enough." Then the old woman frowned. "Regent Sirika and Baron Malgosy died of the Fireblood. They have noble blood, but not royal. Their attitude was selfish and evil. They were arrogant enough to think I'd be forced to save them, but that's no basis for me to intervene on their behalf. No one forces me to do anything. They ended up killing themselves with their own poison."

Katelin leaned back against her pillows. No more Aunt Sirika or Baron Malgosy. She'd never known Anestra Castle without her aunt prowling and scowling within it. Was she finally free of that oppressive, bullying, tormenting presence? Could she imagine her life without it?

Then a worrying thought occurred to her, and she looked out the bedroom window of the woodland cottage. "If Sirika and Malgosy have just died, does that mean the two of them are somewhere here as new arrivals to the Haven?"

Gracie shook her head. "Don't you worry about them, my dear. Those two have gone to a … um … different waiting room, until we judge what should happen to them."

Katelin lay in silence for a while, her thoughts turning to life back in Anestra. Could she enjoy being Queen, with her former enemies removed or brought into submission? She would have Rashelin by her side, to help her with the Anestran Court, with the nobles, ministers and officials. And then there was Zane, of course …

A wide smile spread across her face. Yes, she could imagine that sort of freedom very well.

Gracie wasn't smiling, for her face was still serious. "So,

at this moment, Princess Rashelin is set to become the next Queen of Anestra."

That came as a shock. But of course, if Katelin had died, her reign over, then the Crown would pass to the next in line. How would Rashelin cope with that responsibility? Could she stand up to Tajion and others in the Court? Rashelin would wish Katelin to be there with her as the Queen. And Katelin found herself wishing the same too.

"Let me be clear about the situation, Katelin," Gracie said. "I withdrew the Crown's glory so you were no longer Queen. That is why the Fireblood killed you. Only the Queen's blood is strong enough to withstand the goblet of poison. Your choices, your priorities, saved your friends, but not yourself. Your decision was selfless, but you didn't understand the consequences. Now that you see the bigger picture, I give you the chance to confirm or change your priorities."

Katelin pondered this. The Divine had indeed enabled her to heal herself, and then Zane, after the earthquake. "If I'd chosen to be Queen first, as my highest priority, then my blood would have been strong enough to resist the poison?"

"Yes, it would have been, and it still could be. That's the choice I'm giving you."

"The decision before me now, then, is either Queen, or heaven?"

"I wouldn't put it like that," Gracie said again. "As I said before, it's all a question of timing. Whichever way you choose, your destiny is always Queen and then heaven. The only difference is whether the Queen part is for a year or a lifetime, before you come here."

Katelin took some time to breathe deeply and to think. How highly did she value her life on the Western Coast? Was it worthwhile to undertake a lifetime of hard work and service before coming here to rest? Did she want to give, and love, and make a difference to her people, for longer than the one year she'd already had as Queen?

"So, have you reached your decision?" Gracie asked. "Would you like to return now to Anestra and live out your days there as Queen, or to remain here with me and with all those who have come here before you?"

Katelin knew her answer at once. And it surprised her, given the years she'd dreaded and struggled with her destiny. "I'd like to return to Anestra, please. I'd like to be her Queen."

"This is where I need to be a touch stern with you, Katelin, my dear."

A shiver coursed through Katelin at the thought of the Divine needing to be in any way stern with her.

"All your life you've wrestled with your destiny of being Queen," Gracie went on. "I understand and accept that, because it's such an important and responsible role. You were a girl, but now you're a young woman. You've been hesitant, reluctant, half-hearted, dithering, often wishing you were anywhere else. Being Queen requires a serious, lifelong commitment. It involves tasks you wouldn't normally choose, such as meetings and paperwork. It includes trying your very hardest to get on with those you don't naturally like, such as those nobles, courtiers and ministers. They are all your subjects, and this is the role. Are you still willing to accept it?"

Katelin swallowed hard. She felt like a small child in front of her tutor's desk, being told off and instructed to try harder in future. From anyone else, she would have bristled at this lecture, but this was the Divine she was listening to.

"In addition," Gracie continued, "will you please stop trying to do everything on your own, and in your own strength? Yes, of course, to be a good Queen of a great Kingdom is a task beyond the strength and skills of any one person. That is why I give you friends and advisers, like Rashelin and the Court. That is why I give you the Crown, with access to all my wisdom and experience, my compassion and patience, my glory and power. Please will you humble your pride, and curb all your self-reliance, and allow others to help you to fulfil your destiny?"

The lessons were sinking in, one by one. She needed to take this more seriously. Her life and role were not a game, but a task sufficiently worthwhile for her to spend all her energy and lifetime to get it right. Although she was pivotal to the whole future of the Kingdom, there was no way she could accomplish it all alone.

Her voice was small. "Do you mean that if I try to get to know the nobles, ministers and courtiers of Anestra, then they might be willing to work with me, rather than against me?"

"My dear Katelin," Gracie exclaimed, "they will be thrilled and honoured to get to know you, and to be counted as your friends. Once they can trust you to seek only the very best for the Kingdom, they'll do anything you ask of them. To your credit, you're devoted to the poorer, working people of Anestra, and all we ask is that you include your nobles and the Court within the circle of your subjects who are worthy of your respect, service and love."

Katelin tried to adjust her thinking. She'd taken the time to visit her people within the city of Anestra, so why couldn't she do the same around the noble estates and country houses? If she got to know the different families, and spent time with them personally, that would lead to fewer misunderstandings or awkward moments at Court.

"Yes, I can do that," Katelin responded. "I can do all you've said."

Gracie smiled, and then made a show of examining her fingernails. "Are you sure?" she teased. "I mean, I seem to remember some complaints about 'why was I born a Princess' and never wanting to be Queen. Have you changed your mind about that now?"

"Yes, Gracie, I have. I'm sorry about how much I complained. I realise now that none of us get to choose when or where we're born, or which family we're born into.

I hope I've learned simply to make the most of what you've given me."

The old lady nodded. "So, may I be clear about this, once and for all? You're willing to accept your destiny?"

Katelin lifted her chin. "No. I don't just accept it. I choose it. I choose to be Queen of Anestra for the rest of my life. As long as you and others help me."

Gracie laughed. "That's my girl, Katelin. And please remember this: I am always proud of you. I love you more than I can ever express or you can ever grasp. I will be with you and give you all the help I can, every day of your life."

Katelin smiled back. "Thank you. And I'll keep you to that."

Gracie took Katelin's hand and squeezed it. "This is a solemn moment," she said. "One that you must remember for the rest of your life on the Western Coast. Do you, Katelin, daughter of Etharan and Emmelis, choose to be Queen of Anestra for the remainder of your days, to work at your duties to the best of your abilities, accepting the help of others, loving and serving your people, until I call you home?"

"I do, and I pray that you will help me, and for the Kingdom to prosper in every way."

Gracie's deep blue eyes shone. "Then I hereby restore you to the Queenship of Anestra and the Western Coast. The Crown will display my glory for you again, and I grant to your blood its full strength to overcome the Trial by Poison. As soon as you wish, you may return to your life."

Gracie released her hand, leaned forward, and embraced her with warmth and strength. Katelin long remembered that moment and smiled whenever anyone mentioned the Divine's loving arms.

When they sat back, Katelin said, "Before I go, may I ask you about a couple of other things? You know that Zane and I managed to discover that we love each other. I can't ask you to tell us our future, but is he a good man?"

"Yes," Gracie replied. "Zane is a good man and he loves you very much. Are you going to ask me for more than that?"

Katelin laughed. "Excellent." She glanced out of the bedroom window towards the forest meadow. "And one more thing. Can I have another wash in that wonderful stream of yours before I go back to Anestra?"

Gracie chuckled. "Yes, of course. That's a great idea. It'll clean away the last traces of the Fireblood. Come on, let's go and do that now."

## 22

## QUEEN

Katelin lay curled on the ground of the cold, dark cavern.

The air smelled of smoke and ash. Her body felt stiff, as though she'd lain there for a while, or tensed her muscles for too long. She flexed her arms and legs in a slow uncurling and raised herself to her feet. She listened.

All was still.

No thundering beating of her heart. No rushing of air into her lungs. It was the eternal peace of death.

She looked about. The cavern floor and walls had been scorched and blackened. A few wisps of smoke and ash hung in the stillness. There was no life here.

Something caught her eye near her boot. Her standing up had disturbed the ashes enough to reveal something buried within them. It looked like metal.

Katelin crouched down and eased the ash and dust away from it. It was a dagger, with a tarnished hilt, but with the blade still polished and bright.

It was her dagger.

She curled her fingers around the hilt and lifted it. The blade glinted in the darkness, shining with its own, inner light. It reminded her of sunlight on Ocean waves, the foam and spray of a waterfall, or the curl of a breaker.

The ashes at her feet shifted. She stepped back, for the ground had become soft and damp. A bubble of water popped up into the cavern.

And so the spring began.

The ashen floor darkened with a trickle of water from beneath, filling a puddle, and then a small pool. The water overflowed and began to run in rivulets wherever it could find a passage across the scorched and dusty ground. The ash dissolved into its flow, and Katelin let the new stream wash clean the dirt on her boots.

The spring kept flowing. Further and wider its waters spread, softening, cleansing and renewing the chamber. With magical swiftness, it climbed up the cavern walls, bringing colour, warmth and life. The waters brought with them a movement, a rustle, a breeze, that grew louder and stronger.

Then came the first roar of thunder. The cavern echoed with the majestic boom of a heartbeat.

Katelin smiled as she felt her lifeblood spread. Up her neck to her head. Across her shoulders. Down her arms to the tips of her fingers. Down her torso and legs to her toes.

Katelin laughed, and filled her lungs with the heady scents of life-giving air. She reached out to caress the deep red, warm, pulsing wall of her own heart …

… and she was back in her body.

The smoothness of the cavern wall was the sheet on the bed, as she ran her fingers over it. The breath that filled her body contained all the smells of Anestra Castle.

She kept her eyes closed, listening. The Castle was quiet. There were distant sounds in the courtyard, and further off in the city. They were the normal sounds of daily life. People going about their work, greeting their friends, holding conversations.

She was back.

But her body felt sore and weak. In the Haven, she'd had a magical strength and healing, while this mortal body still needed time to heal and strengthen. But she could give it that time. She had the whole of the rest of her life to look forward to.

But wait. Was that the sound of someone breathing? It was slow, deep and even, as of someone asleep. Katelin opened her eyelids a crack.

She lay in her bedroom in the royal apartments. The

room was empty except for Zane slumped in a chair near the bed. She regarded his ruggedly handsome face for a moment, his untidy black hair, his stubbled cheeks and chin. For he was fast asleep, his head resting on his chest.

Katelin closed her eyes and cleared her throat. She heard Zane stir.

"Well, I think I need to hire a new night watchman," she said. "The one I have now keeps falling asleep."

Then came the unmistakeable sound of Zane falling off his chair.

Katelin cracked open one eye and peered over that side of her bed. Zane came back into view, clambering up from the floor.

"Kat!" he gasped. "You're alive!"

"Lucky for you," Katelin replied. "The next ruler of Anestra might not be so lenient towards those who are supposed to keep watch over her."

"But you're dead," Zane spluttered. "I've been keeping vigil until they bury you."

"Well, good morning," she breathed. "I'm sorry it's been a long night."

Tears were rolling down his face, so that she softened and couldn't keep on teasing him. "Come here," she whispered.

Zane's strong arms encircled her and lifted her from the mattress before she could say, "Careful, careful."

But it was wonderful to be held like this, with her face in Zane's hair, her arms wrapped around his shoulders and back.

At last Zane lowered her back onto the bed and knelt on the floor beside her, so that his face stayed close to hers.

Katelin lifted a hand and touched his cheek. "How are you, Zane? How have things been?"

Zane drew a shaky breath and didn't bother to wipe his face. He wagged a finger at her. "I told you never to do this to me again, didn't I? Leaving me thinking you were dead. I had a few hours in hell while waiting for you above Ryebald's Cleft, and now this. I don't like it, my lady Kat. We accepted you'd died, lying so cold and still. But I couldn't conceive of life without you, even though there was no hope. I needed you to come back to me, Kat. And you have."

"I said I'd see you in the morning, didn't I?" She cracked her face into a smile, but it seemed an effort, as though she hadn't done that for a while. She raised her fingers to smooth out the lines on his forehead. "But I'm sorry I've worried you so much."

"The main thing is that you're back now. How did you survive the poison?"

"The Divine helped me," Katelin said, and realised how much she needed to explain to him. "Have I been asleep for a while?"

Zane nodded. "One long day and night. I've tried not to sleep, wanting every minute with you until they took you to your grave. But the exhaustion caught up with me after all."

"So Rashelin and Tajion survived, but Sirika and Malgosy died of the poison, is that right?"

Zane stared at her. "Yes. But you've only just woken up. How do you know that?"

"Ah." Katelin gave him a sly smile. "That would be because the Divine told me."

Zane gaped, struggling to speak. "That … the … the Divine?"

She patted his arm. "There's quite a lot I need to explain to you." She shifted her head on the pillow to gaze at him directly. "Do you remember I told you about meeting an old cleric woman by the name of Gracie in the Manniswood? Well, it turns out that she is the Divine herself, or at least the Divine come down to the Western Coast to meet and help me."

Katelin smiled at the stupefied, incredulous look on his face.

"No wonder her bread and water tasted so good," Zane said. "And that she managed to heal you."

"Gracie also said you're a good man, and that you love me very much, so I'm afraid you have a lot to live up to."

Zane opened and closed his mouth a few times, and then swallowed hard. He also looked a little abashed, which Katelin thought endearing.

"Yes, um, about that," Zane mumbled. "Listen, I know that I love you, but I've been thinking that maybe you only said it because you thought you needed to repeat it back, and that you were about to die anyway, and so it wouldn't make any difference. So, I won't hold you to it. If you've changed your mind."

Tears sprang to her eyes. She started to blink them away, but decided she didn't mind if Zane saw them. "You silly bread-stealer, and outlaw, and life-saver. No, I haven't changed my mind. I said it because I meant it. Part of why I've come back to Anestra is so I can be with you, and share something of a life together. But I've also come back to be Queen. Can you accept me as that?"

Zane nodded. "I've been thinking about that too. If it means I can spend time with you, then I'll adjust." His dark eyes regarded her for a moment, and she looked deep into them. "I've never known anyone with such fire within them as you've got, Kat. You're exhilarating to be around, and inspiring, and wise, and a natural leader ..."

"Hold on, hold on." Katelin laughed. "I don't need to listen to all of this. If you don't shut up soon I'm going to have to kiss you."

His lips parted, as though he suddenly wanted to do the same. But then they shaped into his lopsided smile. "Well, I need to find some other role here, seeing that I've been dismissed from my post as night watchman."

Katelin tilted her head, regarding him. "Oh, I don't know. If all you're going to do is sleep, then perhaps I'll keep you as my night watchman after all."

They caught each other's smiles, and the laughter in their eyes, and leaned closer to kiss.

In the days and weeks that followed, Queen Katelin's strength came back to her, until she was itching to help her stricken people. Anestra city was still in the ruins of the earthquake and flood, and she accommodated as many of the people in the Castle as she could.

It rained steadily for days after Katelin's awakening, and the farmers assured her this was good, to wash the salt and seawater out of the fields. The food stocks in the Castle were diminishing, and they needed to get everything growing again.

As soon as Prince Tajion was well enough, he disappeared back to his country estate of Mannismill in the south. Both Katelin and Rashelin were glad to be rid of him from the city, with the unpleasant memories he carried for them. Tajion took away the body of his mother, Sirika, to bury her with his father at Mannismill, and the last of the Malgosians did the same with their Baron, burying him at Malgosy Castle in the forest.

Zane kept busy with his timberwork, constructing temporary shelters for people from whatever fallen trees or planks he could salvage. Under-Father Ruis and the clerics of the Divine did what they could for the injured and bereaved, keeping a list of those citizens who were missing, presumed washed out to sea in the flood.

As soon as she felt well enough, Queen Katelin summoned all her nobles, ministers and officials to the Hall of the Court. To confirm for everyone the outcome of the Trial by Poison, she wore her sacred relic of the Crown of Anestra and was relieved to see it blaze forth with Divine glory more brightly than ever before.

She addressed them, apologising if she had not met their expectations so far, or had disappointed them. She called for a new beginning, to reunite and rebuild the Kingdom after all the traumas of the last year. She promised to set aside time to get to know them and asked everyone to devote their best efforts to working together. With their help, and that of the Divine, she was sure that Anestra and the Old Kingdom had their best years yet to come.

Her words were met with widespread approval, and Katelin resolved that by friendship and trust, she would share and delegate her many responsibilities for the benefit of them all.

One day, Zane mentioned to Katelin that his friends Rish and Arch had returned to Anestra with the two children they'd met on the night of the flood, Jen and Cal. After some time living in the forest, they'd come back to the city to search for the children's missing mother, Marla, and to start to rebuild their home.

This gave Katelin an excuse to get out of the Castle and her work for the Kingdom and get her hands dirty again. She and Zane even managed to persuade Princess Rashelin to don some old clothes and help them clear rubble from the family's former home in Spring Channel. Katelin smiled when the Princess kept brushing away the dust and dirt all over her, and teased her that at least she could have a warm bath afterwards.

People kept stopping in the street and telling Katelin how thrilled they were to see her back and well again. Among them were the old silversmith Nanpa Arger, his wife and small grandson Rudo, who paused to say hello on their way back to the ruins of their Silver Cottage in Artisan Street.

Zane, Rish and Arch were doing much of the heavy work, sorting through broken bricks and stone, keeping what could be re-used, and carting the rest down to the harbour. Katelin and her ministers had announced that debris from the city's ruined houses would be used to rebuild the damaged breakwater in Anestra Bay.

Katelin and Rashelin helped the children, Jen and Cal, to

sort through the belongings of their former home. They came across dust-covered clothing, broken parts of furniture, kitchen utensils, cups and plates, and decided which could be repaired and what must be discarded and replaced. There were bittersweet joys as the children found their old toys under the rubble, but then the delight of reunion was tempered with dismay at how damaged or broken they were.

Most heart-breaking of all was when Katelin explained to the young girl and boy that no trace of their mother, Marla, had been found among the dead. She must have been washed out into the Ocean during the flood and drowned there.

Jen and Cal surprised and impressed her by taking the news well. They'd guessed it already, because their uncles Arch and Rish had prepared them to expect the loss. There were tears, but the children had each other, and their uncles, and Katelin and Rashelin did their best to comfort and console.

When they stopped work for an afternoon drink and biscuit, they all gathered in a clear space in the former home. The sun had come out, drying the worst of the rain and mud, and they sat in the shade of the one remaining wall. Katelin smiled to see that Princess Rashelin and the blond-haired Rish seemed to be chatting and getting on well, smiling and laughing together.

Katelin ached to do something more for this family, realising that their grief and loss were repeated many times over throughout the city. What could she do? Then an idea came to her.

"Jen and Cal," she called, "come and sit with me." The girl and boy came over and perched on blocks of stone near her. As they did so, Katelin gave a wink to Zane and Rashelin to prepare them for what she was about to say.

"You know, you two," Queen Katelin began, "I've been thinking it might get quiet in Anestra Castle soon. We're looking after lots of people there at present, but we're repairing and rebuilding their homes so they can all move back into their own places. Once they've gone, I'm going to miss having all of them around."

Katelin smiled to see the puzzled looks on Zane's and Rashelin's faces. Where was she going with this? Rish and Arch were listening to her too.

"In fact," she went on, "I think what Anestra needs is some new young Play Princesses and Princes to bring some life back into the Castle. I wonder if we can think of any girls or boys from around here who might like to do that for me."

A spark of excitement ignited in their eyes. Their little faces lit up, but at the same time, there was doubt about whether they were allowed to jump up and down, shouting, 'Me, me, me!'

She put them out of their uncertainty. "So, Jen and Cal, can I ask if you would be interested in becoming the first of my new Anestran Play Princesses and Princes?"

The grins spread across their faces. They glanced at their uncles, to see if it was all right to say 'yes'. But Arch and Rish were beaming as broadly as Rashelin and Zane. All uncertainty gone, Jen and Cal jumped up and ran about and hugged each other and shouted, "Yes, yes, yes!"

"Now wait a minute," Katelin said, when they'd finally calmed down a little. "I need to explain to you about the duties of the young Play Princesses and Princes. Because we ought to find some others to join you. We'll search Anestra city and invite all the other children who have lost their father or mother, or both, and see if they want to join us. Some will be younger, and some will be older than you, but we'll see if we can all look after each other and make some new friends. Would that be good?"

Jen and Cal nodded, and it lifted Katelin's heart to see some light and hope in their faces. "Now let me think about what your duties should be," she said. They were too young to know that she teased them, so she started with, "There are lots of towers, and rooms, and battlements, and dungeons, and they will all need to be explored."

Their little eyes widened, and Cal burst out with, "Can we do dressing up?"

Princess Rashelin joined in to answer that one. "Oh yes, my young Play Prince, there are whole rooms full of clothes for boys and girls of all ages just waiting to be dressed up in."

"What about all the armour and weapons?" Jen asked. "Will we get to have a look at those, too?"

"Oh no," Zane said, with his lopsided smile, and Jen's face fell. So he added at once, "Not just look at them. I would say they must wear the armour and try out all the weapons, wouldn't you? Safely, of course," he added, when Arch and Rish seemed about to speak.

"In fact, I think the Queen would teach you archery herself," Katelin said. "And Zane here could teach the older children swordsmanship."

"And don't forget the horse-riding," Rashelin put in. "There would definitely need to be lots of horse-riding."

Jen and Cal were looking between each other, and all the adults, not sure which to get most excited about first.

"And expeditions to the forest," added Zane. "We'll fit in plenty of those."

"But I don't want you to think it will be all play, Jen and Cal," Katelin said, "because we have cleric tutors there who can teach you about letters and numbers, about reading, and writing and counting, and all the other things you need to learn, about different crafts, history, the Divine, and so on. Would it be all right if we fitted those things into your days at the Castle too?"

Jen and Cal nodded to her, trying their hardest to be serious, but unable to wipe away the grins plastered across their faces.

"And if you're all well behaved," Katelin finished, "I

think from time to time we could climb aboard one of the navy's ships and go off for a long voyage on the Ocean. What do you think?"

Jen and Cal clapped their hands, dancing about. "Yes, yes, yes!"

"Do you need to think about it, Jen and Cal, or would you like to become my first new Play Princess and Prince?"

Jen and Cal rushed over to their uncles, pleading for their permission, and while they did so, Rashelin and Zane gave Katelin a slow nod and wide smile of approval.

The permission of the uncles gained, Jen and Cal returned to stand in front of Queen Katelin. She took them each by the hand, and said, "Play Princess Jen, Play Prince Cal, by my authority as Queen of Anestra, I hereby admit you to your new positions as young Play Princess and Prince of the Old Kingdom."

They bowed before her, and Katelin nodded her head in return.

But Jen was biting her lip. "Is there something worrying you, Play Princess Jen?" Katelin asked.

"Won't any of them in the Castle mind? It's just that there are lots of important people in the Castle, like nobles and guards and Court people, and won't they shout at us and tell us off if we're noisy?"

Katelin sighed. "Yes, Play Princess Jen, I'm afraid there are people in the Castle who think they're more important than you children are." She gave the girl a wink and lowered her voice like a conspirator. "But you see, that's the great thing about me being Queen. I'm the one who's in charge, and I'll do my best to explain why you're welcome there. They need a very good reason to disagree with me, so that should be the end of it. All right?"

Jen looked relieved, and then ran off with Cal into Spring Channel, where the adults could hear the two children chattering in excitement about all they might do in the Castle.

Katelin stood up, ready to resume work, because they'd finished their drinks. Her heart was encouraged that she'd thought of something to lighten the lives of her citizens.

As she looked around, a figure caught her eye. An old lady stood near the top of Spring Channel, watching her. Her silver hair was tied back, and Katelin knew her at once.

"Gracie," she breathed.

The woman walked down the hill and gave Katelin a smile from the street as she passed.

"I'll be back soon," Katelin said to the others, and hurried out of the ruined cottage after Gracie.

She caught up with the old woman as they reached Harbourside, and Gracie motioned for them to sit on the edge of the harbour. They lowered themselves to sit on an undamaged stretch of stonework and swung their legs as the waves lapped beneath them. In the Bay, there were still some fishing boats, wrecked by the flood, that they hadn't managed to salvage yet. On one side, men carted barrow-loads of rubble along to where stonemasons were repairing the breakwater.

"That was a brilliant touch with the children," Gracie began. "I love it."

"Thank you," Katelin said. "I want to give them the best childhood we can. I think they deserve that much, after all they've been through."

"I agree, and if anyone can stir up the Anestran Court to know what's most important, maybe these young people can."

They were quiet for a while until Katelin asked, "Why are you here, Gracie? Is something wrong? Is there something you need to tell me?"

"No, not at all." Gracie smiled at her. "Please don't think that whenever I appear there's something the matter. I'd like to pop in from time to time, if I may, and see how you're getting along."

"Of course," Katelin replied. "This is your city, and your

world, so you can pop in and visit whenever and wherever you like."

Gracie leaned closer and lowered her voice. "To tell you the truth, Katelin dear, I'm enjoying your new Anestra so much I can't keep away. I've looked forward to your time for so long that I don't want to miss anything."

Katelin gulped, but couldn't think of anything to say in response to that. She looked over to their right, up at Temple Hill, where work had begun to make safe the white marble pillars of the Temple of the Divine. The collapsed roof was being dismantled and lowered so they could rebuild the whole place from the pillars up.

"We're working hard to repair your Temple, Gracie," Katelin said. "We'll try to make it as impressive and beautiful as it was before."

The old lady looked sideways at her. "Do you think the restoration of my Temple is the uppermost of my concerns? I would say that over the last year or two you've learned some most important lessons in that regard."

Katelin frowned. What did Gracie mean? Which lessons was she on about? She looked back at the old lady and saw over her shoulder the groups of Anestran people labouring to clear the rubble from their homes.

"Um ... do you mean something about the people being more important than the buildings?"

Gracie beamed. "Exactly. I knew you understood. Because your heart has the right attitudes. You care far more about these wonderful people in Anestra than you do about Temples and Castles. Yes, they all need places to live and work, but your heart is that the people should be safe and happy and fulfilled. That, my dear, is what will make you the greatest of our Queens. And I love it."

"Thank you," Katelin said again, and was pleased that she understood at last what was uppermost in the Divine's heart.

They sat for a while in the afternoon sunshine, watching

as the sun lowered itself towards its golden path across the Ocean's waves. With the devastation of earthquake and flood all around her, a question nagged at the back of Katelin's mind. Since she had the Divine, the White Goddess, the Life Weaver herself, sitting next to her, this seemed the time to ask it.

"Gracie, why are there earthquakes, and flooding waves, which cause so much death and destruction, when you're so powerful, and you love us so much?"

The old lady beside her gave a deep sigh, and Katelin turned to look at her. Gracie looked sadder than Katelin had ever seen her.

"Yes, that was one of my hardest decisions, Katelin. It breaks my heart when people suffer pain and grieve for their loved ones. I make it up to each one of them in the next life. But you need to know an answer for this world and for this life."

Gracie paused, and they both looked out to the Ocean. "It's because the world itself is alive, you see. The world lives and breathes and produces plants and creatures in such amazing variety and richness. We enjoy that life, and we're part of it. But life means changing, and growing, and moving. An earthquake is a moving of the world, and that causes a flooding wave across the sea. Anestra lives by and off the Ocean and is vulnerable to the changes within it."

Gracie looked at Katelin and went on. "The alternative was a dead world. One without change or moving or growing. But that would be a cold, dark, lifeless one, and I couldn't choose that. It would be a still, calm, peaceful world, but it would be the stillness of the tomb. Which would you choose, Katelin?"

"I'd choose life," Katelin murmured. "Yes, I want a living world, with all that's wondrous and beautiful in it, and to learn to live with the cost of a changing, growing, moving earth."

Gracie laid a hand on Katelin's arm. "Just make sure, my

dear girl, that you enjoy all the goodness and beauty within it while you can, to balance up the costs of the suffering. It's only living life to the full that makes all the rest of it worthwhile."

"Thank you, Gracie. I will."

The sun was sinking when Katelin asked her last question. "Can you promise me something, please, Gracie?"

The old lady chuckled. "Yes, of course I will, if I can."

Katelin turned to hold the old lady's eye and was surprised to feel a tear starting in her own. "Can you promise me that Anestra will enjoy some peace for a while now?"

Gracie regarded her with a look of understanding and compassion.

Katelin wanted to explain. "You see, my people have had the years of the Regency, and then the Lassenite invasion, and Ilbassi Plague, and losing their King, and my aunt usurping the throne, and an earthquake and flood, and now we need to rebuild, so I'm asking if we can all have a rest for a while, please."

Gracie squeezed her arm and nodded. "Yes, Katelin, I know, I understand."

The old lady gazed out to sea, and Katelin wondered whether in fact she was looking into the future.

"Yes, my dear," Gracie said at last. "Anestra will have peace, at least for a while. I can't promise that for ever, but you will have time now to rebuild, and regrow, and recover. I know you'll do a wonderful job as Queen in peacetime, just as much as you have done through this year of turmoil."

"Thank you, Gracie," Katelin said.

They both stood up from the harbour wall, as though understanding their conversation was over. Katelin felt awkward, not knowing what to say.

Gracie reached and embraced her. "Well done, my child," she said. "Thank you and keep going, Queen Katelin the Great. Don't forget to ask me if you need anything."

Katelin squeezed her in return. "Thank you so much, Gracie. Or should I call you, my White Goddess, my Life Weaver, my Divine?"

As Katelin released her arms, Gracie gave her one last smile, one last twinkle of her deep blue eyes, and was gone.

Queen Katelin the Great breathed a sigh and looked out to where the sun was setting into the Western Ocean.

She turned and started walking up Spring Channel towards the city and the Castle.

For she had work to do.

If you like the *Destiny's Rebel* trilogy, you might also enjoy
the first in the Immortality series, *Cave of Immortality*:

**What price for eternal youth?**

Seventeen-year-old Roza doesn't know
she has a secret power.

When an ancient warlock kidnaps her because he needs
her for a potion he is brewing,
he discovers her unique and powerful gift.
But revealing her ability would plunge the whole Sapien
Empire into civil war to possess and control it.

Roza's valley is threatened with destruction,
and if her power is the only way to save it,
how can she keep it secret?

# ACKNOWLEDGEMENTS

Writing a book is a long-term project, and I thank those who have kept me going through the years of not just this book, but the whole *Destiny's Rebel* trilogy.

First thanks go to my wife Ann and our teenagers Mark and Rachel, who allow me the time and space to dream, wonder, think, type, wrestle, gaze out of the window, and otherwise create these stories. I couldn't ask for a more understanding and supportive family.

Next thanks go to the talented team at Books to Treasure: to publisher and editor Adrianne Fitzpatrick, who took the risk on me, to co-editor Ruth Jolly and cover artist Emma Graham. I will always be amazed at what we've produced together.

My heartfelt thanks go to those who showed an early interest in reading what I created, particularly my fellow writers in the Association of Christian Writers (ACW) and the Society of Children's Book Writers and Illustrators (SCBWI), who gave their suggestions and feedback. Those readers who enjoyed and reviewed my first books, and said they couldn't wait for the next, have kept me going even more.

I'd also like to encourage aspiring authors, including the young people in the schools I visit, especially at the Warriner in Bloxham and at North Oxfordshire Academy in Banbury. Please keep reading and writing. Yes, our task is a long adventure, and sometimes it seems an impossibly difficult one. I pray we'll come to see that creating our characters, worlds and stories can be the most enjoyable, frustrating and satisfying of life's endeavours, with the writing itself becoming its own reward.

And my ultimate thanks go to the Divine, for everything.

*Philip S Davies, 2018.*

# ABOUT THE AUTHOR

Philip S Davies came to faith in the Divine at the age of eighteen, and has served as a cleric since 1997. In his family home in Oxfordshire, his study overlooks fields and a valley like those around Anestra.

Philip's debut novels, *Destiny's Rebel* and *Destiny's Revenge*, were Shortlisted as Finalists for the prestigious Crystal Kite Award from the international Society of Children's Book Writers and Illustrators in Los Angeles, and they were both Number One Bestsellers in Teenage and Young Adult Fiction at Blackwell's Bookshop in Oxford.

You can find Philip at: www.philipsdavies.com